MISERY BOY

a novel by

Rose Servis

7.13 Books
Brooklyn

First Edition
1 2 3 4 5 6 7 8 9

Cover art: Drew Shimomura

Library of Congress Cataloging-in-Publication Data

ISBN: 978-1-7333672-2-6
LCCN: 2020930236

When, by a supreme decree of Evil's Expiation,
The Poet appears in the World, this-worn out City,
His terrified mother cries in exasperation
With shrivelled hands toward God, who takes her in pity:

"Ah! that I had not a knot of vipers in reversed revulsion
Begotten rather than this infamous derision!
Cursed be forever the midnight of convulsion
When my womb conceived my expiation and my vision!"

—Baudelaire, "Benediction," *Flowers of Evil*.
Trans. Albert Boni

MONDAY

MONDAY MORNING, in his last week of college, Edward woke up in Christiane's bed, no Christiane. A note on her pillow.

Don't forget – 10 A.M.!

Minutes later he was out the door, flask and notebook in hand. He exited the apartment building, stepping into a cramped, dusty alley. Broad shadows obscured all but the thin band of light he walked along. His face was hot, and his hands were trembling. His cigarette was crumbling in his teeth. He spat it out and continued spitting out little bits of paper as he propelled his body forward, telling himself Christiane wouldn't have started the final exam without him. *She's waiting for me, of course she's waiting for me,* he thought as he sucked in his upper lip and sucked air through his nose, drawing his breath into the back of his head. When his lungs were full, he uncapped the flask, pouring the drink in his mouth as he released his breath in little increments out his nose.

Then, whether from the drink or for a different reason, Edward began to feel like Edward again. The feeling was almost reassuring. He couldn't quite shake the dread he'd felt upon seeing Christiane's empty space in the bed. She could have woken him, but she'd left for campus instead. Why?

Edward made it to the end of the alley, where it intersected with the street that wrapped around the college. He crossed the street and began walking up the grassy knoll, zigzagging because it was too steep to go straight. Halfway up, he began to get dizzy and queasy from all the turns. He shuddered from the fear that he was about to vomit. He fell to his hands and knees and, after taking a moment to let his stomach settle, began crawling. Little tufts of grass and dirt came up with his fingers as he climbed. He found the exercise soothing. When he reached the top, his jeans and jacket sleeves were wet and slimy. He stared for a moment at the green stains. The color was astounding. Bright, bright, fucking hell it was bright. Neon lights running up his body.

He walked to the Modern Languages Building. Sitting down at the bench outside the front entrance, he reached into his jacket to retrieve the cigarette that he had promised himself, just one before he went in to take the test. He took one from the pack and put it in his mouth. But his matches—where were they? He patted his jacket, his pants pockets, the cloud in his head thickening as each place turned up empty.

A throat cleared. He looked up. A girl was standing in front of him, arm extended, the brass bangles on her wrist lightly pinging. She held a shiny lighter. He leaned forward, just as her hand withdrew.

"You're sucking on the wrong end." She pulled the cigarette from his lips, turned it around and replaced it. Edward blushed as she held out the lighter again. Inhaling, eyes closed, nodding, mumbling thanks, feeling what?—not blubbering, not *tears* in his eyes. Ah christ, Edward, you baby.

When he opened his eyes, he was alone. The students he'd seen outside the building were gone. His gaze scaled the building, and he tried to figure out if Christiane's classroom was on this side or the other, if Christiane, standing in front of a window, could see him sitting on the bench, looking up at her. He was pretty sure the classroom was on the other side and her window had a view of the parking lot and not the benches. But he could see the other reality just as clearly: the exams, held to her chest, almost spilled from her arms when she looked out the window and saw him. Her face, tense with worry, dissolved into an unusual smile. She turned from the window and faced her students—*What are we waiting for? Santa with his bag full of A's? Let us begin!*

Edward leaned forward on the bench, elbows on his knees, the cigarette shitting ash on his shoes. He had to go up. He had to go up right now and take his final. It wasn't just a question of failing the class, not graduating, ruining his summer with additional murderous hours of coursework and classes: he'd disappoint Christiane. He'd made promises. Last night, ah christ, he'd promised her. The champagne, two fucking bottles. Christiane had gotten the job at Harvard. He said he'd go with her.

He groaned aloud. As he replayed all the things that were said last night and all the stupid things he'd agreed to do, his groan turned into abysmal, guttural chuckling and his expression changed into the same look of ironic humiliation that he'd just imagined on Christiane's face. Pulling out another cigarette and lighting it off the other, he remembered that he had already decided his course of action—take the final, graduate, go to fucking Cambridge. But now, sitting on the bench, he again had to choose what to do. He was at a turning point, the same turning point he had come to last night. Absurd life. Why come to a decision if he had to come to that decision all over again the next day? The obvious solution, of course, was to stop making decisions and just go do something. Other people seemed to do things. But Edward couldn't do something until he was certain of how it would end, but once he knew, he felt bored and dissatisfied, already circling back to the point where he started: what should he do?

He hung his head, his eyes focusing on the turkey in his lap. In his agitation, he must have picked up and opened a magazine that someone had left on the bench. The smoke exiting his nostrils and striking the ad intensified the illusion that the turkey was roasting right in front of him. The turkey, naked and defenseless, plucked of its feathers and disemboweled, with its wings splayed back and its legs sticking up and beigeish stuffing coming out its ass, was surrounded by red arrows that indicated circulating heat. Below the turkey was a description of the Farberware Convection Oven. Scanning two columns of text, he read, "Save Time, Work, and Money," "The Choicest Choices," and "Exclusive Probe-A-Matic Control." When his eyes worked their way to the tagline at the top of the page, he caught himself before he swallowed his cigarette. The tagline read: "Farberware found that the best way to get something done is to go around in circles."

He wanted to jump up and pace about. He wanted to laugh out loud and scream obscenities. The randomness of it, the fucking chance, of finding that ad, with that message, right at this moment, right next to him! Beautiful! Wonderful! Those goddamned copy-writers really knew Edward! Yeah boy they had his number. Chuckling to himself, he pulled a red felt-tip pen out of his jacket pocket. He uncapped it and continued scanning the ad. When he came to a word he liked, he underlined it and moved on. After underlining a dozen or so words, he looked back at the first line of the ad: "The Farberware Convection Oven is taking cooking in a totally new direction."

Above this line, Edward scribbled—*enough circles, Oven. achieve something superior when inside is ordinary.*

He liked to rewrite ads to show how completely fucking mean-ingless they were. He used only the words in the ad, used each word only once, and kept going until he had used up all the words and written an entirely new version of the ad on top of the old one. He'd done this since he was a kid, something fun to do with the ads in the copies of *Good Housekeeping* his mom left lying around the house. It calmed him, the distracted focus of it. He was barely aware of what he was writing—*need walls to circulate circles—be you constantly surrounded you air constantly over*—and after jotting down the last line—*Poultry moist envious*—he tossed the magazine aside.

He walked to the food cart outside the Main Library to get the donuts with the chocolate filling. He ordered one and ate it where he stood and ordered another and ate it as he walked down a narrow path of wood chips to the back of the library, where tall lilac bushes demarcated what was known on campus as the *Secret Garden*. Edward, who refused to go into a place so adorable, lay on the lawn in the shade of the lilacs and closed his eyes. He burped.

The leaves above his ears shuddered. A croaky old voice exclaimed, "Oh my goodness! What was that?"

Edward's eyes opened to slits.

The voice of another old lady answered her. "I think, Trudy, you're pretending you weren't just burping."

"That wasn't me!"

"Dear, there's no one else around."

He recognized the high, raspy voices of the Motts, the ancient sisters who managed the Main Library. From the way the leaves shook each time they spoke, Edward figured the old ladies were sitting on a bench directly on the other side of the bushes. He would have to get up. These two were unrepentant gossips, and he wanted a nap. But they said no more, falling into asthmatic breathing that he found quite pacifying, like dueling dishwashers on steam cycle. He looked at the sky, hanging low to the earth, appearing even at its apex to droop; he searched for the sun, couldn't find it... His eyelids closed, his breathing slowed, his chest, like the murky sky, dwindled into its contents. Edward's mind shrunk into a small corner of his skull and, looking up, on the other side, blinking at the feet of the old Mott sisters, it wasn't surprised to find itself so measurable, material, and small. Like a dutiful pet, his mind climbed the bench and curled up in the cozy space between the old ladies and waited for them to notice it. It wanted nothing more than for the sisters to speak in the gentle voice of purrs that resembled its own and to scratch the terrible itch between its ears. It pressed the itch against one sister's arm, but her hand withdrew into her lap. It turned away from her, slipping behind the other sister's back, and she responded by scooting her bottom up the bench. The old sisters, completely ignoring it, began speaking to each other in monstrous voices. Its ears flattened, and its tail hair stood on end. It hissed, struggling to banish the voices from its head. It wanted whirrs, chirrups, and other mild, mothering noises, and if it couldn't get that, then it didn't want anything. It leapt from the bench and dove into the bushes. The voices pursued, covering up its body, becoming another body it couldn't escape: its tail shrunk, its coat tore, its vision blurred, and Edward's mind expanded in a brightening tomb.

He blinked up at the cloudy sky: low, close, overbearing. The old ladies' voices, loud in his ears. They were deep in some argument.

"It's the feminine sensibility. You see it in all his poems."

"You get a feminine sensibility from all that? It's hardly poetry!"

"Hardly poetry?"

"He just mixes real poems up."

A small smile came to Edward's lips. He knew exactly who they were talking about.

"Hmph. There's more to Roger Ackroyd's poetry than that and you know it."

"I admit that what he did with 'The Waste Land' was interesting. But what was the point of mixing up *Tender Buttons*? It's pure gibberish to begin with!"

"It's absolutely marvelous."

"You're entitled—"

"I am, thank you very much."

It was a conversation about Roger Ackroyd, the millionth Edward had overheard in the past year. He adjusted his body into a more comfortable position in the grass, lacing his fingers under his head and once more closing his eyes. But he no longer felt like napping. He was thinking about his favorite Roger Ackroyd poem, "The Waste Land," recalling the opening stanzas as if they were at once both a calming prayer and an amusing joke:

A TIME
Now swell
And so a only. Where shadow againe.

So no sun rest—
I red the brown and drank the were vines

Thinking her in my sits
As that I the What said.
Oh I vanity the agony remember
we raised folly empty What cock still was many.
The sea,
The people lightning. in a was late, nearly never it road in
whisper dirty as
The snarl
When you silence at road
Sighs, of night.
ahead horoscope tight. father's shouting downward from the
shore

Twit girl."
—Yet she addresses.

Perceived in is hands.

With some of the Ackroyd poems (usually the shorter ones), you could see something of the original poems that they came from—the remnant of an image, the echo of a theme. But this mix-up was perfect. You could see nothing of T.S. Eliot's poem in it. Edward, who would have been happy to recall all 844 lines of it, found that his thoughts were interrupted as the sisters' argument grew more heated—

"I'll just say this: it's good to finally learn your *true feelings* about Roger Ackroyd. To think, after all this time, you never respected him."

"It's not his *poetry* I respect."

"What then?"

"Why, the mystery!"

Edward grinned. He had to agree with her—the mystery was what he dug about Roger Ackroyd, too. Nothing could be known about the Poet. What he looked like, what his age was, his true name, these were all impossible things to know. The only thing known about Roger Ackroyd was that he was a student at the university, a thing that was, in fact, known *not* because Roger had admitted it, but because only students submitted articles, letters, et cetera, to the paper. It was the mystery of Roger Ackroyd that made his poetry so *interesting* to people on campus: he inspired hate or admiration in one moment, total indifference the next. His readers (students and professors, mostly) referred to the poems as *mix-ups* if they liked them and *rip-offs* if they didn't. Some said that the poetry was proof of the decline of literature and the impossibility of artistic creation in the modern age. Parroting the reading from their lit theory classes, they'd say, *The so-called Ackroydian poetic expression expresses both the destruction of expression and what the destruction of expression challenges—which is, of course, everything—yet it does not express even that!* Or else people said the same exact same thing only to conclude that his poems proved the life of words and the possibility of creation, that Roger Ackroyd was a genius.

"Speaking of *mystery*—there was another letter from Mystery Girl this morning."

"How wonderful!"

"Yes, I found it tucked inside *Dumb Witness*."

"And how is she doing this week?"

Edward covered his mouth with his hand, stifling a yawn. The grass under his neck was starting to make him itchy.

"I don't remember what her letter said word for word. I

peeked at it before sticking it back in the book. You know how I'm always worried about someone coming."

"Yes, we've been very good snoops this year."

"How terrible it would be after all this time to get caught!"

"Yes, and it would quite ruin the mystery!"

Edward covered his face with his forearms, as if that could do anything to block out their endless chatter.

"Funny you should say that. In *this* letter, Mystery Girl finally told Roger that she'd like to meet him."

Edward's eyes snapped open, his hands fell to his sides.

"It was bound to happen. They've been writing to each other for eight months."

His heartbeat quickened. They weren't talking about—they couldn't mean—

"You know, I discovered the first letter, if you remember."

"Mm, yes, you never fail to remind me."

"I was going through all the old mystery books to throw out the ones with molding, and there it was—"

"*In a fusty old Agatha Christie.*"

"—a love letter written and signed by none other than—"

The two ladies chimed together, "*Roger Ackroyd!!*"

Edward's fingers dug into the soil.

"You thought someone just left an old letter in there. But I knew it was in the book on purpose."

"Hm, yes. You are truly remarkable."

"My girl, I just read the clues! The date was recent, there was no address. Yes, I knew that letter was put in that book for someone to find it. And I was right. One week later Roger Ackroyd's letter was gone and a reply from Mystery Girl was inside."

"But here's what I don't get."

"Tell me."

"How did he know to find the letters in the books? Awfully serendipitous if Roger Ackroyd just opened up a library book one day and found a letter addressed to him."

"Oh, of course he didn't! Mystery Girl probably mailed her first letter to the school paper and they established the system with the books *after* that."

"Do you think *they* even know who Roger Ackroyd is?"

"The editor? Surely."

Edward remained on his back in a state of shock, gripping the ground, gritting his teeth, restricted to shallow breathing by a stabbing pain in his chest. *Get up! Walk away!* he told himself, and then a second later: *What good would that do?* He couldn't get away from what he had just heard. His future had eroded. He was stuck here, in the gloomiest moment, wondering, *What the hell?* Some girl was writing letters to Roger Ackroyd? Roger Ackroyd was writing letters back?

How was that possible?

Staggering to his feet, staring blindly into the leaves, he barked at the bushes, "Stay there! Don't move!"

He raced around the garden, peering into each entrance, scanning the empty galleries and glancing down their pathways. He kept running, looking into more entrances and seeing more empty benches, until he had gone all the way around the garden without spotting the sisters, ending up where he started. He hollered, "Are you still there?"

They didn't sound to him the least bit startled by the unfamiliar voice shouting at them. They giggled amongst themselves, before replying, "Who's there?"—a question that struck him as pointless and impossible to answer, especially to them, and at this time.

"Do you know him?" he responded.

"Who?"

He had never said the name aloud before, not even as quiet words to himself: "The Poet!"

They were silent for some time before answering. "We have never met him."

This was a point people were constantly confusing. They believed that an author was a thinking, feeling, breathing, conscious being. Wrong. Words naming an absence, *that* was Roger Ackroyd, but this stupid school didn't seem to understand the author's function: Roger Ackroyd *wasn't*. He *represented*. He didn't tell, he showed. He was riddle, *the refusal to be anything*.

Edward asked, "How could you meet him? He isn't real!"

"Isn't real?"

"I mean he isn't a person. That's just a pen name."

The old sisters tittered. "Roger Ackroyd writes poetry! And he's in love!"

Edward crossed his arms. "Fine. I want to meet him then. How can I find him?" But he heard them getting up, their feet scraping across the gravel, their voices trailing behind them: "We have never met him…"

He followed them from the other side of the lilac bushes, tracking their movements by the shadows through the leaves. Did they know he was there? He was unpleasantly aware that they might want him to follow them. Beyond the garden was the lawn; beyond that, the library. He drew back to the bushes, just as they stepped onto the path of wood chips that cut through the lawn. Through the leaves, he watched the sisters linger: bodies turned toward the other, heads slowly turning side to side. One whispered, "Do you see him?"

Then the clouds broke. There was a moment of intense sunlight, when the view flared up and became terribly shiny—the grass, the sky, the buildings retouched in a brilliant polish. The sisters, wearing identical yellow dresses, vanished in the golden view, only reappearing when, after that frantic, sunny moment, the clouds fused back together again. It became dark, almost black, and he spotted them at the library entrance, their dresses flickering like lights deep inside a cave. He smelled dust and wet leaves and heard and saw in no order the flash and crack of the arriving storm. He stepped into the lawn as it began to rain.

The grass was slick under his feet. As he ran, the ground seemed to slide underneath and keep him as feverishly immobile as a hamster running in a wheel until, finally, his feet touched pavement. He had reached the sidewalk under the awning of the library entrance. He shook out his hair and peeled off his jacket. The water that dripped from it made a brief puddle on the walk, then was quickly absorbed by the creeping tide behind him. He stepped forward, closer to the door, where the ground was slightly elevated and still dry. He was shaking. He was cold? Water dripped from his chin, falling on his shirt. He wiped his face. Its sharp heat surprised him. And his heart, as he pressed his palm against it, beat with hard, hollow thuds. He looked behind him, into the rain, and could hardly see through it. Turning to the door, he felt cowardly, compelled to go forward, not to find the sisters, not for any truth, but because he wanted to get dry. He draped his jacket over his shoulder and pushed through the door.

On the main floor, every table was taken and the sofas were packed. The quiet here was twitchy. Traces of voices. Short, dry coughs. Every few seconds, a chair squeaked, a paper tore. After a minute of wandering, he spotted the old ladies—their identical silver bobs had disappeared behind the stairwell door. He stepped over a student asleep on his books and then squeezed between two tables. At the stairwell door, he held his breath and turned the knob.

Walking up the stairs, he stayed a floor below them, taking care with each step. The sisters' voices echoed down the shaft, but he couldn't make out any words. The first clear sound he heard was the abrupt slam of the door at the top. He ran the rest of the way up.

He didn't expect to see the sisters when he slipped through the door, slowly closing it with a soft click. But turning around, he sucked in his breath, seeing them down the aisle, just ten feet away. He kept his breath held, waiting for them to notice him. But as they reached for the top shelf at the same time, their hands collided and their bracelets got caught. Edward slipped behind the bookshelf as the sisters busied themselves with the untangling of their bracelets, taking turns scolding the other.

He saw them through the gap between the books and shelf. One of the old ladies held an orange book. She parted its pages to reveal the white envelope tucked inside. Was that it, the letter? As she opened the envelope and pulled out a folded page, Edward closed his eyes. His heart—god, fuck! It was beating so hard! He tried to suck in his breath as slowly and silently as possible, but the air seemed to go only as far as his throat before it sputtered out his nostrils. He tried again, visualizing the air tunneling down to the pit of his stomach. Air filled him. His head began to clear. And when he exhaled, his heartbeat slowed. His eyes opened. The sisters were folding the letter back up. They slipped it into the envelope, murmuring, "Goodbye, Mystery Girl! Goodbye, Roger Ackroyd!"

He went for the book as soon as the sisters were through the door. Among the series of blue spines, he spotted an orange one. He pulled the book out—heavy, a bit oily. A little white dog on the cover. Agatha Christie. *Dumb Witness*. The pages loosened, hanging by threads, as he flipped open the cover.

His hands shook as he took the letter out and read—

May 18, 1980

Dear Roger,

I have a confession to make to you. I am very fat and I have a huge purple birth-mark in the center of my face.

Ha-ha. Just kidding. But it's awesome you don't care what I look like because I don't care what you look like. I really do think that true love is blind.

So yes I DO think that it's about freaking time we got around to meeting each other. It's been 8 MONTHS since I wrote to you after reading your freaky

Waste Land poem. The Student Drama Coali-
tion is putting on BLUE OF NOON. How
about you come to the last show on the
20th? You'll recognize me by my green
sequined dress. Fingers crossed that
it'll be love at first sight!

Ha-ha, just kidding. You know I'm already
crazy about you.

XOXOXOX — Your Mystery Girl

What the hell was with her casual tone? Forget that a girl was writing *Roger* and that she loved him. Forget that *Roger* was writing her back and that he apparently loved her. The flippancy with which this ditz addressed the Poet, like he was just some guy, and then to sign her name as *Your Mystery Girl*—*his* mystery girl? It was a joke! It was goddamn awful! It was... Edward moaned and leaned against the bookshelf.

What should he do? What *could* he?

He could write his own letter. Put it in the book. Writing anonymously, he'd say, *It's come to my attention that you have been writing someone who claims to be the poet Roger Ackroyd. I know a few things about the Poet in question, and I should tell you that you're being duped—this person you're writing isn't who you think he is...* But why would she believe him? Who was one anonymous person to tell another anonymous person that the anonymous person she was writing was a phony?

He abandoned that idea. He would write instead as Roger Ackroyd, the real one. *This person whom you have been writing and who has been writing you is not the real Roger Ackroyd. I am the real Roger Ackroyd, and I want you to stop writing to this poser!* But what would that solve? That kind of letter would have the same effect as the first: who was the real Roger Ackroyd to tell her about the fake one?

To come forward as himself, as Edward who wrote under the pen name Roger Ackroyd, and then to provide *the evidence* (drafts of the published poems, drafts of the new ones) seemed to be the only way to convince her—and this was something that Edward would not do. Edward was *not* Roger Ackroyd. How could he be a thing that had no existence? Roger Ackroyd was nothing to Edward: a name, absent and sovereign, to appear before each one of his poems, while Edward, the writer, could remain unknown to the readers, pure secret. No reader could point her finger at Edward and claim that, having read his poetry, she had entered into a special understanding of him, one that he, as the source of that understanding, could never hope to obtain. Let her say that about *Roger*—let her say she knew him! Roger Ackroyd, the perfect prank of him, allowed Edward to write nothing, and as he wrote nothing, call himself nothing, and when the writing appeared in the world as a published work, as *something*, he discovered it not as its maker, but its only possible true reader, and so faced his work with an attitude that was something like objectivity. Few writers today (honestly he could think of none) had such a relationship with their work, could view themselves from such a distance. The distance between Edward and the work was equivalent to the distance between Edward and the world and, while he often felt that there was something daunting and maybe disquieting about that distance, he was in control of it and it owed its existence to him. Who else knew, after all, the truth about Roger Ackroyd? No one. Edward should have been able to relax behind his secret—shouldn't he feel calm and powerful and free?—but he didn't, not any longer, or at any rate he wouldn't anytime soon, because of the death sentence in his hands, declaring that Roger Ackroyd was no longer his.

Edward's eyes widened. He looked down at the letter.

"It doesn't matter if I write to her. *He's* coming for this!"

Edward stuffed the letter back in the book and put the book back on the shelf. He walked to the opposite end of the room and without a chair to sit on, leaned against the wall and slid down to the floor. He had a clean line of sight to the letter. He would wait. He would wait for the fake Roger Ackroyd to come and then... what? What would he do?

"Eddie?" A voice called out. "Eddie *Moses?*"

Recognizing the voice, he jolted forward, then slowly turned his head. Ted walked toward him, hands stuffed in pockets, his jaw working a huge wad of gum.

Ted stopped in front of him, blocking Edward's view of the stairwell door. Edward leaned to the right to see past him.

Ted asked, "Are you *studying*, man? Where's your—"

"Yeah, sure, how long have you been up here?"

Ted popped his gum. "Dunno."

"How'd you get in?"

"How'd *you* get in?

Edward pointed. Ted looked back at the door.

"Nah." Ted shook his head.

Edward's eyes widened. "You mean there's another way in?"

Ted laughed. "Eddie fucking Moses. I heard someone talking to himself and I was like, it's got to be him." Ted looked back in the direction he'd come from and waved at a girl walking toward them. "Jennifer, this is Eddie."

The girl came up, and Ted slipped his arm around her. She was short and pretty. Ted had dated a million like her. "Hey Eddie," Ted nodded. "You should tell Jennifer one of your stories."

Fucking Ted, always hassling him. Edward shook his head and continued staring at the door.

"Tell her the one about the dogs."

Edward's brow furrowed.

"You know. The barf story."

"Are you kidding?" Edward asked. "No way."

"Come on." Ted waited. "Are you *busy?*"

Edward gestured at the door. "I'm just... There's this..." His hand dropped to his lap. What excuse could he possibly give him?

Ted whispered to Jennifer, "You're going to love this."

Edward began the story unpleasantly, in a mumbling, luster-less voice. "So Jim, this friend of ours from high school, his parents were out of town…"

Ted started laughing.

"…And we got six cases of beer to last us the holiday weekend." Edward kept his eyes on the door, not bothering to see if Jennifer was smiling or looking interested or even listening. "But two hours after they pull out of the driveway, we get a call. It's Jim's parents saying that the trip's been canceled. They'll be back first thing in the morning."

"Wait." Jennifer interrupted. She pressed her index finger into Ted's shoulder. "Where were you during all this?"

"The lake," Ted said.

Edward continued. "So we look around at all the beer we have stacked in the kitchen and… Come on, Ted."

Ted had a huge, stupid grin on his face. "No, no. You're doing great."

"We look at all the beer and Jim says, *We got like twelve hours to drink this*, and I don't know. I'm fifteen. I've never been drunk before."

"Eddie was the class nerd," Ted explained. "He was—"

"But Jim," Edward was now glaring at Ted, "has been waiting for this weekend for months. He cracks open a beer, downs it, then wipes his mouth and says—"

"Hold up." Ted held up his hand. "You're forgetting something."

"What?"

"Eli came over."

Edward shrugged. "Yeah. *Maybe*. I don't really remember. The night is a blur after five p.m. But anyway, Jim remembers that he has to feed the dogs. He's got these two dogs, these longhaired chows. They're nice dogs. And so while Jim is feeding them—"

"Eli."

Edward stared at Ted. "Huh?"

"Eli was feeding them."

"Look, I'm sorry, but regardless of whether Eli was there or not—which, as I have always said, *I don't remember*—but regardless of that, he did not feed the dogs. He's allergic to dogs, and if he were there, he would have been nowhere near the dogs, probably in the basement or upstairs bedroom."

"Eli told me he fed them."

"No way Eli touched shit those dogs have touched, OK? He gets one hair on him and his throat swells to the thickness of a—"

"All right, all right. Eli is a liar."

"I didn't say that!"

"Just tell the story, man."

They glared at each other.

Jennifer said, "So…"

Ted cleared his throat. "The dogs are hungry."

Edward snorted.

"And Edward is drunk. He's had like twenty beers—"

"Maybe four. I've had maybe four beers."

Ted shook his head. "You're fucking up the story, man."

"So Jim's feeding the dogs and they're chomping on the food and I'm feeling shitty. And I turn to Jim, who's blasted. He's staring down his beer can like it's the pit of hell. What can I do to cheer this guy up? I say to Jim—*Man, I know this sounds weird, but can I puke on your dog?* And he looks up and says—*Jules or Dahlia?* Five minutes later we're all in the backyard, me and Jim and the dogs. I'm running around and the dogs are running around and I'm puking on the dogs and the dogs are jumping on each other, trying to eat the puke off each other, rolling around in the grass, trying to eat the puke off the grass. When I wake up, some hours later, I'm lying in Jim's parents' bed. Jim's with me and we're covered in puke. The dogs are also in the bed, eating the puke off us. And that's the story. Yeah."

Ted was busting up, red-faced, clutching his head.

Jennifer's nose was scrunched up. "I don't get it."

They stared at her.

"I puked on the dogs."

"He puked on the dogs."

She frowned. "But like…don't you feel bad about it?"

Ted smiled at her. "The thing you gotta understand is that was the best night of those dogs' lives. To this day, when they see Eddie…"

Edward tried to look around Ted, but he had moved too far to the side. "Hey man, I can't see."

Ted looked down at him. "You can't *see*?"

"You're blocking my view of the door."

Ted leaned to the left. "I *am*?"

Edward leaned to the right, and Ted stepped in front of him. He leaned to the left, and Ted stepped back.

"Cut it out!" Edward tried to stand, but Ted pushed his head down.

In that moment, over Ted's laughter, Edward heard the stairwell door slam.

He scrambled across the carpet and then jumped to his feet. He ran over to the door and opened it. Peering into the stairwell he saw no one, and listening for footfalls he heard none. He turned and looked up at the shelf where the orange book should be. His eyes darted across the blue spines, the blue spines, the blue…

"Oh my god." Edward's hands ran down his face. "It's gone."

Ted laughed. "What?"

He pointed at Ted. "You kept me from seeing!"

Ted looked at Jennifer. She held up her hands.

Now Edward was walking over. "Do you have it? Do you fucking have it?"

"Christ, Eddie. Chill—"

"Let me see!"

Edward ripped Ted's backpack off his shoulders and held it tight. Ted's arms flailed out, striking his shoulder, his jaw, but failing to reclaim the pack in Edward's arms.

Edward could hear Ted shouting at him as he ran down the stairs. And when his feet hit the first-floor landing, he didn't turn around to see how far Ted was behind him. He pushed through the door and squeezed between tables, hopping over a guy asleep on the floor, colliding with a girl just stepping through the library entrance. His chin connected with her forehead and his teeth gnashed together and he groaned, she gasped. He clutched his jaw, tripping over her books to push past her.

The sky misted on his shoulders as he slogged through mud and slimy grass, crossing the lawn, finally reaching the Secret Garden. He turned into the first entrance he came to and jogged down a path, following twists and turns until he reached a bench and flopped onto it. His chest was heaving. He gulped down air but couldn't get enough and started coughing. His throat was dry and burning. He looked for his jacket, but didn't have it. Then he looked down at his lap. His breathing slowed. He stared at Ted's backpack.

"Fuck, man!"

He pushed it off his lap, burying his face in his hands. He was such a shithead, so stupid. Obviously the letter wasn't in there. Obviously Ted hadn't taken the orange book and put it in his backpack. *Don't check, don't even*, Edward told himself. *Don't you dare go through...* His hands slid down his face. The backpack was sitting in an inky puddle. He lurched forward, snatching it up, groaning at the sight of grimy water sliding down the vinyl. Ted, oh—Ted would kill him. *First you steal my backpack, then you fuck it up? You asshole, you piece of...* Edward shook the bag and slapped it, turned it around in his hands, shaking and slapping and gazing at every inch with glassy concentration until he figured he'd shaken or slapped out every last bit of moisture or grime he could; and then he placed it next to him on the bench, placed his hand over his mouth, and thought, *What would be great right now is a fucking cigarette*. He knew he'd find some in Ted's backpack. But there was no way he was going through it. It was unthinkable now to unzip the pockets and go through them as he had done countless times before. He would not allow himself to do it, even though it'd be only to get the cigarettes that were definitely in there. They were in the outer pocket. You could see the outline of the pack sort of crushed.

"What a fuck-up," he yelled and bit his fist, agitated knowing that he needed to do what he couldn't do, because he needed to think but couldn't, not when the things he needed for writing were in the pockets of the jacket in the library with Ted. Goddamnit. He couldn't think through anything without his *smokes, pen, notebook*. With this backpack and without his *smokes, pen, notebook* he was at least centuries away from thinking one clear-headed thought about anything. Useless and mentally paralyzed, Edward picked up the backpack and stood up from the bench, thinking only *smokes, pen, notebook*, as he stepped out of the damp, steaming garden and into the green, sun-drenched lawn.

Edward walked back over to the library and got within sight of the entrance, when he veered abruptly. He sat on the short wall and leaned forward, his elbows on his knees and his hands clasped together. He watched the entrance for Ted. After a time, no one coming in or out the door, he looked down and saw that his hands were swollen and discolored, twisting between his knees. He separated his hands and rubbed them up and down his legs...his fingertips paled, his knuckles turned red, and a loud clap of the door caused his hands to slide fast and grip the wall's edge.

Two girls were coming out of the library. They stopped and grabbed each other. "Sun!" one said and lifted her chin with pleasure in the sunshine. Under her arm was a book. It was small, bright— yellow. It was yellow. The Agatha Christie book had been orange—

Edward looked back at the entrance, no longer watching for Ted. His eyes were peeled for the fake Roger Ackroyd. A guy walked out, walking hard on his heels with his hands in his pockets and his elbows stuck out. Like a creep. Someone familiar? The guy glanced—and then was dangerously glaring at Edward who suddenly felt better, felt the blood rushing to his legs. *Is this it, am I ready?*

Edward squeezed his fists, longing to hold a blunt, solid—No, look at *his* hands. Empty. No orange book. No bag to carry it in.

"What?" the guy yelled; hateful eyes. Edward's own gaze felt stuffed, like burning light bulbs or bloody strawberries were crammed in the sockets. A rabid thought was eating away at the others: what if he didn't find the poser with the orange book? If he didn't get his hands on Mystery Girl's letter?

Could he remember what it said?

"Freak," the guy spat, walking on.

Edward couldn't wait for Ted, couldn't wait for his *smokes, pen*—he had to remember now, right now, every word of Mystery Girl's letter: she had freckles? She wasn't fat, she'd said that, strangely. What else? *Dear Roger. Your poems are freaky. Let's meet.* And she suggested a place, a time, but where, but when? A goddamn play. Closing Night. What goddamn play? *Let's meet at mm-hm on Closing Night. I'll wear a green sequined dress.* The dress! Thank god he remembered! What goddamn play?

Out of the air came the bell toll—one, two, three o'clock... The doors banged open—stayed open, held by shoulders, elbows, hands. Edward was desperate now to spot the poser with the orange book in his hands. He glanced at faces and then at hands—girls he ignored, staring longest and hardest at the guys, fixating on their faces and forgetting until the last moment to look at their hands.

A dark shimmer at the side of his vision. He saw a girl sitting next to him. Pretty girl. He knew her. That was Katie, smoking in silence. He felt relief. As good as seeing his sister, as if someone who loved him were sitting there. Her white thighs were bare and crossed. One arm hugged her tiny stomach; the other held the cigarette at her ear. Then her head whipped around. She looked straight at him.

"You." She blinked. "Hi. How long have you been sitting there?"

He snorted. "Me?"

"What?"

"You sat next to me," he said.

Katie's eyebrows shot up, and she chewed her bottom lip. Then he watched her stab her earlobe with the burning cigarette. Screaming, she threw it to the pavement. Her eyes widened. "That was my last one!" She hung her head. "I guess you think I'm wasted."

"Are you?"

She shook her head. "Do you have your flask? Or did you drink it all?"

"I don't have anything. I lost my jacket."

"Well, I know that!" she exclaimed. "I just saw Ted."

Edward looked around. "You saw Ted just now? Where?"

"Outside the Student Union. It was about…oh, I don't know. How long have I been sitting here?" She shrugged and rubbed her bleary eyes. "You won't find him. He was on his way to take a final. Hey, aren't *you* in that class?"

He shook his head. "Yes, no, I mean—I am in that class, but in a different section. We had our final last Friday."

"So you're all done then?"

He nodded. But then the blood drained from his face. He was in a daze, a ringing in his head louder than anything. He pulled the backpack off his shoulders and unzipped the front pocket. His hands were shaking as he took out Ted's cigarettes.

"I missed my last final."

She threw her head back and laughed. Any other girl would ask him what he was going to do about it. But Katie wiped the tears from her eyes and leaned in to bum a cigarette from him. He breathed in the smell of her hair and his mouth filled with the taste of vanilla frosting and he looked for the blobby mole on her neck, thinking that the last time he'd been this close, he'd licked it. She leaned back, and he saw her brown hair was the same non-cut, thick and curly, springing out from behind her ears. In her right ear, she had three hoops and a diamond stud. His favorite part of her face—her chipped front tooth with the tea stains—was caught on her bottom lip as they stared at each other through the smoke. He liked Katie. He'd forgotten that. The first Roger

Ackroyd poem, a mix-up of Charles Bukowski's horrific "So You Want to be a Writer," he'd written while she slept in his bunk freshman year. She didn't wonder what he was up to then, she didn't wonder now, and he liked that best about her.

"So, Eddie—the dirty joke you told? The one that got you fired from the newspaper? I never did get to hear it."

"I didn't get fired because of a joke," he said coolly. "I got fired because Ryan Brewer is a prig."

"Right, totally. I appreciate the distinction you're making. But the thing is," she leaned toward him, "*nobody* can agree on what the joke was. You hear all these versions of it floating around in the newsroom."

He frowned. "Versions?"

"Like…" Katie razzed her lips. "OK, and this is lame, but a guy is on his way to the bar to get a drink with his buddies when he sees this girl tied up to the train tracks. He runs over to her, unties her, and they fuck. When he gets to the bar, his friends ask why he's late, and he brags about all the sex he just had. His friends ask him, *But did you get any head?* and the guy says, *No, I couldn't find it.*"

Edward scowled. "Not even close."

"Tell me! If you tell me I'll stand right next to Ryan Brewer at the staff party this Wednesday and repeat it in my loudest voice."

"In that case… no, obviously."

She put a hand on her hip. "What's your problem?"

"Ryan is a prig. But don't you owe him? I thought his uncle or something got you an internship at the uh Wall…the um…"

"*Wall Street Journal?*"

"Sure."

Her bottom lip popped out. "Please tell me? Pretty please? I'm not even going to the party. Please? Please? Please—"

He didn't have time for this. He cracked his neck and—

"Don't go!" Katie grabbed his arm. "I know a better joke. It's silly, but I like it. My ex used to tell it to me, to cheer me up." She was looking straight at him, blinking rapidly, now rushing through it—

"A writer is sitting at a bar, reading over the first draft of his novel. As he reads, he keeps hearing a voice that's complimenting him. *Nice dialogue! Nice metaphor! Nice allusion!* The writer looks around, but nobody's there. Then the writer hears a different voice. This one says, *Hey asshole, you can't write for shit!* The writer's really upset by this and runs... Aw, hey, Eddie!"

Edward was standing now.

"You tell it!" She squeezed his hand. But he pulled away. She called after him.

"Hey, you tell it to me!"

He kept on the sidewalk. Shoulders hit him, bags hit him, someone yelled, "Hey, watch it!" What was the big idea, Katie saying he used to tell her that joke to cheer her up? The way she'd mentioned it you'd think he told the joke all the time. You'd think that it was something special between them, a private intimacy, when really it was something he had told her only once, three years ago, in the presence of about a dozen other people who, like them, were all standing outside the Icehouse Theater.

When the writer hears the second voice, the one saying he can't write, he runs over to the bartender. Hey! I'm hearing voices! The bartender shakes his head. That's just the peanuts and the jukebox you're hearing. —The peanuts and the jukebox? —Yeah, the peanuts are complimentary, but the jukebox is out of order! —*And the whole joke,* he had told Katie, *is an example of what's bad about praise and good about criticism. Praise is like bar peanuts, stale, bland, free. It fills us up and takes away our hunger. Whereas criticism,* he had told Katie, *tells you what's broken and gives you a reason to do anything.*

Then Edward had thrown down his cigarette, getting ready to go back inside the theater, because intermission was over and he'd wanted to see how this abnormal production of *The Birds* was going to pan out. Hitchcock had used real and mechanical birds in his film, but this director was using *lasers.* Red and white lasers flashed at high frequencies across the stage to signal a bird attack. It was great, wonderful really, the only things missing

were the *laser noises*. What were they thinking, forgetting the
laser noises? Maybe he should go backstage and suggest they add
some. *How awesome would it be if in the final scene the whole audito-
rium went black so we couldn't see our noses and we heard these noises,
all these laser noises starting up just before the lights started flashing?*
And Katie had said—

    Ugh, don't you like anything?

    He couldn't believe she had said this to him. Their rela-
tionship, he realized, was rapidly deteriorating. Maybe not the
first time she'd said it, but then he might have said something to
provoke her. He might have said, *your argument in the second para-
graph needs more supporting evidence from the text,* or he might have
said, *your short story would benefit from being put in a drawer and left
there for some time,* and her nose would scrunch up—*Ugh, don't you
like anything?* The important thing, he knew, was not to get angry
when she complained about him. He must explain to her clearly,
calmly, why criticism was a good thing.

    So, the joke about peanuts. *Praise is harmful and tasteless and sick-
ening like bar peanuts, but criticism is our best defense against ourselves, it
tells us what's broken, you know, why you suck.* Inside, *The Birds* was
starting back up, but outside, Katie was crying. Inside, people were
enjoying this imaginative adaptation, but outside the Icehouse
Theater, he'd have to light another because Katie was really
wailing: *Edward, dammit, you always criticize me and it's really hard to
be around someone who thinks I'm shitty at what matters most to me in
the world.* For some reason she had decided the joke was about her.
Probably to pick a fight she thought he was thinking of her when
he said, *You can't write.* Actually, he hadn't been thinking about
her writing, actually not everything was about her writing, but he
didn't really feel like telling her, he said to her, before going back
inside the Icehouse Theater, that she was dead wrong because he
was completely out of his mind tired of dating a writer. *Who cares,
Katie, if you're talented at writing? Do you want to write? Do you really
want to? Yeah? More than anything? Great! Fucking write then.*

Edward unzipped his fly. He pissed in a urinal in the bathroom in the Student Union, hating that people's opinions mattered to Katie. She was his first real girlfriend, the one who taught him girls think the truth is how you feel about something. Every girl since Katie had been a continuation of Katie, an attempt to end the argument that had begun with her. He had come close with Christiane to finding a girl who placed more meaning on reason than on the planets. But even Christiane had grown quiet and sullen and said, the one time he'd mentioned Katie, *You're still in love with her then?*

In the last stall of the bathroom, perched on the tank, he smoked another one of Ted's cigarettes. *True love is blind*, the letter had said, *it'll be love at first sight.* Probably Mystery Girl would get along with Katie. Probably they'd be best friends. For all he knew, Mystery Girl *was* Katie. *The writing is shitty enough*, he thought, as his eyes narrowed on the cock on the wall. There was a tiny black fly, no bigger than a pea, drawn on the tip. His finger scratched his eyelid—and he had an idea, a really good one, thanks to Katie.

The Icehouse Theater wasn't a far walk, just a few blocks from campus. He'd go there right now and see what play they were putting on. If there was no play, or if he didn't recognize it as the one mentioned in Mystery Girl's letter, he'd check elsewhere—churches, senior center, high school. But it wouldn't come to all that because the Icehouse Theater was the only place in town to see *real theater*.

He stepped out of the Student Union and into the bright, muggy day. The chapel bell hammered out four o'clock. His stomach growled. A minute later, on Main Street, he stopped under the awning of a corner store and checked Ted's backpack for something to eat. A banana, a stick of chewing gum, anything, he was starving, had he eaten today?

No food in the backpack. And Ted's wallet, when he checked it for money, was picked clean. He pulled out Ted's student ID and

read the name on it: *Teddy*. It depressed him to be reminded that
Ted's real name wasn't Theodore, but Teddy. Tapping the card
with his fingernail, he thought how it was one thing to be given
the wrong name, to be a Margaret when nothing about your face
said *Poor Midge*, but it's another thing entirely when your name
was self-mutilation. Ted's mom was hostile like that. Naming him
Teddy was an act of aggression.

Edward threw the wallet back in the backpack. He no longer
wanted to eat. He wanted to vomit, remembering the time in the
eighth grade when another boy, not one of their friends, had said
Ted's mom was sexy, you know? —*Very fuckable.* Ted's response
had been disastrous, blushing, staring at his shoes, while the other
boy screamed, *Did ya hear what Ted said? Did ya hear him? He said*—
and Edward punched the kid in the face before he could repeat
what Ted had said. And the next day, before the first bell, Edward
kicked the kid's ass a second time as a reminder to never repeat
what Ted had said. It was simple what Ted had said. It was fucking
unbelievable. Blushing, staring at his shoes, Ted had said, *I know.*

Edward picked up his pace as he rounded the corner. Even
if Ted got his name legally changed, even if every ID and public
document read the name *Ted*, it wouldn't matter. His mom would
still call him *Teddy*. He'd still be *Teddy*. *He'd still think of himself as
that,* Edward thought looking up at the Icehouse Theater.

The building in front of him was a tall, sinister cube, all the
windows boarded up, and no visible doors. Across the red brick
front, someone had spray-painted in black, two-foot letters—IS
IT OK IF I SLEEP HERE?—with arrows pointing all around. He
walked around to the side, where a metal staircase led to a door
midway up the wall. Beginning to climb he kept his hands in his
pockets, not wanting to touch the handrail and its curling flakes of
bright orange rust.

He reached the top of the stairs. A poster was taped to the
door. The image was dark and grainy, at first very difficult to make
out, but looking closer he saw a woman, naked, sitting in a chair

turned backwards, her legs spread wide, her pussy visible in the cross rails. She was fingering herself.

The image was superimposed over four lines of text.

I dreamed of a flower
That would not die,
I dreamed of a love
That would not fade.

His eyes moved to the bottom of the poster, where the text was clearly printed.

Blue of Noon, May 17-22, 8 p.m.

That was it. Fucking shit. The play. Mystery Girl would be there, wearing a green sequined dress. Straightening up from the poster, he reached for the doorknob. But it wouldn't turn. He rattled it. Then knocked. And then began pounding—the door pulled back. A girl leaned against it, sipping from a coffee mug. She had a thick neck and very black eyes. The message scrawled in permanent marker on her mug: *Shakespeare sucks.*

She said, "Come on, dude. What?"

He nodded at the poster behind her left shoulder. "What is this? Some kind of porno?"

She scowled, stepping away from the door. His hand went up, punching the door back open.

"Hold on. I want to buy a ticket."

She glared. "You can't."

"Why?"

Her lips curled. "No one from *the community.*"

"No one from *the community?*"

Her eyes widened. "Hey! This one listens!"

He glared at her, face burning. "I'm not a *hick.*"

"Aren't you?"

"A farm boy with a backpack? Is that something you see a lot of around here?"

She looked him up and down. "Eh, whatever. I'm not sorry. We've been getting a lot of push back from *the locals*. It's been really hard. And this morning, the dean came by and shut us down."

"You mean…"

She leaned against the door. "I mean he *shut us down*. No more performances. A lot of us are graduating this year and *Blue of Noon* was our last show. And yeah, the play has *sex* in it. It's Bataille. Like, what do you expect? We knew *the locals* would have a problem with it, but we never thought our own college would."

He ran his hands down his face. "I don't believe this."

"Ha, you have no idea, buster." The girl pressed her lips together, her eyes passing over his face. "OK, look. We're putting on one last show. Tomorrow evening, 8 p.m. *Not here*, obviously. At a house nearby…" She pulled back from the door. "I'll write down the address for you. Just a sec."

The door slammed shut. Edward stared at the porno poster. *If you think this girl is bad, just wait until you meet Mystery Girl. If you think she's a terrible person, get ready for the girl in green sequins. She wants to meet you at the theater. She wants your first meeting to be an artistic occasion. She is the reason why you're putting up with—*

The door opened.

"Here," the girl handed him a small card. "This is the address. And like, try to come early. If we hit capacity, and I think we will, we'll have to turn people away."

Edward examined the address handwritten on the card. *1526 S. Dunbar Road.* That was outside of town. Kind of far. And Mystery Girl might not even hear about the venue change.

"So you're telling people about this?" Edward asked. "People who bought tickets and still want to see the show?"

"Within reason. The place isn't huge. But yeah," she gave a loose shrug, "if you aren't a square, you're invited. But *come early*."

Agitated, restless, resisting the urge to strip off Ted's backpack and search it again for food, Edward lingered on the sidewalk outside the theater, wondering where to go, what to do, to eat. He was hungry. Starving. He needed cash for food. But Ted had his wallet. Ted had all his shit.

Well, that settles it.

He began walking in the direction of Ted's apartment, technically their apartment, but some time had passed since Edward had come around. The last few months had been weird. Too many nights spent at Christiane's. But he would be *home* again, opening the refrigerator, in less than ten minutes. He smiled, imagining the sandwich he would make for himself: roast beef, or better yet, pastrami, salami, with pickles and mustard and swiss on rye. No, a soft bun. With mayo and—

A horn honked. Then again.

Beep-beep!

A lime-green Chevette trailed him. The driver's side window rolled down.

"Hey," a joyful voice called out, "I thought it was you!"

The car rolled to a stop alongside him. Edward squinted and stooped, trying to get a look at the woman in the driver's seat. She wore oversized sunglasses and a scarf around her head. Dark red lips. He wondered how he knew her. Had they fucked? She looked familiar enough.

"Where ya headed?" she asked.

"Here," he said. "But I was going there." He tipped his head to the right. "But now I'm just standing around."

She cackled. "You nut!"

Her teeth were very white. Her shoulders and cleavage were dark orange. But he didn't know her. Did he? The purse in the passenger's seat looked familiar, beige with brown trim, the same as his mom's. And hanging from the rearview mirror was one of those medallions, the kind Catholics carried around for protection—*Saint Christopher's*. So, she wouldn't have gone to his high school. Maybe Central Catholic?

The woman touched her throat. "So…"

Edward swallowed. "So yeah, so…"

The woman pushed her sunglasses up her nose. She asked him, "Did you go see your mother this morning?"

Ah fuck. Friend of his mom. God fuck this was getting old. This was the problem with his mom always talking about him to people. Completely fucking random people knew who he was, and he didn't know who they were, and he couldn't ignore them because he was *Josephina Moses's boy—a very nice young man.*

"I didn't see her, no," he said, feeling a yawn coming up.

She nodded. "Yeah. I'm feeling that too. Couldn't get out of bed, called in hooky to work. It's no good feeling this tired. I'd probably still be in bed if I wasn't so starving."

Her skin was finely wrinkled—breasts, neck, face. He saw that now.

"Right," he said.

Her tongue wet her lips. "So, what do you think? Too soon to get a bite? Dolce Vita is just around the corner."

He frowned, suddenly confused. "Huh?"

The woman laughed. "I'll even buy you a drink. Sounds like we both need one." Her smile grew. "Hey, my treat." She leaned back in the seat, and Edward stepped back from the curb. The bright green Chevette sped forward, zooming down the road. Edward gave a shrug. He stepped forward, in the opposite direction of Dolce Vita and that woman's car.

He went a few steps. His stomach twisted with hunger pains.

"Eh," he decided, turning on a heel.

Inside Dolce Vita, he told the waitress, "Two whiskeys."

The waitress laid the towel on the counter and crossed her arms.

"We only do one at a time over here," she said.

"But I'm meeting someone!"

The waitress snorted. "Yeah, we'll see."

She left him with one drink. He sipped it, half-sat and half-stood at the bar, keeping both eyes on the door to the street. Each time a car drove by, the door shuddered in the frame, and he lurched forward, expecting to see the woman walk in.

Two drive-bys. Three. After the fourth, Edward pushed his drink forward and slumped against into his hands. Christ… she wasn't coming. The whole thing was a joke. She didn't know him, and he didn't know her. And he had this drink to pay for, this drink he couldn't pay for. The drink was going straight to his head. He was feeling nice. Dreamy. It wouldn't last for long, it'd turn on him, unless he got some food in him. Chicken fingers, extra ketchup. Yeah. That was exactly what he needed. He'd order that, call the waitress over and order that. No, fuck. What was he thinking? He couldn't. The woman wasn't here yet. He had to wait for her. It was rude not to. Everything he did, every rude thing he did, would get back to *his mom*. He was really at this bar with *his mom*. Ostensibly he wasn't. But really—

Edward lurched back, terrified, as a beige blur slammed down on the bar.

"I had to pee!" the woman yelled. "Thanks for waiting. Did you get a drink already?" She squinted at his glass. "What's that? Gin?"

He rubbed his eyes. "That's straight whiskey!"

The waitress called over, "Hey honey, you want a G&T?"

"No," the woman said, curling a finger at Edward's drink. "I'll have me one of those."

Now she adjusted herself on the stool, rolled her shoulders, crossed her pin-thin legs at the ankles. He was certain now that he'd never seen her before this afternoon. She looked younger than his mom, in her 40s, possibly early 40s, but that might have been a trick of the light on her skin: the fake tan made her neck look almost flawless. The scarf was gone. Her hair clung to her nape like strips of glimmering tinsel. He tried not to stare at her huge and totally wrinkly hands.

He had to think of something to say to her now. What did anybody talk about?

She asked him, "Do you come around here much?"

He shrugged. "You?"

She held her drink against her breastbone, eyes wandering the bar. "Used to. Not so much anymore. Back when I knew some people at the university, we were always at the Dolce. Not anymore—I'm all *growed up* now." She took a sip and added, "Lord, I'm babbling. Just like last night."

Edward lifted his eyes from the menu. "Last night?" he asked, gazing at her.

The woman nodded. "Yeah, hey—do you know what you want to order?"

Edward followed her gaze to the waitress, arms folded, behind the bar.

"Do you have chicken fingers?" Edward asked her.

The waitress said, "Yeah, for twelve and under. Are you twelve and under?"

Splitting laughter in his ear. "Honey, just get the burger!"

The waitress left with their orders, two burgers, what a fucking joke. He wanted the chicken fingers. Edward knocked his empty drink around, only looking up when the woman said—

"Remind me—you're from around here, right?"

"Yeah," he muttered.

"*Yaaah?* What're you saying it like that for—*yaaah.*"

He shrugged. "After high school I wanted to get *out*."

"But…?"

His head shook. "But instead I'm here. Exactly a mile away from my parents, sister, aunts, uncles, cousins, all fourteen million of them…my gran…"

"Wow," she said. "That's really something. I haven't been home in years."

Edward snorted, lifting his empty glass. "Cheers."

"Oh no. I never meant to leave! I thought moving to Michigan was only temporary. But then I had the baby—"

"Oh!" Edward rolled his eyes. "You know my dad!"

"Sorry?"

Edward nodded. "My dad delivered your kid!"

The woman bit her lip. "A, uh, Dr. Moses did the delivery?"

"Right on. He's about to retire, you know."

"Dr. Moses?"

"Later this year," he said. "No big deal. He doesn't even want a party."

She hesitated. "But your father, you were saying he... Sorry, what were you saying?"

Edward sighed with relief, staring at the steaming plates of food in the waitress's hands. A plate dropped in front of him. He picked up the fat, dribbling burger.

"Oh, this is *good*," the woman said.

"You haven't tried it," he said, chewing.

"No, *this*. Us." And Edward felt a hand on his thigh. "Blind dates are usually such a crapshoot. But given how last night went, I guess our friends know us pretty well."

Her eyebrows wiggled up and down as she said that last part. It was difficult now to not laugh. To chew his burger calmly. And now that he had swallowed his food, to explain.

"Here's the thing..." Edward said. "I don't know what you're talking about."

She cocked her head.

He took another bite. "We didn't hook up last night."

Her hand clenched his thigh. "What?"

"I thought you were a friend of my mom when I first ran into you. That's why I agreed to lunch. But I don't know you. You don't know me."

"This isn't funny," she said, snatching her hand back.

"Like, what do you think my name is?" he asked.

"Stop!"

"No really, what's my name? Dale, Dan, Bill, Bob? Tell me, because I don't have a clue."

The woman groaned. "What? Why are you doing this? I

mean, we had such a great time last night. I never ask guys back to my place. I don't do that. But last night was…you were just…" She slapped the table. "I *trusted* you!" She slumped in her seat, muttering miserably, "It's your eyes."

"My eyes?" Edward cried.

"They are so freaking blue."

"These?" He pointed. "These look blue to you?"

"Yeah, they're blue!"

"My eyes are brown. Like…brown. Here, look." He grabbed the little candle off the bar top. He moved the flame from eye to eye. "Blue…? Or *brown*?"

"Stop!" She pulled his hand down. "Stop," she said in a quieter voice. "You're acting…" Her voice dropped into muttering. In the soft bubble-up of words, he thought he heard her say a name.

"What'd you just call me?" he cried.

She looked away.

"Did you just call me—what do you think my name is?"

She threw her napkin down. "You're sick to do this. You're a very sick person." She slid off the stool.

"Hey, what's my fucking name?" he called after her, but the woman hurried out of the restaurant, leaving him there.

Edward remained turned in his seat, watching the door. He waited for it to reopen and for the woman to come back in. But she wasn't coming back. And he couldn't turn around, couldn't look ahead, so afraid of seeing the waitress on the other side of the bar, frowning at him, holding out the unpaid check. The restaurant was quiet. He could hear the clatter of dishes in the kitchen, the car tires rolling down the street. Out of the corner of his eye, he spied a couple in the corner booth, watching him curiously. He looked away, back at his half-eaten burger, eyeing the teeth marks in the soft sesame bun, the threads of torn, red beef. So yummy. Too bad he wouldn't get to finish it. He had to look up now. Look up now. He couldn't look up now. Look up, Edward! Look up, shithead!

He jerked his head up, blinking at the rows of liquor bottles, the spectrum of ambers and blues and saw…no waitress. He looked up the bar—down the bar—no waitress!

Now he was slinking around tables and chairs, eyes on the exit, then breaking into daylight, feet pounding pavement, running, turning a corner, running. He looked down and saw Ted's backpack in his arms, hugging it! He didn't remember grabbing it, but there it was! He was beautiful! He was goddamned amazing sometimes, he could've left it there, he nearly left it there, and he'd be screwed, so fucking fucked, if he had. He imagined the waitress back there, looking around, thinking, *What the hell? Where'd that kid get to?* She checked the bathroom, didn't find him. The couple in the corner booth called out, Oh he's long gone, he booked it. *WHAT?? The waitress walked over to them. WHAT???? He tricked that woman he was with, too. He's scum, that guy. A real creep!* Ribs heaving, head pounding, Edward felt sick thinking of what they were saying about him back at the restaurant. Trick her? He didn't trick her! If somebody said they knew you, that was it. It was all over for you. From that point on, there was nothing you could say or do to convince them you were someone other than whatever the hell they thought.

He was nearly to McGregor Street and his apartment, when he had to stop and lean against a wall. He didn't want to puke. He wasn't even drunk. He had to puke and he wasn't even wasted. It was terrible having to puke when you were sober. You felt it all. Vulnerable. Like a little kid again, as he straightened, spat, and wiped his jaw. He was hungry now, possibly even hungrier than before. He could laugh at the whole thing. He could just fucking kill himself. He took steps around the corner, arriving at his and Ted's apartment building. He thumbed the buzzer for 4F. Nobody answered. He pulled the backpack to the front of him and riffled through it for Ted's keys.

A voice from above, someone harassing him. Edward looked up, saw a guy hanging out of a window, shirtless, smoking a joint.

"4F?" the guy called down.

"It's fine, it's fine." Edward waved the keys in the air.

"4F?" the guy repeated.

"I have a key!" He shoved the key in the lock.

"4F???"

"*Yes!*" Edward screamed, banging on the door. "Shit fuck, jesus…"

And there the guy was, standing in the doorway to some third-floor apartment, as Edward came up the stairs. He didn't know the man. He'd never seen him before in his life, but he knew the guy's type from his red eyes and sunken chest and freckly bony shoulders and little teeth and dope-stink and weak goatee. What had the girl at the Icehouse Theater called his type? *A member of the community.*

The man nodded, looking at Edward's feet. "Hey bud, looks like ya dropped something."

Edward stepped over the small mailer in his way, no doubt filled with shitty weed.

"Sorry," he called over his shoulder. "We're a pills-and-booze-*only* apartment."

His anxiety only increased inside 4F, when, standing in front of the open refrigerator, Edward observed Tupperware containers in careful stacks, each labeled with the initials EF.

He thought about it. EF. EF.

Eli? *Eli* was keeping food in their refrigerator? How long had that been going on? Edward tried to figure the last time he'd been by the apartment. A few weeks? A month? He wasn't over at Christiane's every night—sometimes he camped out in his gran's basement, her damp, dank, secluded, silent basement, that fantastic, fantastic basement, although Gran didn't know. Edward shut the refrigerator door. The arrangement of magnets was the same, *thank god*. But he slid Popeye off the freezer door and pocketed him, suddenly worried about the safety of his things, not just Popeye but what he kept, oh shit, in his bedroom…

Edward left the kitchen and crossed the living room, entering his bedroom. He saw his bed, his dresser, his desk, his rug, but none of his clothes, his books, his notebooks, his very important, private notebooks. He picked a piece of mail off the desk and read the name on the front—

Eli Firkin.

"Motherfucker," Edward muttered, tossing the letter aside. Eli Firkin had moved into his bedroom—Eli was sleeping *less than four feet* from Edward's shoebox of Roger Ackroyd poems. Edward took a chair to the closet and stood on it to reach the highest shelf. His hands trembled as they moved across the dusty surface, groping its depths. If Eli found the poems, would he know what they were? Eli didn't attend college with them—stocked shelves at Kroger— but he could have taken the poems to Ted.

Hey, Ted-Bear, what're all these papers in this box here?

Edward's fingertips grazed the edge of the shoebox, but he couldn't do more than nudge it further back. He pulled his hand out and grabbed a wire hanger off the rack. This time, using the hanger as a hook, he was able to coax the shoebox forward...

The bulk fell into his hands. His eyes ran across it, fingers ran across it, looking and feeling for any rips in the quarter-inch thick skin of duct tape that kept the lid secure. OK. It felt OK. The shoebox didn't appear to have been fucked with.

He walked out of the bedroom and into the living room and lay down on the couch with his eyes fixed on the ceiling and blinked madly as he breathed in his nose and out his mouth, telling himself *in out, in out, in*.... It wasn't true, it hadn't happened. But he imagined it anyway. Eli gave Ted the shoebox. Ted looked through it. The papers, Ted recognized, were all early Ackroyd. *Eddie? This whole time the Poet was Eddie?* Edward could hear Ted clearly. His skin crawled as Ted shouted, "Eddie, you asshole! You great gaping—"

Edward's eyes snapped open. A knocking on the door. Goddammit! He jumped up, and over, opened the door, and...

No one. Looking both ways, no one and no one. He closed the

door and waited, breath held, for the knocking to stop. It stopped, gradually, only vibrations, no perceptible sound, just a blur of wood as the door, the entire wall, trembled. Edward walked back to the couch and lay back down...

A munch. Crunch. *Munch crunch slurp.* He looked out into the room and saw a black dog chewing on a human face.

Edward sat up on the couch, pulling the prickly afghan off his head. A dream, he thought.

The apartment was very quiet.

The refrigerator turned on.

In the kitchen, Edward wrote Ted a note: *I want my jacket.*

With the shoebox tucked under his arm and a fresh cigarette behind his ear, Edward turned the doorknob to leave. He got halfway over the threshold when he stopped, staring down at the floor.

Ted was up against the wall, eyes closed, drooling on himself. Napping. Wearing the jacket. Edward considered closing the door quietly. Instead, he extended his arm, opening it more widely, then—

Slam! Ted lurched forward at the clap of the door. He looked up, bleary-eyed and blinking at Edward. He wiped his mouth, muttering, "You! I've been knocking for an hour!"

Edward leaned a shoulder against the closed door. "An *hour?*"

"Kevin saw you go up!"

"*Kevin?*"

"Third floor!" Ted reached up for the knob and rattled it. He looked up, glaring at Edward. "Where's the key?"

Edward grinned. "Oops."

Ted gaped at him. "How am I supposed to get in?"

"Dunno, Ted... Maybe *Eli* can let you in."

They glared at each other.

"I can't believe—" Edward began.

"You haven't paid rent in months, you piece of shit."

"He's using all my stuff!"

Ted squeezed his eyes shut. "Eddie, you know what I like

best about you? It's not your I.Q., your very fucking average I.Q. You're a giving person. Totally selfless. A total fucking…what're they called? A boddi what?"

Edward chewed on his thumbnail. "Bodhisattva," he said.

Settling back into the wall, Ted crossed his arms and nodded. "Right, right…"

Edward spat out a little sliver of nail. "You know what I like best about me?"

Ted squinted at him. "What?"

"I'm sexy."

Ted covered his face, shaking his head.

"I'm a really sexy guy," Edward said, holding back a smile. "Listen, do you remember Anne Marie? From Central Catholic?"

"You mean *Annie*?" Ted asked.

"Yes. Do you remember her mom?"

Ted frowned. "Was she hot?"

"Yes. What's her name?"

Ted shrugged. "Why?"

Edward cleared his throat. "Annie's mom stopped me on the street today. She thought I was somebody else."

"Who?"

Edward scratched his jaw, grinning. "The guy who fucked her brains out last night."

Ted lost it, laughing, flopped across the floor, basically wept.

Eli came up the stairs. He stopped and swayed on the final step. "Hey guys, what's so funny? Hey, what are you laughing about?"

Ted wiped his eyes, still wheezing with laughter. "Eli! How's it hanging! Got your keys?"

"Great, uh-huh, terrific! Hey, what's the joke?"

"You got some keys, Eli?" Ted asked him.

"Oh no, did you lock yourself out?"

"Eli, Eli, Eli," Ted said.

"What?"

"*Your keys, man?*"

Eli unlocked the door. Ted went in, followed by Edward who eyed the jacket around Ted's shoulders.

"My jacket?" Edward asked.

"My backpack?" Ted asked.

Eli followed after them. "But what was the joke?"

In the kitchen, Ted rifled through his backpack, while Edward watched from the doorway. Opening his wallet up, Ted hollered, "Hey! Where're all my twenties?" He laughed. "Nah, just messing!"

Eli squeezed into the doorway alongside Edward. He eyed the shoebox in Edward's hands.

"That's really taped-up. You really got that taped-up. How many rolls is that? You need some garden shears to get into that."

Ted snorted. "Blowtorch more likely."

"What's in it?" Eli asked.

"Nothing. It's trash. I'm tossing it." Edward walked to the table. He picked up his jacket, felt the pockets.

Wallet, notebook, pen, smokes...

"Where's my flask?"

Ted still had his eyes on the shoebox. "You know, no one cares what you write in your *diary*, man. All that duct tape is *superfluous*."

Edward said, "Wow. Awesome word, man. Are you like a writer or something?"

Ted sneered. "Yeah man. I *am*."

Edward nodded. "Wow man. You must be so good at it."

"I'm *all right*."

Eli, too, was eyeing the shoebox. "Is it trash? Really? Because I'm expecting a package from Kevin."

Ted rolled his eyes. "Christ, Eli, what'd I tell you? If you want some weed, I'll get it for you."

"But Kevin—"

"Takes your money and doesn't give you shit for it. Every time you buy from him, this happens."

Eli frowned. "No. Kevin's all right."

"He's *all right*? Really, Eli?"

Ted turned to Edward. "So last Friday, right? We're at Kevin's, chilling at his apartment. And Eli gets up from the couch and says, *I got to piss bro!* But Kevin doesn't hear him right. He hears Eli say, *I got a pistol!* So Kevin, he yells, *Yeah I got one too!* and pulls out a fucking nine."

Eli grinned. "Ted got so scared. He was so scared. He ran out of the room."

Ted looked back ahead. "You pissed your pants!"

Eli laughed. "I know, I know. I was so frightened."

Edward walked over to the kitchen window and looked out. Night was rising quick off the ground and the few dim streetlamps weren't enough to light anything. He shivered. This windowpane, as his forehead pressed against it, felt cool, almost cold. He didn't want to go back out there. Just looking out the window had given him the chills, they were running up his arms, his neck—he couldn't go. Ted and Eli would think he wanted his old room back, but if he could just sleep on the couch. If he could just, somehow, explain.

Edward looked back over at them. Their voices were low.

"Did you tell him?" Eli whispered.

Ted shook his head. "He doesn't care."

"He just doesn't know," Eli said quietly.

"Know what?" Edward looked between them. "What?"

Ted stubbed out his cigarette. "Katie pulled some shady shit with the school paper. And now she won't be doing an internship at the *Wall Street Journal*."

Edward waited.

"What she did isn't evil," Ted said. "Not necessarily. More like *sad*. What she did is sad."

Edward yawned. "Christ, what'd she do?"

"She wrote a bunch of fake letters to the editor."

Edward snort-laughed. "What?"

"A lot of them were about how amazing of an opinion columnist she is. You know, *your articles are amazing, your writing is awesome.* That kind of shit. But she wrote at least fifty letters—"

"Fifty?" Edward exclaimed.

"—that basically shat on the other columnists. She made up a bunch of fake names to do it, and she would have gotten away with it, too, if we hadn't gotten an anonymous tip. Katie denied it of course when we asked her about it. But then last night, she turned up here at the apartment, asking for you."

Edward felt cold. "Me?"

"Don't worry," Ted said, "I didn't tell her you we're at your girlfriend's. She came inside to wait for you. Couple drinks later, she confessed to everything."

Edward ran his hands through his hair. *Idiot, you complete fucking...* Why hadn't he made the connection between Roger Ackroyd and the paper until now? If you wanted to get a letter to Roger Ackroyd, what would you do? You would write to the Culture Columnist who was Katie, or to the Letters Editor who was Ted, or to the Copy Editor who was Edward (up until he was fired four months ago), or you would go straight to the top, the Editor-in-Chief, maybe you'd ask Ryan Brewer to *pass a letter along to Roger Ackroyd.*

Edward cleared his throat. "So how does it work? Do you read every letter the paper gets?"

Ted shrugged. "Eh, depends on my mood."

"What if someone writes to Roger Ackroyd?"

"Ackroyd? I dunno. Nothing."

"*Nothing?*"

Ted shifted, looking uncomfortable. "I give them to Ryan. He deals with them." He narrowed his eyes. "What are you getting at? Did you even hear me about Katie?"

Eli piped up. "Who's Roger Ackroyd?"

Ted looked over at Eli. "He's…" Then he paused. He looked at Edward. "Oh shit."

Edward was already shaking his head. "No. No way."

"It's an interesting thought. She *did* make up all those personas."

Edward groaned. "Katie's no poet!"

Ted pointed. "You thought of it!"

"No, I didn't! I was thinking about the Poet's fan mail, that someone on staff, like Ryan, might be reading it." Edward studied Ted's face. "Come on, you were never tempted?"

Ted rolled his eyes. "Please, I'm not obsessed with Ackroyd like you are."

"*Obsessed?*"

Ted drummed his fingers against the table. "But Katie writes the poetry? Katie is Ackroyd? Does that even make sense?"

Eli looked between them. "Who is he?"

"Or maybe *I'm* Roger Ackroyd! Did you ever think of that?" Ted cried.

"Hey, come on," Eli said. "Why won't anyone tell me?"

Ted nodded. "Exactly, Eli. Why won't anybody say? Why are we still wondering who Ackroyd is after four years? You know, I could go to the paper tomorrow and say it's me, it's been me this whole time, and who'd contradict me?"

"The actual poet?" Edward said, voice breaking.

Ted grinned. "Wonderful. Then we'd finally know."

Edward shoved his hands in his pockets. "Cool," he said, walking around the table. "Really cool." He reached the door.

"You're forgetting something," Ted called.

Edward kept walking.

"Your diary?"

The shoebox, shit. Edward paused in the living room.

"Trash," he called back, lamely.

"Oh right," Ted said, his voice loud and sarcastic. "Then you won't mind if I…"

"Go for it," he muttered and walked through the living

room. As he opened the front door, he heard the sound of the shoebox hitting the bottom of the trash can. He stepped into the hall, trembling, both excited and filled with dread. He'd called Ted's bluff, holy shit! He actually let him trash the shoebox—fuck. He pulled out a cigarette, forgetting to light it as he walked down the stairs. He'd come back for it tomorrow, when Ted was in class and Eli was at work, when they both were out of the apartment he'd get it out of the trash… Then he'd take the shoebox to campus. He'd go to the newsroom, find Ryan—*Hey Ryan, quick question, kinda random: what do you do with the letters sent to Roger Ackroyd? Do you just read them, or do you write back to them, too?* And if Ryan turned red, if he so much as paled… or if his eyes widened, if he even blinked, then Edward would be happy, so fucking happy to have found Ryan out.

Outside of the apartment, a sharp whistle broke his thoughts. Edward looked up, expecting to see Ted hanging out a window. Instead, something soft hit the crown of his head. He swore in surprise, rubbing his head, as a voice called down, "PB&J, my man! Hell yes, oh yeah!"

Edward remembered him now: Kevin, third floor, dude called it *PB&J*, Edward's kind of lifestyle, nothing but *pills, booze, and jams.* He's basically sweet this guy, brain fried by pot and shrooms and acid. Might be the same Kev that lady talked about whenever she played bridge with his mother…*my Kev you know he works at the gas station maybe you've seen him at the one on Forester and 8th the Shell not the Texaco that's a block away and always a half cent higher than the Shell where my Kev works you know so it ends up being a better value in the long*…but Edward had never clarified.

He looked around for the thing that had hit him. There, an envelope at his feet. It looked different from what Kevin had tried to give him earlier when they'd crossed paths in the hall. That package had been bulky—definitely Eli's shitty weed. But this envelope rattled. Pills? He slipped it into the inner pocket of his jacket, pleased that he now had a good excuse to come back to the apartment tomorrow. *Shoebox, what? No…I'm just dropping by the pills Kevin accidentally gave me.*

Edward pulled his jacket tighter, stepping into the street. A song came murmuring from one of the houses, an infant let out a long, lonesome wail. Where could he go tonight? His gran's basement at the edge of town… No, that's where he went to write poetry, and tonight—he almost laughed—was no night for that. Ah hell, it had been a rotten spring for writing poetry. The winter had been good. Spent all of January down in Gran's basement with nothing but his smokes and pen and notebook and a thermos of boiling hot ginseng tea, but this spring had been his most blocked period to date, not a line, not a fucking yen to write one. What was the problem? Did he know? This business with the fake Roger Ackroyd was obviously karma, a wake-up call to get his shit together because weeks had passed, no, it really had been months since he'd spent a night away from Christiane's bed. *There. That's it, man. Why don't you feel like writing? Why don't you ever feel like writing? Christiane. It's Christiane. Christiane's the goddamn problem. What are you going to do about it?*

Edward's pace slowed. He stopped, looking around. This was the alley that led to Christiane's building. And the dog barking a few houses down, wailing behind the fence, was the one he often heard from inside Christiane's apartment. He stepped closer until he was in front of the dog. Edward's enduring presence seemed to enrage it more. The barks became more frenzied, higher pitched, the dog began mashing its snout into the chain links…

A light came on in the back porch.

"Hey, you there!"

The dog writhed against the fence.

"Are you crazy?"

The fence creaked and groaned.

"Get out of here!"

The fence pitched forward.

"Get out of here! Out of here! Get—"

Down the alley, hands in his pockets, staring at the dark movements of his feet, Edward could still hear the dog but he was free
of that, grinning and free of that. He could do anything right now,
anything he wanted to. How different everything was from last night
when he was riddled with dread about the future. Just last night
everything was decided for him: you pass your finals, you graduate
and spend your life with Christiane in fucking Cambridge. There
would be kids. He could count on that. She said she wasn't sure she
wanted them but he knew there'd be two or three and how could he
afford that? Last night, over a second bottle of champagne, Christiane
had asked him what he'd do once they were living in Cambridge. He
shrugged and said, *There's always law school.* Christ, jesus, he actually
said that out loud with conviction as if it were an actual consider-
ation and not his mediocre impression of an asshole. That's fucked
up. That's fucked up. That's really fucked up. Just last night he was
going to give Roger Ackroyd up for Cambridge. He was going to
walk away from it all, as if it didn't matter, all for Cambridge. But if
today had taught him anything, it was that Roger Ackroyd mattered.
Edward couldn't give him up. It was fucking brilliant, actually, that
Edward had missed class, had missed the final, had probably flunked
Christiane's class. Fucking brilliant he had saved himself.

He reached the overflowing trash cans near the back exit of
Christiane's apartment building, not far from a mass of useless bicycles
all chained together. A sign on the back door read KEEP SHUT, and
a brick kept it open. He pushed through, passing into an oozy yellow
space, a corridor filled with hot, moist air and flickering light and
cooking smells, oil and onion and meat. Climbing the stairs, he heard
crying babies, laugh tracks, opera. A little girl in a doorway stared at
him. That spooked him, made him jump. He hated how kids just
stared at you. He didn't know what it meant: they ogled you with
wide unblinking eyes. It made him want to stare back, make faces,
and he did that, he made a face at the little girl—stretched his lips,
scrunched his nose—but it didn't shame her, she didn't look elsewhere. The little girl's gaze followed him up the last flight.

He now stood at Christiane's door. Sucked in his breath. Knocked twice. And, as seconds passed, he wondered if he could really do this. She might open the door and slam it back in his face before he could get a word in.

He'd write her a note. Really, a note was perfect, far better than a conversation. No questions, no discussion. There were at least two people in a conversation, there was no one in a note. Reading was a choice, you did that to yourself, so the person who read becomes the person who imagined, *Sorry, this isn't working out.* You made it actual, you were complicit, *Sorry, this isn't working out.*

The door opened—Edward reached for his pen, Christiane stared at him—he shoved the pen back in his pocket.

"Oh," he said to her, the most profoundly stupid thing he could begin with.

Her hand fell from the door. She turned.

"Come in, stay awhile." Was she angry? Her German accent made her words sound clipped and formal, but no more than usual. He watched her trip on a moving box. She swore in German, then looked back at him with a wry smile.

"Edward?"

Now she sounded bemused. As he stepped inside, he felt a twist of fear. *Please let her be angry. At least let her be angry.* It was always difficult to break up with someone who played it like there wasn't a problem. Better to end things screaming—or bleakly, in oppressive silence. Mutual rage helped spread the guilt around.

He closed the door behind him and stepped into the kitchen. She was sitting at the table. There was a pot of coffee there and a stack of papers. She pulled one of the papers off the top and began marking it up, willy-nilly it seemed, with her red pen.

"If you have come to take your final, you are too late," she said, scribbling.

"I know."

"As you can see, I am grading them right now."

He set his jaw.

She looked up. "Why did you do it? Why?" Very lightly she hit her fist against the table. "Where did you go today?"

He shook his head.

"What?" she exclaimed. "What does this possibly mean? You shake your head like this is somehow meaningful. Do you mean nothing, you did nothing today? Or you can't tell me?"

He said, voice flat, "I can't tell you."

"Why?"

He looked at his hands. He was holding them up, and he didn't know why. He closed them to fists and let them drop.

"There's no way I can tell *why I can't tell you* without, you know, *telling you.*"

Christiane gritted her teeth. "*Try!*"

"A man…" Edward faltered, "goes into the woods…"

Christiane gaped at him. "OK?"

"He goes into the woods to meet the fairy, right? And the fairy tells him if he dances a certain way, right there in the woods, he will feel the happiest he's ever felt. The man says that's silly, but the fairy says just do it like this. And so the man does the dance, right there in the woods, and he feels amazing, the happiest he's ever felt. And the fairy tells the man that he'll always feel that way if he dances that way, right there, as long as he doesn't tell anyone about it."

"Is that it?" Christiane exclaimed.

Edward shook his head.

"The man is still thinking about how happy he felt when he goes to sleep that night. And when he wakes up the next morning, he thinks to himself, *Geez, I gotta go do the Wood Dance!* But on his way to the woods, his brother stops him and asks where he's going. *I'm off to do the Wood Dance*, the man says. His brother asks, *What's that?*, but the man says, *I can't tell you*, and continues on alone to the woods, to that place, to dance in that way. But when the man starts dancing, nothing happens. The Wood Dance doesn't do anything for him anymore."

Now Edward waited for Christiane to say something.

She reached for her smokes.

"Cigarette?" she asked.

"No," he said. "I quit."

"You what?"

"I quit. I'm quitting. I don't want one."

Her face contorted. "I don't understand you. Since when did you quit? When did you decide this?"

He shook his head. "My story? Were you even listening?"

She gave him a lopsided smile. "Oh yes. A man believes he'll be very happy so long as he engages in a secret obsessive-compulsive practice about which he can tell no one. But then the man makes a mistake: he gives the practice a name."

Edward scratched his head. Hadn't the fairy called it the Wood Dance to begin with? But whatever, that wasn't the point.

He said, "You lost me, Chris. It doesn't matter who names the dance."

She lit her cigarette. "It doesn't?"

"His mistake wasn't to *name* it."

Smoke curled from her nostrils. "No?"

"His mistake was telling his brother about it."

She leaned forward. "You think?"

"Yes!"

"Can you be sure?"

He groaned.

She remained pitched forward on her elbows. "I'm just thinking of something, OK? I'm sorry, but listen. What if when the fairy says tell no one, the fairy also means *you*—you cannot tell yourself about this dance, you cannot try to claim it as your own. You cannot do the things that are indications of ownership, in this case, the act of *naming* the dance."

He rubbed his eyes. "But that's the point. The dance *is* his, but other people misunderstand the simplest things that you say. So by not telling anyone about what's most important to you, you're protecting that thing that's yours."

She sighed. "The fairy, don't you see? It mocks the man's desire for control."

Edward's face grew hot.

"It doesn't matter—" she stopped, seeing his face. "Um..." She blinked rapidly and then let out a low, nervous moan. She was laughing? Some species of it. He turned his back to her, walking over to the kitchen sink. He filled a mug from the tap and gulped it down. Turning back around, he saw that Christiane was no longer looking at him: she was puffing away at her cigarette, eyes downcast, seeming to read one of the papers in front of her. Her right hand clicked and unclicked another red pen.

A minute, maybe two, passed. At last she said, "You're not coming with me to Cambridge."

"No," he agreed.

Her eyes shot up. "Oh, let me finish! You're not coming with me to Cambridge because you will fail my class. You will fail to graduate. This amazes me: rather than tell me you don't want to be with me, you would fail my class, fail to graduate, I think you are..." she said a few words in German. "Um..." she twisted her lips. "I'm trying to say you are a *warm-showerer*? Is this something you say in English?"

He knew what she meant. She'd said it before.

"Wimp," he said. "Sissy, wuss, candy-ass..."

Her eyebrow arched. "Candy-ass? I don't understand this."

"I'm very fragile, Christiane. And you're right, I love warm showers."

Her hand flew to her mouth. She was smiling, trying to hide it. A moment later, her hand dropped to the table. Her face was straight, but her eyes had changed. They looked, god what? Hopeful?

"Hey," he said, stepping toward her.

"What?"

"You got ink on your face."

"Hm?"

He rubbed her cheek with his thumb, still wet from filling up the mug.

"There," he said. "It's gone."

She blushed now. Sighing, "Please, please…"

He held his breath, as thoughts flashed toward a different ending—Christiane naked in bed. He kisses her neck…

"*Go*," she breathed, and then repeated it, twisting the butt of her cigarette in the ashtray. The glint in her eyes wasn't anything hopeful, just anger, pure anger, that's how it always ended: his chest in a knot again. Where there was a warm flow, an opening to somewhere else, her bed maybe, there was now a hard enclosure. He stepped back from the table, embarrassed, hands up. He crushed clothes and shoes and empty cigarette packs, muttering *Sorry, sorry…* She was still repeating *Go*, might have been screaming it, but his ears were closed. Too much, no more. He couldn't fit another thing in his head today. So let her yell and have her fit. After all, this was exactly how he'd wanted it: no goodbye, just a fuck you.

Out the door. Forgot to close it. Halfway down the hall it slammed. He jumped—bit his tongue. Salty tears, blood in his mouth, *Oh god*, he thought, coming down the stairs, *that kid, she's still there*. In the doorway, peering out at him. He made a grim, ugly face at the brat, grimmer and uglier than the one he'd given her on the way up.

And you know what the girl did? Nothing, she did nothing. She didn't look away and continued staring right at him. What did it take to keep people off your back? To keep them from watching your every movement? Yip, yap, growl, howl—did he have to *bark* at her? Yowling at the girl like a wild dog, he watched her erupt into giggles as he passed her. She fell to her hands and knees.

She too cried out—

"Hawoooooh!"

His heart rose up. Just a little girl, just a little one. He pushed open the apartment building's front door.

Outside, in the cold, windy yard, his mood turned black: there was nowhere left to go, he realized, but down, down, further until he reached his gran's basement.

TUESDAY

EDWARD AWOKE. Had he just dreamed? He couldn't remember. Something about lying in bed in his childhood home, trying to masturbate but nothing came. Now the memory or dream dissolved into dimly lit objects and arranged themselves in fixed positions above him. He stared up at wicker baskets hanging from the rafters of the ceiling, while grabbing his dick, finishing.

He moved on reflex, no thoughts to accomplish, no decisions to make. He slid off a sock. Cleaned up what he could. Then he lifted his achy body up from the sleeping bag and stumbled around the baskets on the floor, the baskets in boxes and the baskets in other baskets until he was standing in front of the basin sink, turning on the tap.

He pissed in it. Then lathered his chest and armpits with the wet bar soap and mopped up the suds with a towel. Now he smelled like artificial cherry and mildew. Grimacing, tossing the towel aside, he cupped his hands under the cold stream and splashed his face. The cold caused him to hoot in shock. He shook and blubbered his cheeks—he froze: a creak, a groan, a whelp of floorboards above him, and then his ears picked up a succession of mucculent coughs. With water dripping down his chin onto his bare chest, he groped for the tap, turned it off.

Gran was up already? He heard her, in the kitchen above, talking to herself.

"Oh god. Oh my god..."

Back at his sleeping area, he put on clothes and stuffed the one cummy sock in his pocket. He zipped up his jacket. The sleeping bag he rolled up and repacked inside the large Maytag box that held his dead pop-pop's camping gear. Looking around, he checked that no traces remained of his overnight stay.

He went to the basement stairs. There were two. He stood between them, reminding himself which was which. A mistake would be terrible. The left stairs went up to Gran's kitchen where she would just be sitting down at the breakfast table with her muddy Taster's Choice and various pink and white pills. If he went up those stairs, stepping out into the fluorescent light... Gran would see him. She wouldn't scream in surprise—she'd just go white.

The right staircase led him out into the backyard, dark and cool this morning. The door closed behind him with a feeble groan. The lock stuck at first. Then the key went back under the pot of desiccated thistles, and he was down on all fours, feeling the new shoots against his palms, passing under the kitchen window where Gran usually sat.

Reaching the side yard, he stood up and walked among dead rose bushes—

That car in the driveway. He paused. It wasn't blue. Gran's car was blue. This might be blue, but it wasn't. It was covered in grime, totally filthy. He could practically hear Gran, as if she were standing right next to him. *Whose car is that? That's your car. No, whose car is that? Your car, that's your car,* as he walked around the car, *that's how little your family cares about you. We let your car get like this. Can't even see the color, it's blue, you wouldn't know, you couldn't guess. You'd say blue because of a very distant memory, but all you could say with certainty about your filthy little coupe is that it's car-shaped...*

As a murmuring, a voice interrupted his thoughts. A television playing? But Gran rarely had it on this early. He looked across the lawn, in through the living room's picture window, which was, this morning, a golden rectangle. Every lamp was lit. All billion table

lamps—the *torchiere*, the *port-o-call*, even the goddamn *six-way*. On
the end table was a glittering martini glass, a jeweled jar of olives pits.
Gran had made a night of it then. Stayed up late watching assholes
sell knives and jewelry. Or else she looked out the window, saw the
filthy car, and spent the night consumed with dire thoughts—oh
god, god! What the neighbors must think of her!

Edward ran up the porch, tried the door—

He popped his head in, peering down the entryway, straight
through to the kitchen nook. Gran wasn't there. Her pills were on
the breakfast table—but instead of her head he saw the window
and a view of the backyard, its bushes and lawn in shambles.

To his right, sounds of the morning news, but no Gran.

To his left, a toilet flushed. He stepped forward, looking down
the dark hall.

The bathroom door was rimmed in light.

"Anybody home?" he called out.

"*Who's that?*" Her voice was muffled.

"Edward," he said.

"*Edward, OK, it's Edward. Give me a minute here!*"

In the kitchen, he opened cupboards, pushing past salt canis-
ters and laxatives for the Ring Dings.

He called out, "You want coffee?"

No reply.

"Gran?"

"*Yeah?*"

"Coffee?" He unwrapped a Ring Ding.

"*Oh—do whatever!*"

He bit into the cake. Something in her voice felt...off. Something about it was a little too...hyper. Like she wasn't breathing,
but frothing. She hadn't even quizzed him, *What, who? What are
you doing here? What are you making me to eat?* Always the first things
out of her mouth, one followed the other and he needn't reply, so
quickly would she say, *There's money in my wallet. Go buy eggs and
cheese and potato chips...* Edward licked the cream and crumbs from

the Ring Ding off his fingers as he walked out of the kitchen and into the hall. A foot away from the bathroom door, he stopped. Smelled...

Oh whoa. Wow. He covered his nose and mouth.

"Gran?" His knuckles rapped against the door.

"*Don't come in!*"

"Gran..."

"*Edward, it's terrible.*"

There was no breath to her voice. No wind.

"Are you decent?"

"*It's never happened like this. I had no time. No warning.*"

"Gran, I'm coming in now."

She moaned. "*Oh god, oh god, oh...*"

He pushed the door open. Her shit was everywhere. It was on everything. It was very black, very thin, like oil. She was standing in the middle of it. Christ, there was so much of it. All over her robe and slippers. And the walls, how the hell had it gotten up there?

She was fully clothed, thank god. Her hands covered her eyes, as she stood a foot from the toilet bowl. "Are you *laughing*?" she gasped.

Just gagging. The smell was unbelievable. What had she eaten?

"Come on." He waved a hand. "Let's get out of here."

"I have to clean it!" she cried out.

"You'll be in here all summer!"

She moaned. "Well, *you* aren't going to clean it!"

He moaned too, realizing he would have to.

So he had her strip off her soiled robe and soiled slippers and throw them in the bathtub. She was in her nightie now, and that was clean—thank God. Christ keep him from undressing her. He had her walk on the clean bath towels he'd spread across the floor, in order to reach the door. Her gnarled feet padded across the towels, and then she grabbed him. They walked together. He got her into the kitchen and sat her down at the table and told her to stay right there, "Hell, don't do anything." He didn't know why he said it so severely. Her eyes filled up with tears. She started to say she was sorry, but he surprised them both by kissing her head, the top of it, at least her hair smelled good, like baby powder, felt like silk, her shit had been smooth too, coating the walls like runny yolks. His stomach turned. *Man, are you trying to gross yourself out?* And he left her there.

In the bathroom, he cleaned it all up with paper towels, three rolls that filled a garbage bag, and while scrubbing all surfaces with watered-down ammonia, a memory came to him. He was at the babysitter's house. He pooped in her bed, and his mom drove him home. She was incensed. *You're too old for this! What's wrong with you?* But he wasn't embarrassed, his mom couldn't shame him. He was incredibly angry at her and had this feeling that it was all over. There was nothing that his mom could say to make things right between them.

While spraying all-purpose cleaner everywhere, he thought that's basically how he felt last night. That's basically what happened at Christiane's. She wanted to shame him, wanted him to feel embarrassed, but she couldn't, he wasn't, so she kicked him out. Edward might as well have been four again. Christiane might as well have been his mother in the driver's seat: *You're too old for this! Too old!* All this really meant was *I don't understand you. Don't tell me, I don't want to know.* Like his mom, Christiane couldn't stand Edward's problems, she couldn't bear them. She said to him, *Tell me all your problems,* when really she wanted him to protect her from his problems and from her problems and from all problems, all of this together. That was the problem with Christiane.

Edward took the soiled laundry down into the basement. *She shits all over me, then tells me I stink.* He took each soiled article of clothing out of the bag and dropped them, slippers and robe and towels, into the machine.

Edward really only felt close to Gran. They shared a code. She knew basically nothing about him and he knew basically nothing about her and the things they did know about each other, they didn't let bother them. Best not to presume anything. And ignore the family rumors. There was no misunderstanding and there could be no misunderstanding and, in this way, he and Gran were connected through their mutual sense of privacy.

Edward dumped detergent in the washer. He twisted the dial, dropped the hatch. While the machine ran, he took his journal out of his jacket pocket and began writing. *Digging deeply into any relationship is digging its grave. You exhume nothing: You grow exhausted, you lie down in your deep hole, and you starve...*

When the timer buzzed, he pulled out the wet tangle of clothes from the wash and stuffed it all in the dryer. He punched the on-button, and the machine began to moan and tremble. He smelled (not) himself. All he could smell was Gran's shit. He didn't see any of it on him, but he couldn't smell anything but Gran's shit. He looked around and saw all the old flannel shirts in the baskets. Forty years of flannel shirts. Sweat stains that were older than him. Ketchup and toothpaste and coffee and grease and chocolate and alcohol and milk and blood and cum and mud and grass stains that were twice, triple, his age. It blew his mind. Gran saved these, all these years she'd kept them. If it weren't so banal, he'd say it was insane. He stripped down to his boxers. Threw his stinking clothes into the basin sink (he couldn't bear to mix them in the washer with the other things)—but his jacket, that smelled, eh, fine. He carefully laid the garment on the washer. Then he walked around baskets and baskets, picking out things to wear.

He chose a green flannel shirt, and walked around, looking for pants. *I should get back in the habit of coming here*, he thought as he stepped into a pair of jeans. *I think better at Gran's.*

Absentmindedly, he began to recite a bit from "The Waste Land," a portion from the second section—

Richmond knew Mrs. her sat DEAD
Reflecting the she, lack the SAID
Oh the moment
Madame violet all and sterile and dead
Drip out to
window, slippers,
ceiling.
Dead
dead
' cold,
nothing said.
Exploring five finger-nails wisest twit Richmond
turns back
said, Der Do
 said,
 DA
DA
said,
 und can a Weialala
HURRY
 You!

in run friends,
beating Alexandria
came William Unshaven,
Sweet Philomel, coming
Sweeney tumbled there on something Unguent,
crying
The of? the shall WHAT
From hermit-thrush of coming cold public THUNDER

Back upstairs, Edward found Gran in the living room, sitting on the sofa, barefooted, in her nightie still. The way she hunched, her head seemed broken at the neck.

He stooped a little to catch her eye. "I got this shirt from the basement. Is it my dad's or Uncle Curt's?"

Her eyes flickered up to him. "Oh, who knows! I could never tell them apart."

She could never tell *what* apart? Her sons? Their shirts?

"My father is the short, hairy one," he reminded her, but Gran's mind was elsewhere. She held in one hand an unlit Marlboro. In her other hand, she held a gold-plated lighter, the one engraved with Pop-Pop's initials. She flicked the lighter on. She flicked it off.

"Listen, kid…" she began.

Then, a car outside, a motor shutting off. A door opened, and they both looked out the picture window.

Gran moaned. "Oh, now what? Who's that?"

Next to Gran's filthy little car was a bright red one. Edward's mom stepped out of it.

"Shit," Edward hissed.

Gran sank into the sofa cushions. "Kid…"

"Yeah?"

"*Don't tell her.*"

His eyebrows rose, as if in question, and her own little stubs shot up.

"Oh you know what I'm talking about!"

He rolled his eyes. "You're nuts to be worried. My mom has seen it all with my—" but he swallowed the word *sister*, realizing that mere embarrassment wasn't the point. Gran's independence was at stake. Her privacy and ability to manage her own life would be lost upon the intervention of someone as dangerous as Josephina Moses.

"But yeah." He coughed. "Sure."

Gran had managed to light the cigarette. Now she frowned at it. Her daughter-in-law was coming up the walk. Her hand extended, waving the cigarette at Edward. "Here, take it!"

"Gee, thanks," he said, picking it from her fingers. The doorbell rang, the front door opened, and Edward was in the kitchen, just approaching the backdoor, when his mom exclaimed—

"*Cripes, Marie! It's nearly noon, and you're still in your PJ's!*"

Now, standing in the tall grass of the backyard, he took a few drags on the Marlboro, then watched it burn down to his fingertips—

The fire nipped him. He flicked the butt into the grass, holding his breath as, behind him, the back door creaked open, banged shut.

There she was, stepping through the grass in her ridiculous clogs.

His mom got a few feet from him and stopped. Her eyes narrowed.

"Is that one of Pop-Pop's old shirts?"

"Hi, Mom," he said. "Nice clogs."

"Uh-huh. Right, right. So, what have you been up to this morning?"

He shrugged. "Not much."

"Come over here for breakfast?"

"Yeah."

"Everything…smells fine to you?"

He looked her in the eyes. "Gran's toilet was backed up."

"And you fixed it," she said, large eyelids snapping.

"I did."

Her eyes rolled. "Fine, you're not talking, she's not talking. Whatever."

But he had to give his mom something. She'd keep sniffing around until he did.

"I…"

His mom turned back around, halfway to the house. "What's that?"

"I broke up with the girl I was seeing."

Her eyes widened. "Oh terrible! I liked Helen."

He frowned. "Helen? I didn't break up with Helen."

She batted her lashes. "So…?"

He shrugged.

"So you're still dating Helen," she said, voice flat.

"No! Christiane, I broke up with Christiane."

Her neck stuck out. "What happened to Helen?"

His head shook. "I don't know Helen, I don't know a single Helen!"

"Edward Allen, come on. You brought her over. Last Thanksgiving she brought a pecan pie."

"Helen?"

"Oh yes she did! The pie was amazing. Absolutely, and I got a *Thank You* card from her. All these months it's been on the fridge."

He said, thinking of his cousin, "That girl came with Peter."

"Well no, Peter was there. Helen was... You sat next to Helen. You two acted like we weren't even there. Like we were all there at the table for the same reason as the veggies and spoons."

Edward shrugged. "Helen was OK. But the new girl Peter is dating is cooler."

"No! Peter broke up with her?"

"Ages ago. Eons. He couldn't stand all the baking. Hey, where's my sister, Ma? Where are you hiding her?"

Her eyes fluttered shut. "Ah crap. That's right." She rolled her wrist around, blinking down at her watch. "Shoot." She looked back at the house. "I've got to pick your sister up from H.U.G.S."

"*H.U.G.S.?* Are you kidding me?" He had an image of his adult sister, short and obese and wrinkled among the young bright children, fighting over Lego blocks.

His mom looked back at him, eyes in little slits. "You don't even know. She helps out. We're saying she's a *volunteer*."

"Dad agreed to this?"

"I need a few hours in the morning! It's not like I tell her she's *going* to daycare. It's like a job for her, she thinks of it as a job, that *she's* watching the children. Ah come on! I get it from you, I get it from your father. You and your father and that old lady in there, you should all just go off on an island together."

Edward laughed.

"See how long you last!" She half-smiled, a wary smile, unsure if he was laughing at her, or maybe just laughing. It was amazing to him that it should always be unclear to her.

She left him, not bothering to go back inside the house, but walking around it, through the side yard. Calling over her shoulder, she hollered, "Don't wake Gran up! She was just starting to doze when I came out here."

As he rubbed his temples, an engine started up. Wheels crunched gravel. Bright red between the houses, his mom's car there, then gone.

He didn't move. Stayed still. Dread, in tiny tendrils, steamed off his shoulders. Faded, in the quiet yard.

Edward went back inside the house.

Opening all cupboards, calling out to Gran, "You want anything?"

No answer.

Swallowing Ring Dings, he walked into the living room—

Gran was up and smoking.

He lit one of her Marlboros and joined her, semi-aware of her soft, rapid panting. She puffed away, chest and cheeks inflating, deflating, while the rest of her body remained very still, rigid, neck and jaw and two tightly sealed eyes.

"I went to H.U.G.S., too, you know," Edward blurted. "That shitty country day camp. Do you remember how old I was? God, I couldn't stand it. The way they white-knuckle the kids' shoulders as they say they say they *love* children, *all* children, *God bless the children!* So messed up. These people think they love children, but they can't stand them. They think it's adults who suck, but really they've got a bad attitude about people. I mean, you've got to be totally pathetic and spiritually stunted to want to yell at my sister all day."

He thought for a moment. His mom, how was she different?

Elbows on his knees, he flicked ash into Gran's pit-filled martini glass. "My mom, on the other hand, is one of those people who say that children are, by and large, totally unremarkable, completely and totally *whatever*—except for her daughter. Her daughter is different.

"And she's right," he said, leaning back. "Viv *is* different, she's *Mom's*. My mom treats her like a little Shih Tzu she can just tuck away or pull out when she needs to. Sometimes she takes Viv out for air. Sometimes she *walks her*, but mostly she just tucks her away and suffocates her.

"And the thing is, Viv is like a little puppy, like in the best way. There's never been a human with more capacity for joy than my sister. She's just like…good."

Gran nodded.

"Right, *you* get it," he said.

"Children are wonderful," she said, "just wonderful."

"No! They are not wonderful. They cannot be wonderful. *A kid* can be wonderful. But all kids are not categorically—" He jumped up, surprised, as the embers of his cigarette fell across his lap, slightly burning him. He swatted at his pants and then the sofa cushions. "Sorry! I think these are Pop-Pop's pants. I think they're OK. I don't see any burns. The sofa seems OK…"

Gran was saying something, murmuring, "But it'll all sort itself out. Once your sister's older…"

"What's that?" he asked, and then his stomach sank: a black burn mark on an embroidered pillow. Ah god, if Gran saw that, she'd freak out. She was murmuring again—*Once your sister's older*, which didn't make sense, of course. Viv *was* older, thirty-five years old. But he wasn't really paying attention, arranging the cushions in such a way that Gran might not discover the burnt one.

"It's the same with old people," he said, putting this pillow here and that pillow there, then trying a whole new arrange-ment. "When people are like, *Aw old people are so cute*. It's a really demeaning thing to say. It's really—"

Gran was snoring, her body slumped back and her head tipped sideways and ah shit, her cigarette slipping out of her fingers. He plucked it from the folds of her nightie. Her eyelids fluttered halfway, but she kept on snoring. Her mouth came partially open. He looked away, slightly annoyed she had conked out on him, and located the throw on the floor. He got it and covered her body from shoulders to toes. Those toes, good god. His stomach flipped at the sight. Purple-grey and swollen. Like small, sporing mushrooms.

He crept out of the living room.

On the kitchen table, next to the pill bottles, he saw the note his mom had left.

Marie.
Your DL expired last month.
NO driving until renewed!!

Gran's driver's license was next to the note. The license was in two pieces. Unbelievable. His fingers pushed one severed half up the table. His mom had actually cut up Gran's license. It wasn't enough for her to forbid Gran from driving, she had to go through her purse and find and cut up her license. What would Gran think when she saw it? Already she was upset about her car being filthy. Hell, Gran would have gotten it washed weeks ago, but couldn't, because uh duh, her license had expired. But here his mom had to come and pull this bullshit power play, rubbing it in Gran's nose, leaving the old girl with even less control of the car situation than she had before. *Bullshit, bullshit, total bull—*

Edward grabbed the notepad and dashed off a note of his own.

Gran.
Your car is filthy.
But we can get it washed togeth

He paused, heart racing, with the pencil point on *togeth*. This wasn't right. His mom's note next to his note, they didn't fit together. Hers cheapened his. He dropped the pen, crumpled his note. Best not to make a big deal of it. Best to just borrow her car and get it cleaned without her.

Gran, I'm borrowing your car. Thanks.

He riffled around Gran's purse for her keys, then remembered they wouldn't be in there—she always kept her car keys in the ignition. *That way, kid, I'll never lose 'em!* He took the bag of sunflower seeds from her purse. The flavor was—yes! It was Dill Pickle! His mouth began to water as he stuffed the bag under his armpit. On his way out, he passed the living room to check if Gran were, as certain members of his witless family liked to put it, *still breathing.* He found her still asleep, snoring powerfully.

Now he was outside, sitting in Gran's car, all ready to go. His seatbelt on, his hands on the steering wheel.

Edward had a thought, then a second thought, which dragged the first thought down immediately. Now a third: he was thinking how this always happened. His negative thoughts dragged all his good thoughts down. Or if they didn't, then his good thoughts were dragged down by the thought that he'd thought through all this before. That was massively depressing. But what had he thought in the first place? *It's lucky I have the car today…* That was it! The good thought! But before he could enjoy it, he was thinking of *all the things I have to do.*

A thin salty slick of perspiration covered Edward's face. He licked his lips. *The thought of ALL suppresses THE GOOD,* he thought. *Shit man, write that down.* Reaching into his jacket pocket, he pulled out his journal. Searching for the first blank sheet, he stopped cold. There, right before the entry he had made while doing laundry, was the to-do list he had made before falling asleep last night:

GET THE SHOEBOX
CONFRONT RYAN

"Shit, shit! Shit cocksucker!"

Edward threw down the notebook, looking up, looking out the—fucking fuck. The windows. He couldn't see out—they were all filthy, grimy, he cranked the driver's window down and then the passenger's and leaned into the back, searching for the cranks but there weren't any: god the windows back here were flip-open. *This is a death trap, I am in a death trap,* he thought, and started the car. He located, a minute passed, the switch for the windshield wipers.

Edward drove to Ted's with the bag of Spitz open between his knees. He grabbed a handful at a time and spat the shells out the open window, sometimes missing and hitting the car door or armrest or even the steering wheel but really not giving a fuck. He could see the road, kinda. Thanks to the wipers, he could peek out a half-rainbow smear of glass. He got to Ted's at 6:30 p.m. Ah what? That couldn't be right. Looking away from the clock in the dashboard, he stuck his head out the window and squinted up at the bright sun that was either burning directly above or a smidgen to the right. So it was noon, around noon. That was really perfect, yeah. He had come at the right time: all the roomies would be out, Ted at class, Eli at work, he could slip in, get the shoebox, unnoticed, easy-peasy cheesy...

Pulling the keys out of the ignition and giving them an ironical little toss and thinking:

No.

No no no.

Not his keys, Gran's keys. His keys weren't in his jacket pocket either. They weren't in his pants. Had he left them...? At Grans? At Christiane's? Ugh, probably. He slumped back in the seat.

He could drive over. He could drive over to her apartment right now and look for his keys. Christiane would be there. She'd be sitting at the table, a red pen in hand, grading the finals. He would just be coming for the keys, but she'd think he was there to make up the final he missed. *Have you come to beg me for a makeup?* No, fuck no. He didn't care about her class. He didn't care if she failed him. "A Couch of One's Own: Psychoanalysis and Writing." Christ, the name alone. He only took it because he'd already read all the novels on the syllabus. It was going to be a class of zero reading and zero thinking. But as it happened, he'd actually learned a valuable lesson, thanks to that class. He'd put time and money toward getting an English degree, and in the end, he saw that it was all worthless. Graduate, don't graduate. It made no difference. In either case, he'd be looking for work next week, finding no employers that would take him, and he'd be forced to crawl back to college to study some subject that was vile to him, like law, or uninteresting to him, like medicine, or one that was both vile and uninteresting, like business, or one that was vile and uninteresting and hypocritical and bad for the world, like teaching. He would kill himself before he taught. Yes. Teachers, all teachers, even the most idealistic teachers who went into the profession swearing they'll be different, earned their keep by bashing in kids' brains until they were insipid and soft-minded enough to cope with capitalism. *I'll have no part in that shit.*

He was still trying to decide what to do when a light went on in the apartment building. Edward counted the windows. Three, four, five—yes! That was his old room! Edward pumped his fist and got out of the car, ran across the street. His thumb hit the buzzer for apartment 4F.

Across the intercom came static, then a voice—

"*Hello? Yes? Is this thing on?*"

"Eli, let me up!"

"*Is that Edward?*"

"Yeah, yeah, buzz me!"

The intercom crackled. Eli seemed to hesitate.

Edward took a deep, deep breath. "Eli, I just need to get something. The shoebox, man. It's in the trash. Can you get it?"

"*Your box isn't here.*"

"WHAT?"

"*Ted took it.*"

"Did he open it?"

"*Well—*"

Edward stared at the intercom. "Eli?"

Nothing.

"Eli man, you gotta keep holding the button down!"

Nothing.

"ELI. HOLD THE BUTTON DOWN."

Then Eli was back, mid-sentence. "*… Kev came by and asked how I was liking* The Ludes *he gave me. And I was like, firstly,* The Ludes? *What's that? Sounds awesome. Secondly, when did you give me these…*"

Edward cut in. "Did you open the shoebox?"

"*… So I'm wondering is it really your diary in there? Because, you know, Kevin said that yesterday he gave you* The Ludes *and I'm wondering if that's the package…*"

Edward walked back toward the car. Unbelievable. Ted had taken the shoebox out of the apartment. But to where? Lunch? The cafeteria? A bar? Why take the shoebox to a bar? Why take the shoebox anywhere at all?

Thinking these things, thinking and thinking and sitting very still in Gran's car with the door closed. Eventually his fingers crawled to the center console and undid the latch. He was flicking the silver lighter, the one with Pop-Pop's initials, flame on, flame off.

The campus?

Edward turned the car on, and started driving in the general direction of campus.

… Eli had wanted to open the shoebox last night. He had wanted to, but Ted hadn't let him.

At a stoplight, red. The light turned green. A horn honked.

… Ted had no interest in the shoebox. And yet he had taken it out of the apartment.

More honking, the light still green. Honking from all sides. Edward frowned.

… There was no reason for Ted to take the shoebox.

Unless… Eli, fuck, fuck! He'd lied, the little fucker. They *had* opened the shoebox, they *had* seen what was inside, and goddamn Ted had taken it to the goddamn newsroom.

He stamped on the gas, zooming under a yellow light.

Edward reached the campus minutes later, whizzing into Visitor's Parking. He glanced at the cars as he zipped down the aisles. Shit, shit fucker: every spot was taken. Looking at the license plates—*Ohio, Ohio, Ohio, Ohio, Ohio.*

"Go back to OHIO, you bucking fuckeyes!" He yelled as he spun the wheel around, now zooming down the first row.

A handicap spot. He pulled in, slammed the brakes, and Gran's handicap decal fell off the rearview mirror. He cut the engine and his gaze cut to the passenger seat, where the precious handicap decal lay. He grabbed it. Hung it up, it fell. He tried again, it fell, tried again, it was hanging, wasn't going to fuckin—it fell. Goddamn. He threw the decal on the dashboard. And then he was out of the car, running up the walk.

Now stopping, turning. Now running *back* to the car. Christ, the windows, he left them down! *Thank god I remembered*, as he ran back over. *Don't want to think about what might've happened. Don't think about it, man. Don't even*, as he thought of how the school was overrun with jerks who would not hesitate to steal a handicap decal or—his blood chilled—Gran's car. *Oh god*, he thought, running his hands down his face, imagining how bad it would feel to come back to the parking lot and see the empty space…*My god. Stolen. Her car's been stolen. Never should have driven it to campus, never should have left Gran's. But you did, you did, you left the windows down! Your fault. All on you! The people here are liars and thieves and you all but invited them to walk all over you! Idiot!…* Edward was vibrating inside the Business Administration building, in the doorway to the newsroom, a small room, throwing his gaze at all the desks crammed in there. These were cold, metal desks, brutal and fascist-looking. Each had a green Selectric and each was covered in papers and pens and books and greasy old food things—pizza boxes, white Styrofoam, brown paper bags. Miserable people. Journalists were disgusting. It took three months away from this place—since he was fired, *freed*—for him to finally see the newsroom for the cesspit it was.

His breath caught. On Ted's desk, between the Doonesbury mug and the Snoopy bobblehead doll and on top of the battered copy of *The Electric Kool-Aid Acid Test*, was the shoebox.

Edward could see, before he even picked up the shoebox, that it was still sheathed in duct tape, rolls and rolls. Could Ted have taken all the tape off, piece by piece, then taped everything back up in exactly the same way? Crazy. But possible! But who had the patience for that? Ted would've said *fuck it* in the first few seconds and reached for a knife.

But *were* there any knives in the apartment? Damn, they didn't even own scissors. And so that's it. That's why Ted brought the shoebox to the newsroom: *there were scissors here.*

OK. Wow. Ted was probably looking for scissors this very moment. Possibly in the supply closet. Both doors were closed.

… Ted inside one room… Ryan inside the other…

Looking around, Edward was suddenly very uncomfortable. Where was everybody? He'd never seen the newsroom deserted like this. There was always somebody here, four in the morning, four in the afternoon, didn't matter when, you couldn't work or think in peace. *Nobody here but us chickens*, Gran would say. Poor Gran. So tired this morning. She had totally conked out. But earlier… *Holy shit*, the bathroom door swung open. Gran knee-deep in shit. On her legs, feet, between her toes. The look on Gran's face. Oh christ he felt so bad for her. He wanted to hug her right now. He wanted her to be OK. Would she be up by now? Was she hungry? Why not get out of here, go see her? Take the car over to the wash, then bring it home. Make Gran lunch. That sounded pretty good to him. Yeah, he was starving.

Damn, I'm so hungry I'd eat that grapefruit on Carl's desk...

Edward took up the grapefruit and peeled it. He tore off a wedge and took a bite and the tang shot through his head and he immediately felt guilty. What was he thinking? He couldn't go back to Gran's. He had accomplished nothing, eh, not nothing, one thing, he'd accomplished *one thing*, the first on his to-do list. He had the shoebox, yes. He had kept Ted from opening it, yes. Ted hadn't learned Edward's secret and he would die without knowing—they all would, they would all die in ignorance, darkness, as to the truth of Roger Ackroyd's identity, and that was how it should be.

But that didn't change the other thing...

Edward's fingernails tore off another segment of grapefruit: horrible. Unthinkable. He could kill that poser, he was pretty sure which poser—Ryan, that prig, of course he was the one pretending to be Roger Ackroyd. Reading the Poet's fan mail. Writing back to that girl, making her fall in love with him. The poser had stolen Edward's identity. Well, basically.

Oh yeah? Prove it.

Edward, imagining Ryan say this, paled.

All the wind rushed out of his lungs. He slumped back in Carl's desk chair, feeling totally defeated, totally fucked. Edward couldn't simply accuse Ryan and expect him to *cave*. No, he had to catch Ryan *doing it*, had to catch Ryan in the act of *replying* to the Poet's fan mail—or, at the very least, he had to catch Ryan *reading it*.

Edward dropped the grapefruit. A letter—a letter written to Ryan and addressed to the Poet. Yeah, that was good, kinda great. Ryan would open the letter, read it, and know he'd been found out. Actually a fucking feasible idea. Ha ha, yeah, you're fucked, Ryan!

Edward rolled a sheet into the typewriter and slammed out—

```
Hi Roger Ackroyd . . . I mean Ryan.
Gotcha, shithead.
Edward.
```

He pulled the sheet out. Read it over. *Gotcha?* Lame. Weak. And why the fuck was there a period after Edward's goddamned name?

Trashed it. Rolled another sheet.

```
Hey, asshole, guess what
```

Too chatty.

```
Dear Asshole,
```

Right. Because Ryan's asshole is dear to you.

```
Fuckface: Quit answering mail that isn't
yours. Edward.
```

Ah shit, that period again. And it should just say *Ryan*, right? None of this *Asshole, Fuckface* shite because like, how else would *Ryan* know that *Ryan*, not The Poet, was the one really being addressed?

Eleven attempts later: Edward was folding up an entirely blank sheet of paper and stuffing it in the envelope addressed to Ryan with Gran's return address, thinking—*Genius!* Ryan would see this and know Edward knew and his knowing Edward knew was enough right now because citrus was for shit. So hungry. Couldn't think straight. He tossed the grapefruit in the trash. Real food—needed it.

Licked and sealed the envelope and intended to write the Poet's name as the addressee but hesitated. *Ah come on, just write it, it's easy, write the goddamned name, you aren't compromising anything, just for chrissakes write the goddamn—*

He scribbled: *Roger Ackroyd*. It was legible, barely. Standing, walking around desks, he made his way to Ryan's office. Held his fist up to knock.

His eyes flickered up to the nameplate, the assignation *Editor-in-Chief*.

He grabbed the knob and pulled the door open.

And in the little room, Edward saw…people. The office was crammed with guys, girls, mostly guys, like Carl sitting on the floor next to Jeff. Christ, they were all here, every writer and reporter and editor on staff. His coworkers—ex-coworkers—were all looking down at the clipboards in their laps. They were filling out this, uh, what was that—a test? Filling it out with identical expressions of exaggerated absorption, brows in knots, mouthing their No. 2 pencils. Ryan wasn't among them. Man, he really wasn't here. Behind Ryan's desk sat a feature writer and the sportswriter. To the first four questions on the form, the sportswriter had checked the boxes, *Yes, Yes, Yes, Yes.*

Edward whispered, "Hey..."

"Shh!" someone hissed—fucking Georgie. Christ, Georgie. She sat on an upturned trash can.

"I'm looking for..." Edward mumbled. "Do you all know where..."

No one was paying any attention to him.

Edward cleared his throat and said, in a booming voice, "Hey kids! What are we all doing?"

Everyone looked up and silently glared. *Eddie, god, he's so inappropriate.* Georgie pressed her middle finger to her lips.

Fucking psychotic, Edward thought. But if Ryan had everyone in his office, he'd have to be nearby. Smoke break? But he didn't smoke. Bathroom?

Edward was winding through desks, headed for the newsroom's back exit, when he stopped and looked back at the office. He'd left the door open. Big mistake. Ryan's overbearing, frankly pervy insistence that all staff meetings be conducted in his tiny office had only one benefit, as far as Edward could tell: after the meeting, Ryan had to sit in an office that smelled terrifically foul. But now, thanks to Edward's fuck-up, the perfectly ripened air dissipated, mixing with the ink and paper and vague cheese smells of the newsroom. Unless Ryan *liked* it when his office stunk. What if he got off on their stink? Ah god. Oh it was too much.

Edward opened the door to the hallway, stepping out.

Voices, vague, echoing.

Near the exit, Ryan and Ted stood talking together, turned

in such a way that you could see the corners of their eyes but not their faces. Hard to tell who was speaking. Both throats wobbled. Long necks tensing, flexing… Edward got the chills imagining their faces without any mouths, a smooth sheet of skin from their chins to their eyes.

Then Ted looked back, nodding at Edward.

"*Fuck you,*" Edward mouthed, just as Ted mouthed, "*You're welcome.*"

Edward's chest tightened. *You're welcome?* A look of surprise, then pure loathing, flashed across Ted's face.

Ryan clapped Ted on the shoulder. "All right, buddy! Catch you later."

Edward ducked back inside, face burning, hands shaking. What was with Ted's hurt expression? *You're welcome?*

At a random desk, Edward chose not to sit or stand, but to lean, sway, bounce in his shoes. He set the shoebox down. He picked it back up. He straightened the letter resting on top of it, and then he pushed the letter off-center so it looked more casually placed.

Ryan came in through the door.

"Eddie Moses. OK, sure. Hi there."

Edward started forward. "I have a letter. I was, am, hoping to get it to… Roger Ackroyd," he finished, in a mutter.

Ryan cocked his head. "Sorry? Didn't catch that?"

Edward's face burned. "I've got a letter for Roger Ackroyd!"

"Hm, yeah, I thought that's what you said."

Edward licked his lips. "So? Can you get it to him?"

Ryan's head lolled around. "Yeah no. Yeah I can't do that for you."

"Why?"

Ryan pushed his glasses up his nose. "Oh Eddie, you have to have *somewhat* of an idea why. The Poet's a private guy. Doesn't like to be bothered."

Liar.

"So what you're saying is," Edward growled, "you *could* give the Poet my letter, but you won't do it."

Ryan grinned. "In so many words."

"Bullshit."

Ryan's smile froze. "Heh?"

"You don't have an address for him! Why are you pretending you do?"

Behind him, Edward heard some tittering, some fucking tee-hees, then a throat cleared. He glanced back. The staff was gathered at the door of Ryan's office, leaning forward to get a good view.

Edward slapped the letter across Ryan's chest.

"Put it with all *the others*," Edward growled.

Edward kicked out of the back door of the building, emerging among the dumpsters. His chest was heaving. There were some cardboard boxes that hadn't been broken down yet. He kicked them, and his foot hit something hard when he expected it to go straight through.

Shooting pain up his leg.

"Fuck!"

"Whoa," a voice said. "Easy, easy…"

Recognized the voice. Smelled the weed. And he looked away from his poor throbbing foot to see her, Katie, between two dumpsters. She was perched on a book carton, legs daintily crossed, thigh on thigh. Such a tiny person. So much hair. In bed with her, he liked to tug on her curls, wrap one around his finger and stretch it out into a long taut strand.

Katie tipped her head back, blowing up a smooth stream of smoke.

"Eddie… What's up?"

The shoebox, shit, he wasn't holding it. He looked around. Behind him, it was tipped on its side. Flattening some weeds growing out of the pavement.

"Just cleared out my desk," he heard Katie say, apropos of what? No question of his, that's for sure. He bent down to pick up the shoebox—in his jacket, he heard a soft crackling, felt a slight stiffness. There was something there. Edward touched his chest, recalling the small envelope in the inner pocket. Earlier today, hadn't Eli mentioned something about 'ludes? *Kevin said he gave them to you.*

Edward straightened, tucking the shoebox under his arm. Should he take one of the pills now? Why not? Half a pill. Just enough to chill out.

But there was Katie, holding out the joint.

"Want some? It's dipped."

In shit, he thought. He muttered, "What are you even doing here?" He'd have to go into the bathroom, take a pill there. He patted his pockets, searching for cigarettes, cigarettes, just one for the road…

His head whipped up. "Katie! What is it?"

She was screaming with laughter, cheeks and chin flaming, curls and breasts shaking, an arm raised up to hold the sherm above her head. Christ, what was her problem? She was so incredibly frightening sometimes, something super scary about her, like under her skin there wasn't just one person, but a fucking mob of egomaniacs and narcissists and maybe one or two actually nice people, but most just a bunch of sociopaths.

"Eddie," she said, catching her breath, "Wait, don't go! I have something to tell you!"

Her face was composed. Sincere, calm, it sickened him.

"I got the internship at the *Wall Street Journal*," she purred.

Oh Katie, you can't help yourself.

"I start this June, right away. I'm actually going to go back to my dorm right now to pack. I won't be around for the graduation ceremony."

He studied his cigarette. With Katie, you needed a team of people behind you, fact-checking everything she said. With Katie, you needed every last friend you had, reminding you to plug your ears with beeswax and run fast.

"That's it? You have nothing to say?" she asked.

He took a drag. He didn't care why she wrote those fake letters to the editor, or why she was lying to him now about the internship. He told her, "You always knew you could do it."

An expression—who could read it?—flashed across her face. She hung her head. "I can't believe you... You were just going to let me lie to you. You were just going to walk away." She looked up. Her voice grew desperate. "I don't understand. I don't understand anything!"

He groaned. "Katie, you're not the victim!" He crossed and uncrossed his arms, unsure if he should bother making the point. "What you did wasn't cool."

Her lips puckered.

He shook his head. "Well, if you can't see why, then I guess the only lesson is *don't get caught.*"

She snorted. "Ha. I'm the one who *told.*"

He blinked in surprise. "Really?"

A small nod. "Ryan and Ted don't know though. They think that *Amanda Pitts, Class of '80* is the person who outed me."

"And Amanda Pitts is...?"

"Another one of mine."

He laughed. "That's, well..." He was going to say *hilarious,* but that would only encourage her.

A smile broke across her face.

"What?" he asked.

"You don't think what I did is that bad!"

He shook his head. "What you did is just so..." He frowned. "I could understand plagiarism. But your thing? It's...well, it's nuts."

The smile dropped from her face. "No more so than Roger Ackroyd," she muttered.

His eyes narrowed. Why bring *that* up? Ted maybe... Did Ted tell her about their conversation in the kitchen?

Slowly Edward said, "The two things are not the same."

She rolled her eyes.

His face heated up. "Someone writes poetry under a literary pseudonym. Someone else talks shit about her friends and coworkers under a series of fake, assumed-to-be-real identities."

She held up her hand. "It's OK. Ryan and Ted already *spelled it out* for me. I got an hour-long lecture on how Roger Ackroyd is *sooo* different."

He nodded. "Right, because there's a public understanding that Roger Ackroyd isn't a real person."

Her eyebrows arched. "Really? Roger Ackroyd is just a name?"

"Whether we're talking about Roger Ackroyd or the person *behind* Roger Ackroyd, identity is a total fictitious thing, created by us, and the beauty of it, the purpose of it, is—"

"I *guess*," Katie interjected. "But most people think that Roger Ackroyd is just some guy. You think he's just some guy."

Edward frowned.

"I mean, is it really so hard to believe that Roger Ackroyd could be a *she*?"

He winced.

"Oh my," she murmured, "you can't bear the thought."

"The actual identity isn't the point," he snapped.

She tossed her head to the side. "Oh, *Eddie*..." Her tone was an insipid singsong. "I think you know there's something at stake here. I mean, Ryan and Ted were ready to throw themselves off the roof this morning when I told them that *I'm* the Poet."

He didn't hear her correctly. "You told them what?"

"I swear, it was same reaction as if I had told a Jesus Freak, *there is no God, your god is fucking dead!*"

"Wait, what did you tell them?"

She smirked. "I'm Roger Ackroyd."

"Katie..." He pointed back at the building. "... Katie, Katie, Katie. Fuck! You have to go in there and tell them you're kidding!"

"I am?"

"Christ, Katie!"

"Hi, yes, that's me."

He covered his eyes. "What did Ryan do?"

"I already told you. He was on his way up the stairs, ready to jump to his death. It just kills those jerks to think that a woman could write all that!"

"Katie!"

"*Edward*."

"This isn't a joke! You can't just go around saying that you're Roger Ackroyd. First of all, it isn't true."

Katie opened her mouth.

"And second of all—" His voice rose above hers. "Second—" His eyes widened. Was Katie writing to Mystery Girl? Was Katie the poser?

She pointed. "Who are *you* to tell *me*—"

"Who knows?"

She blinked. "Who knows what?"

He counted them off on four fingers: "Ryan, Ted, Edward— *me*. Who else knows about this?"

She bit her lip and exhaled. "No one," she said.

His jaw clicked.

"Not yet," she muttered.

His eyes closed. *Oh my fucking god.* "Have you written to anyone?"

"Huh?"

"Roger Ackroyd gets mail. The readers write to him. Have you ever replied?"

She shrugged. "I never bothered with it."

"OK," he exhaled, *OK OK*, "so when you told Ryan—"

She cut him off. "Ugh, you do this! You work everything to death!" She shook her head. "I don't want to talk about this anymore."

Her cheeks puffed away on her dwindling sherm. It was almost burnt to her fingers. Edward continued glaring at her, thinking of the other girl. Mystery Girl was, in his head, very hazy, possibly dark, possibly lovely, but everyone looked dark and lovely when they were blurry. In the letter, Mystery Girl had told the poser to meet her at *Blue of Noon*. Edward's chest tightened. Christ. If only he had kept the orange library book. Then the poser would have never read it. Then Ryan, the poser, wouldn't *be* at the play tonight, scanning the audience, spotting the girl in green sequins.

Hi, are you Mystery Girl? I'm Roger Ackroyd.

But what if Katie went to the play too? What if Katie were in the audience, actually seated right next to Mystery Girl? Then Ryan would freeze up. Seeing the person who he thought was actually Roger Ackroyd would keep Ryan from confronting Mystery Girl.

Wow... Edward exhaled. *That's it. Katie. Freaking Katie. She's the solution.*

"Katie," he said, wiping sweat off his brow, "do you remember that time we went to the Icehouse Theater?"

She stubbed the joint out on her shoe. She shrugged.

"Come on," he said. "I took you."

A long red fingernail scratched the side of her nose. "Eh, was it a play about aliens?"

"*Birds*," he said.

"Nope. Didn't see it."

He sucked in his breath. "Well, actually..." *Nah man, doesn't fucking matter, just drop it.* "...do you, uh, want to see a play with me tonight?"

She shrugged.

"You will?"

She was staring past his shoulder. "Hey, do you want to come back to my dorm?"

He touched his jacket, feeling for the pills. He really needed this now. He absolutely needed this now. He really fucking—

"I've got to use the restroom," he said.

"Sure. My dorm isn't even five minutes away."

"Cool, but..."

She leaned forward and said in a fake whisper, "You only go to certain bathrooms on campus, don't you?"

He said nothing.

A giggle rolled through her. "You only go to one bathroom. You have one special bathroom across all of campus." She was full on convulsing now, arms holding her stomach, hugging herself. "There's one special stall in one special bathroom in one special building on campus, and that's the one that Eddie Moses goes to shit in!"

He opened his mouth. And then he closed it.

She sighed, wiping her eyes. "So where is it?"

He said nothing.

"Oh come on, Eddie! There's no point in having secrets anymore! Graduation is in three days. We're all *leaving*."

His eyes scanned the dumpsters. "I'll meet you back here?"

"You're kidding me!"

"Your dorm room then?"

Her eyes rolled up. "Good grief!" she groaned, all the little tight curls on her head bouncing. "Fine."

OK, he thought, walking. *OK OK*, he thought, walking. *OK OK*, he thought, sitting, standing, flushing the toilet. He sat back down on the bowl in the last stall of the bathroom in the Student Union.

It was what Gran always said as she moved through the house. She touched a wall, *OK*. She went to another, touched another. *OK OK*, her voice moving through the house. He'd be in the basement, staring up at the ceiling. Then the creak of a chair, Gran's body easing in. *OK*, he'd say with her.

She had been OK when he left her this morning, hadn't she? He dropped his head into his hands. Again his stomach roiled.

That thing Gran had said right before he left, she hadn't been in her right mind, she hadn't been *OK*. They'd been in the living room, talking about his sister, and Gran had said that crazy thing: *everything would sort itself out once your sister's older.* It's what the family used to say about Viv when she was younger. *She'll never be normal, but it'll all sort itself out, you know, once your sister's older.*

But nobody said that about Viv anymore. They stopped saying that once Viv was into her twenties. And Edward, still a small kid, noticed the change, realized they weren't waiting for Viv to get older—*Viv is older. She's been older.* The family, hell—they were just waiting Viv out. But one morning they woke up, and *they* were older. And Viv? Just as she always was. Alive.

He lit a cigarette. Gran knew better. But she'd said it anyway: *once your sister's older.* The same shit the family had said years ago. The same weird and senile shit Gran had said just six months ago, after she had those so-called *mini-strokes.* OK. So maybe Edward had fucked up. Maybe he *shouldn't* have left Gran to nap on the sofa. Or maybe…it was nothing, absolutely… He did get upset like this sometimes. Out of nowhere, something flew into his brain and he would think, *Goddamn!* How could you possibly know the difference between what you felt and what was real?

He flicked the cigarette butt into the toilet bowl. Things were OK, they already were! Right? He had worked out a plan with Katie. They were going out tonight—to annihilate Ryan. And Gran, she had been tired this morning, but now she was up! She was watching *General Hospital*, leaning forward on the sofa, asking Rick and Ruby and Dr. Jeff, *What?! What are you doing?*

Edward took a blue pill. Dragged it down with all of his saliva. Probably it was enough. Probably. He stepped out of the bathroom, in search of a payphone.

He called Gran up. It rang and rang. And rang and rang and rang and he hung up. With shaking fingers, he dropped more coins into the slot and dialed his father's office.

The receptionist picked up on the first ring.

"Dr. Moses's office!"

"Is my dad around?"

"Sorry?"

He exhaled. "Is Dr. Moses in?"

"Is this Edward?"

Edward looked over his shoulder, for the clock. "What time is it?" he asked.

"It's two-thirty," she hesitated, finally adding, "p.m.?"

His shoulders loosened. He let out a long breath. *General Hospital* started at 3 p.m. Gran hadn't heard the phone because she was still napping.

The receptionist said, "Hello? Edward?"

Walking down the mall, halfway to Katie's, he stopped to light another cigarette. It was cool Gran didn't pick up because she was napping. He hated waking her up, hated when people woke them both up. Down in the basement, he heard a bang bang bang! He thought, *Who the fuck*, as above Gran shouted, *OK HOLD ON!* Naps. Yeah. He was smiling, imagining falling into the millions of pillows that Katie kept stacked on her bed. Nobody did pillows like Katie. Nobody napped like Katie. He took a drag of his cigarette. Already he was feeling it? He shouldn't be. *Faking yourself out man. Just, like, chill. A good thirty minutes, twenty-five to thirty minutes, that's how long it usually takes to get you…*

Floating through the lovely yellow. Closed and closed his eyes. Aware of his toes. Everything in his toes, all his concentration.

In front of her dormitory, pulling and pulling.

Someone walked by.

"Yeah," the voice said, "you have to push that door."

The voice pushed the door for him. Edward went in and up. He had a great spatial memory. That was the thing about Edward. He was great with space. He had a great mind for where things were located. Someone once told him that cats had that, too, that they were good with space. Birds too. Animals were cool.

He got to her door and knocked and the girl smiled at him.

"Hey, cutie. Katie is a few doors down. The one at the end…"

He flopped down on her bed. Stared up at the ceiling, slowly opening and closing his lids.

Katie was talking to him.

He turned his head to the side. He saw her hip. Right next to him.

A clipboard in her lap.

"Have you filled out one of these yet?" She tapped the end of the pen on the form.

No. He didn't know. What?

"It's the personality test everybody's taking. The administration gave one to every graduating senior. Apparently it's supposed to..." She talked and talked. She clicked the pen. Katie was so tiny. He liked to take one of her curls and stretch it out. He loved doing this.

She said, "Take it with me. You can write your answers next to mine."

He fingered the edge of her blanket.

"These tests aren't evil," she said. "They're not."

He was startled. His hand withdrew. Who said they're evil?

"You."

He shook his head.

"This is the Myers-Briggs," she said. "It's a big deal."

He laughed.

She sighed. "OK, Mr. Smart Guy. What's so wrong with this test?"

He smiled at her. She was really cute. He nuzzled his face into her many pillows. He finally said, "I don't think it's evil." He thought of his mom. "Mostly I don't think anything is evil."

"What about Hitler?"

He laughed again.

"Fuck you," she said. "What about *Pol Pot*?"

"Katie...what *about* Pol Pot?" He rubbed his eyes, trying to think of why he hated the Myers-Briggs. Did he hate it?

He said slowly, "We like tests. We take them, and they tell us, you are this, you are that, you are special..."

She snorted.

"...you belong in this world...and we hear this, and we feel validated. We find that we expect certain things. Of ourselves. Of other people. And we don't question..."

He felt the bed rise.

"...that we should work, work for money..." He lifted his head up. Katie was at her desk, taking the test, probably marking, *Yes, Yes, Yes.* He sighed. Who cares? Who knows? Why bother? It's all so brainless.

He rolled over to his side, burying his face in her pillows. He'd argued with Christiane about this. Three semesters ago. In the first week of the first class he ever took with her. They weren't dating yet. She didn't even know his name, and he only knew hers because it was on the syllabus. She had just passed out a test to figure out what kind of *learning personality* each student had. He sat all the way in the back, so he had to shout a bit for her to hear him.

This isn't helpful. He held up the test. *This doesn't help me understand myself. It won't even help me do what I want. It's just... meaningless.*

Christiane looked up. The whole class went quiet. All the students were horrified, gaping at Edward like who was this loser? He reached for his jacket, thinking, *Fuck this,* and started to rise from his desk. But he stopped. Christiane was speaking.

Hm. Yes. I think I know what you mean. It would be nice to live in a world in which we don't have to rely on self-classifications. In such a world, we could just do whatever, be whatever. But you don't live in that world. You can't do whatever you want. And these classifications aren't meaningless. They offer you an available commitment to the present that is useful and workable. And that's all we can hope for—to understand ourselves and others in a way that is appropriate to the world we live in.

Sliding back into his seat, he felt a rush to the head, felt that he was falling, then the back of his head brushed the wall. He said, *There you go. That's the problem. These tests reinforce ideas about the world that we've already internalized. When do we get to be different?*

Actually truly—not from each other, but from what we expect from ourselves? I mean, don't you get tired of yourself, Christiane?

She flushed, but he didn't think she was flustered by his argument. She said, *There is no other world to escape to. This is it. You are here. But say you try to escape. What is your game plan? Your strategy to resist your culture would inevitably lead you to consider yourself a contrarian, no? And to be contrarian, this would be so difficult.*

Her smile deepened. She looked straight into his eyes. *I mean, I know this. It is exhausting. And it is expensive to live and eat and express yourself outside of culture, so not only are you tired, you're broke...*

"Edward?" Katie said.

He mumbled into the pillow.

"What do you think?" she asked.

He lifted his head. "About?"

She flushed. "About what I just said?"

He shook his head. "Um."

She winced.

"Tell me again," he said.

She chewed her lip.

"You're basically insensitive."

He rubbed his eyes, a yawn building in him. "Why not call a spade a spade, Katie? I'm an asshole casserole."

He thought he could hear Katie laughing. *That's confusing*, he thought. But never mind. A yawn overtook him, he was closing his eyes. *Just a little nap, a small one.....................................*

....
....
....
....

The black clouds built up on the horizon. The wind shifted, moving the black clouds his way. The black clouds hovered over the building. That's the building he wanted to live in. The smell of the pines. And the...peaches, was that peaches? The sound and feeling of pinecones crunching underfoot. Down the highway that went to the building. That's the building he wanted to live in. He's getting close. He's walking in—There's a desk, a toilet. Everything he needed. His life was easy here. It was easy to get things done. He wrote alone. But someone was at his desk—Christiane was in the building! Ah fuck, ah fuck!

Edward yanked the pillow off his head and blinked up at the ceiling. The images of his dream faded away, replaced by loud music, Talking Heads, vibrating the headboard, coming in through the walls and not out of some nightmare.

He sat up, looked for Katie in the bed next to him. There was no Katie. Just the discrete indentation where her body had lain. Eyes searching the room—tidy, clean—he recalled that Katie was someone who hid her messes, the carpet would be vacuumed and the pens would be in a line on the desk, but open the closet and you'd be creamed by an avalanche of sweaters.

The door to the bathroom was rimmed with light.

Katie had to be in there, listening to this music. She probably put it on because it was his *favorite music*, a notion she had because of a concert they'd attended freshman year. And true, Edward loved every note, every word, every breath, every fucking thing about *Talking Heads in New York in 1976*, but he was hating what he was hearing—he was hating *Talking Heads in Katie's dorm room*. He wasn't listening to music. Recorded music wasn't music: it was a purchase. An object. You consumed it endlessly, until you threw it away. Recorded music—like cheap paperbacks or prints of *masterworks*—was perverse to him. He could enjoy these things only when he forgot they were objects produced for mass consumption. The people he knew—his friends, family, neighbors—all consumed art, they didn't care about having an experience with it. Their consumption of art and especially of music was compulsive and undifferentiated from all the other times they'd scratched an itch, utterly antithetical to having an experience. Which was the important thing about music. The only thing that mattered. Edward loved concerts. His favorite thing about going to concerts was the phenomenon that they were together, all of them, and their lives and bodies made the music. People together at a dinner party with music playing in the background, or shoppers and workers together in a supermarket with music playing in the background, or even more worthless, Edward and his fucking ex-girl-friend together in a college dormitory with music playing in the background, filled him with revulsion.

And then, as if in sync with his thoughts, the album switched to Talking Heads' *Fear of Music*. The first song, "I Zimbra," began deafeningly behind the bathroom door, the recorded drums and guitar and voices bumping, bouncing, into the room and into his head. He kicked off the blankets and jumped out of bed. Head rush. And he fell back, jostling the nightstand, disorder-ing the objects there, as everything around him grew white and crumbly and nauseating. He held onto the nightstand, steadying himself against it, closing his eyes, opening them up, waiting for the world to come back: it came back, he wasn't quite steady, but he could see, he could walk, was now walking across the carpet toward the bathroom, arriving to the door just as David Byrne's Dadaist chanting transformed into a message for Edward and Edward alone—

Fuck you! You're a nut job!

Shouting Katie's name, shaking the knob, finding the knob loose, he turned it, opened the door wide, wide. He saw...

Girl on toilet.

"HELLO?" she screeched.

Then she reached out and punched the door shut.

Ah, the suitemate. Katie shared the bathroom with a suitem-ate. Ah yes, well—fucking lock the door next time, *psycho*, and he looked around Katie's room, expecting to see her in the shadows, spying and laughing and loving this hilarious game. His gaze landed on Katie's desk. There, a telephone—a pink hulking mass of plastic and cord. He went to it. Lifted the receiver. But who the fuck should he call? *Katie? Hey, where are you?* And on the other end, she'd snort-laugh. *Don't you know, dum-dum? You called me.*

The dial tone droned on. His fingertips sat on the rotary. He saw, below the dial, that Katie had written her own telephone number in black marker. He could tell by the smudged ink and faded areas around more distinct, sharp-edged lines, that she had written and rewritten it many times over in the last four years.

Edward grinned. Katie had such a terrible memory. Always forgetting things. If she wasn't late, then she wasn't coming. And always a lie about why she had gotten *held up* (and always that, always *held up*, she claimed to forget nothing). He kind of loved that about her. Nothing could change her. Time changed people, other people changed people, but there was nothing changing Katie, clearly, since she had tried being other people, and three years later she was the same girl. Forgetting her phone number. Forgetting their plans.

He dropped the phone in the cradle. The play started at 8 p.m. Glancing out the window, he saw the blinds were drawn. But that was clearly sunshine creeping through the slats. *OK OK. It's still early. There's still time. Find a clock. Where's a clock? Does Katie really not have a fucking clock?*

There, on the nightstand. Katie had moved it out of place—turned it around to face the wall.

He leapt for it. Read—7:50 p.m.

His eyes widened.

"Fuck you!" he yelled.

And at once the girl in the bathroom shouted back, *"No fuck you, you fucking butt-wipe!"*

"*OK,*" he mouthed, "*OK OK,*" and looked around the room for his clothes, snatching up pants and shirt and socks and shoes and jacket and remembering, in the last moment, the shoebox. He tried to remember what plan they had made for the evening. It was possible Katie hadn't ditched him. They had agreed to meet at the Icehouse. Right? She had something to do, and she was going to meet up with him after. Right? Shoes on, clothes on, shoebox tucked under his arm, Edward walked to the parking lot. A bounce in his step. A little, spirited *hmmm* from his lips. He went over his plan for tonight. Play this right, and he could get Ryan and Katie to both back off.

All he had to do was take them aside, separately... *So Ryan, hey. Seems like Katie found out you're pretending to be Roger Ackroyd. But don't worry, she won't rat you out. Just get her that internship with your uncle and, of course, drop the act you're playing. You're not Roger Ackroyd.*

Then he'd go to Katie. *So, listen. Ryan is willing to clear your name with his uncle if you stop kidding around—you're not Roger Ackroyd.*

Edward stepped quickly toward the parking lot, thinking how they were sure to agree to these conditions. Ryan would agree because he self-identified with *doing the right thing*, which basically meant he was horribly frightened of confrontation and even more frightened of looking bad in front of others, especially in front of people he envied and feared. And Katie would agree because she was desperate for a speedy resolution and volatile of will and never stuck to any of her decisions, so was frighteningly quick to forgive, one of the worst people in the world at holding a grudge or any other sort of personal promise no matter how severely (but rightly, in this case) she had been treated by complete shitheads. And that didn't make her a *good person* of course, just someone who was incredibly desperate to climax, desperate for release.

Edward gave his head a shake, rubbed his eyes. That wasn't his own voice in his head. That was Talking Heads. A shiver ran through him. What did you hear when you heard a song in your head? It wasn't music. What was it? Did anyone know? Why weren't more people weirded-out by this? Edward was humming. Just a single suspended note while he stared ahead. Stared at a parking lot. The student parking lot. The wrong fucking lot.

And when he made it to the right lot, finally, he threw the shoebox into the trunk and himself behind the wheel and drove to the Icehouse Theater, immediately surprised to see that there were no cars and no people in front of the building. No signs of life, no lights.

No Katie.

Talking Heads played on in his head.

Which song?

And then it dawned on him.

Calmly he reached into his jacket pocket. He pulled out the little card in there and held it in front of him.

1526 S. Dunbar Road. Tuesday, 8 p.m. at Jonathan's.

He moaned and was speeding the car down the road toward South Dunbar. He definitely hadn't told Katie this address. He had no memory of telling her or not telling her that address, but oh he knew he hadn't told her anything. What would he do? Ryan would be there, but Katie wouldn't. He would see Ryan there, and he would just have to—

"What?" He clenched the wheel. "What do I do?"

Beat the shit out of Ryan.

"Ah bullshit," he moaned. "Ah oh, ah oh this is bull…"

Edward zoomed past fields now, the houses growing further apart from one another and further from the road, further afield, settled deep in green and gold next to dilapidated barns and tin silos. He remembered driving down this road with Gran. When about? Oh, a year or so ago. And Gran looked out the window. *Look at all this farmland! Would you look at it!* They all looked, even his sister Viv. And yeah, there was a lot. Nothing else but. Just lawns and lawns and lawns of cropped grass that the sky went straight down to. Edward shook his head. *Same old shit.*

Gran, though, couldn't believe it. What she saw amazed her. She looked at the land as if it were new, instead of what it was: all she knew. He couldn't understand that. It made no sense. What did she see? What possibly?

The car approached 1526 S. Dunbar.

There was nowhere to park. Cars everywhere. On the road, in the road, double-parked. The road began to turn. Now he was driving toward a dark horizon, with a bloody sunset in his rearview mirror.

And still no spaces. He pressed the gas, speeding past the lineup of cars.

Behind the last car, he parked.

… Sprinting down the road.

Terrified that the play might have already started, that it was too late: they'd met each other. The girl in green sequins was just now saying his name.

Roger!

… Two girls were passing out programs, in the driveway to 1526 S Dunbar.

"Did I miss it?" Edward panted.

"As you can *see*…" she rocked her head back. People were milling behind her, on the wide grassy lawn.

"We're running about fifteen minutes behind," the other one said.

Edward straightened. Stepped forward.

"Hey! Your ticket?"

He stopped. Reaching into his jacket, he took out the card.

"That isn't a ticket," she said. She pointed down at her feet, at a box, it was overflowing with little slips.

"I don't…" Edward started to say, and then he realized what was going on—something similar to what had happened yesterday with the girl at the Icehouse. "*Hey*. I go to Monroe," he said, looking between them. "I'm a student, OK? And I was told that this card would get me in."

Her eyelids fluttered, a lazy eye roll.

"Gimme," she said.

He handed the card over with shaking fingers. "Thanks," he murmured, too grateful to tell her to fuck herself.

He stuffed his hands in his pockets, slightly stooping, and walked down the drive. The sunset was behind them, sending slanted golden rays across the lawn. He could see everyone clearly. He could see all their shining faces, their bare arms and legs and happy bodies in the warm evening. A girl in green sequins would definitely stand out in this crowd of people wearing cutoffs and worn tees and thong sandals. And Ryan, who never wore less than slacks and a button-up, would definitely pop out as the resident nerd. But he wasn't here. Mystery Girl wasn't here. *Not yet*, he told himself, reaching the end of the driveway, staring up at the farmhouse in front of him. White clapboard. Big, typical, old-looking. Three stories tall, if you counted the attic. The porch was wraparound, no railing to it, just tall, alabaster columns spaced about ten feet apart, three to the left, three to the right. Something strange about that porch. There was a dining room table on it. And a roulette wheel. Those lamps weren't lamps. Light stands. The porch had been converted into a stage.

He walked between the porch and lawn and came out the other side. As before, he tried to see every face as he walked. Where was Ryan? Not there. There? Nope. He gritted his teeth. He wasn't anywhere—*not yet*.

Or maybe…

Maybe Ryan wasn't coming.

Edward felt sick, even more scared, to think that he had miscalculated everything. The poser was Ryan. It had to be Ryan. Right? Everything pointed to Ryan, every clue practically screamed *Ryan, Ryan*—Ryan ran the paper, Ryan personally vetted all of Roger Ackroyd's fan mail. One day he got a letter from a cute-sounding girl who called herself *Mystery Girl*, and he decided, what the hay, to reply to her. *But don't send your reply to the paper! Put it in an Agatha Christie library book. Get it? To increase the mystery!* Eight months later, Mystery Girl asked to meet him. Did Ryan flake? Ryan was a pussy, a milksop, a total dorkasaurus, but this was what he had been working toward for eight long months. Ryan was scared, but also thrilled. If he met her, he'd blow it, if he didn't meet her, he'd blow it. Didn't want to meet her, totally wanted to. Decided to meet her, only to meet, guess who?

Whoa! Katie man. Katie! Fucking everything up, that's Katie. She freaked Ryan out with her bullshit Roger Ackroyd confession and now he was not coming. OK. What to do? Like, that's fucking great you know, actually solved everything, except who's to say that Ryan actually was the person pretending to be Roger Ackroyd?

Edward was excited again, truly enraged, striding over to the girls in the driveway passing out the programs. They were bent over, picking up programs, a sea of them across the gravel.

He asked, "Is there a phone around here?"

They didn't look up. "In the house!"

He jogged back up the driveway. Katie, all he could think about was Katie, that Katie wasn't here and Ryan wasn't here. Katie should be here and Ryan should be here and they both weren't here. Where the fuck was Katie? Why had she stood him up?

Edward hopped the porch steps. Walking around the dining room table and the roulette wheel…

The front door was closed.

Should he knock?

Eh, fuck it, turned the knob, slipped inside the house. It was dark. Almost impossible to see. All he could make out was the outline of windows—broad windows wrapping around the room, covered by dark curtains that let in only a little light… A large room. Actually, not too dark. He could see well enough, and he saw nothing. There really was nothing to see. A staircase came down into the center of the room, splitting it into two halves. To the right, in that half, a chair, only a chair, one of those chairs with the funny backs, with *wings*, situated in the center of the room. To the left, in that half, no wing chairs, no seating of any kind. Voices, footsteps, activity, indistinct and chaotic, above this room, beyond this room… He glanced ahead. To the left of the staircase, the dim mouth of a hall. A little way in, an old rotary telephone mounted above an end table. Next to it was a large pickle jar filled with coins.

A sign read, *Make a call? Drop a dime.*

He pulled out his wallet. A dollar bill, all he had left. His hands plunged into the pickle jar, sifting through cold coins for exact

change. He exchanged the bill for the coins, then made the call.
With the phone ringing in his ear now, he almost didn't hear the
soft voice say—

"A hundred and five cents."

He looked over his shoulder. There was someone there. She
wore a silk kimono and smoked out a window. Her thighs were
crossed and bare.

"You dropped a dollar and took a hundred and five cents."
She flicked out the cigarette. Dark red hair, bone white skin, and
the kimono was almost coming undone in front.

Edward opened and closed his mouth. The phone. Still ringing
in his ear. He noticed it and frowned, somewhat stupefied by the
harsh and literally alarming sound.

But now the redhead was getting up from the windowsill,
walking toward him—

She stopped within inches of him. Her eyes were lime-green.
God, fuck, they were. Her wrist brushed his arm hair. Her ivory
fingers plucked two coins from the pile and dropped them, *clink,
clink,* in the jar.

"Ninety cents," she said and moseyed up the stairs.

Face flaming, staring at the cigarette smoke still clinging to the
half-drawn curtain, he thought—he thought—the phone. Still ringing.

The answering machine kicked on.

"*Hello, you've reached Marie Moses…*"

He pulled the phone from his ear. Shit, Gran? Didn't mean to
call her. He cut the connection.

Dropped in more coins. Dialing Katie now.

She picked up on the first ring.

"Hello!"

"It's Edward. Did Ryan tell you not to come to this play?" he
asked.

"Excuse me?"

"Did Ryan tell you—"

"Ryan's there? At the play?" A sharp intake of breath. "You

mean you invited me to a play where you knew I'd run into—"

"No, no." Edward groaned. "Ryan's not here. He's not here. And what do you care? You're not here either! He's not here and you're not here—"

"I'm hanging up now."

"Katie!"

"What?

"Where were you? You were supposed to come to this thing with me!"

"I was next door with my suitemate. We were listening to music."

Edward's head dropped against the wall. When he looked up, he saw he'd already put the receiver on the hook. Fingers shaking, he dialed another number.

"Hello?"

"Mom?" he croaked.

"Edward, I'm so glad you called. I forgot to ask you when I saw you earlier about possibly getting some extra tickets for the graduation ceremony this *Friday*. Your Aunt Amy is driving down from Grand Rapids *tonight* to get everything ready for the graduation party this coming *Saturday*, and Uncle Joe also will come down probably *Friday*, so it would be great if you could see about getting some extra tickets, just *two* extra would be nice, they'd be for your aunt and uncle if that makes a difference, although if you think you could weasel *a few more* then we can get your Great Aunt Jane in the audience. You know how she loves a ceremony."

"I, uh…what?"

"I'm just asking is all. If you don't think you can do it—"

"You want two extra tickets?"

"Three extra. Three or four. Two at a minimum. Three would be ideal, or four."

"I can ask…"

"Perfect. OK, hun. I've got to go—"

"Mom!"

"What?"

"I've been trying to get ahold of you," he said.

"You have?"

"Well, I've been calling Dad."

She sighed. "Your father had a very difficult delivery this after-noon, twins, they came out all right but the second one—"

"Gran had an accident," Edward blurted.

His mom didn't skip a beat. "OK—did you call someone? Are you there with her now?"

"It happened this morning."

"What? Why didn't you say something?" Her voice rose. "Oh my god did she fall?"

"She didn't fall. She had *an accident*."

A pause.

"You mean she pooped," his mom said.

"Yes."

"OK. How did it come out?"

"Seriously?"

"Yes, seriously, this is serious! Was it a pig-in-the-blanket sort of deal or—"

"It was everywhere, on everything."

His mom was silent.

"I cleaned it up and all, and she was fine, you saw her. But she hasn't been answering her phone."

His mom said, voice soft, "I remember. I remember that she was out of breath. Ah god, she was really winded today. I asked her, you know I asked her if she felt all right, and she—oh god I thought she was just sneaking cigarettes, but I didn't think to ask if she felt any chest pains or…"

His mom's voice broke off. The line crackled.

Then her voice came into his ear, low and venomous.

"Edward, you really messed up."

The line was cut. She hung up? He frowned, not quite believ-ing the dial tone. The phone drifted…ended up in the… He felt numb. Huh. Nothing. He walked away, out the front door, into blinding light, christ. Soaking the deck and pillars, the table, his eyes, blinded by a red and yellow sunset. Stumbling to the dining room table and pressing his hands on the wood, leaning into the heat, sensing more than seeing the swarming people on the lawn. *I have an announcement*, he imagined saying. The people on the lawn would fall into a hush. *I have an announcement*, he would say, and their silence would grow to a boil. Tantalizing to think they were all his. What they would do for a distraction, if it's a good enough one... *I have an announcement*, but what? Did he really have nothing to say to them? No, it wasn't that simple. Their voices rose up into a deafening roar.

He walked down into the crowd with his eyes full of black spots from the light. He went into the center of them all, and stopped and stood, arms folded, turning around and around, looking at the tops of their heads. He looked for sandy blonde hair, thick and more or less straight except for the little curls growing over his ears and down his nape. Those curls always looked wet. *Gotta say something to you, Ryan. I've been thinking about it for years and I can't hold back any longer...CUT YOUR HAIR.*

A drumming, tapping. Some guys all in black were setting up a microphone on the porch. "Check, check, check, well *hello* everybody..." Edward could see the crew on the porch and that didn't strike him as strange. But then it struck him as strange. He looked around at the lawn and realized that no one was blocking his view—everybody on the lawn was seated and silent and looking up at him.

Edward sat at once, on the grass. Static and horrific screeching came across the microphone, and then a guy on the porch was speaking: he's the director, he's excited to be here. He wants to welcome them all.

"And thank you very much for coming..."

Edward looked from side to side, trying to determine a clear path out of the audience. But he was surrounded. The girl in green sequins might be walking up the drive right now, and he'd have no way of knowing because he couldn't see beyond the people around him. He wrapped his arms around his knees. Hang tight, man.

"And now, to situate the play in the context of the world we live in…" the director said, talking with a vaguely but not possibly British accent. He held the mike in one hand and an unreasonable stack of index cards in the other. He was struggling to manage both, and when he flipped to the next card, he scuffed the mike.

"The war is between us and our bodies," the director said. "Our bodies out there in the world. These bodies are written about, idolized, and punished. They are visible to us, but we do not have access to them. We are medicalized to ourselves. This medical contraption that carries us. Or we look with longing to the incorporeal corporeal, the printed, spoken of, glorified representation of…oh, um." The director flipped through the cards. "That bit was supposed to go…well."

Edward laughed out loud. The people around him looked over, glared.

The director cleared his throat into the mike. "OK, um. A quote from Sade, whom you all know: 'There is no God. Nature suffice unto herself; in no wise hath she need of an author.'"

"And uh, lastly, I'm supposed to inform you all that the farmhouse is off-limits. And that includes, um, phone calls, bathroom breaks, emergency or otherwise. You'll have to go—" He covered the microphone, conferring with the guy next to him. He removed his hand from the mike.

"Yeah so basically just walk straight down the road that way and turn into the McDonald's parking lot after about three miles."

Light laughter.

"Or," he gestured out to the fields around them.

Loud laughter.

"Yeah. Sure, guys. Without further ado, we got *Blue of Noon* for you here."

Edward jumped up at once and made a dash for the driveway, a dash that lasted all of two steps and then became a fucking slow-going and circuitous endeavor, with Edward tripping over this guy on a towel, hopping around this girl on a towel, stopping and walking around this girl and guy and guy and girl on a goddamn Persian rug, catching angry glares from everybody because apparently the play was starting. There was an actor on the porch speaking the opening lines: "The blank head in which *I* am has become so frightened and greedy that only my death could satisfy it."

Wow, sounds like a fun play, he thought, at last emerging from the audience and stepping out to the driveway. He glanced over at the porch, where the lone actor held out his hands, gesturing expansively.

"Several days ago, I came to a city that looked like the setting for a tragedy…"

Blah, blah, fuckity blah, the guy yammered on and on and Edward turned away from the stage.

He watched the audience and not the play. He watched their faces, solemn and sincere and totally receptive to the *heightened reality* being presented to them. These were the same people who spoke of the Icehouse Theater and Roger Ackroyd in the same breath, chalking up both the plays and poetry to *really groundbreaking—it's avant-garde at its best*. But what did actors and Roger Ackroyd have in common? Actors wanted to attain something, entertain or teach, and Roger didn't. Actors wanted to uncover the world—or maybe they wanted to cover up the world? Edward forgot which—but Roger wanted to push his audience off a cliff. Now compare that to what these fools on stage were doing. You couldn't. They reminded you of someone. But Roger wasn't like that, he was nothing and no one and totally real.

The lawn and surrounding fields grew dim, and the stage grew brighter. The world went black, and the stage gleamed. It was dark now. Night now. No lights in the field or in the road, the only light was the jewel-bright stage. Edward flicked his lighter. A glowing ember. Thinking to himself, any minute now—any minute—he'd hear Ryan: *Hey, buddy, how's it hanging?*

On stage, a woman grabbed her bright green skirts and pulled them up to her lacy underwear, revealing a bare white thigh spewing neon-bright blood all over the floor. A silver fork was in her thigh, stuck deeply in her flesh, and blood spewed. Edward stopped breathing. There had been an accident? Shit, someone should—but then a man in a tuxedo knelt in front of the bloody thigh and put his lips on the wound. Sucking up the blood. His hands crawled up her legs, disappearing under her skirts. The girl's eyes closed, drunkenly. These were actors. This was a play. That was really nuts there. For a second Edward thought she was actually stabbed. The guy sucking her thigh pulled away. The folds of her dress fell down to the floor. Edward grunted—that dress was green, sparkling, sequined, holy shit, Mystery Girl, that's—*Mystery Girl has red hair.* She wasn't a blonde. She had red hair. This meant absolutely nothing and yet he couldn't stop thinking, not blonde. Not what he had imagined. Blonde, brown, red, what the fuck did it matter but it mattered somehow.

And he knew her, too. From here, from today. She was that girl in the silk kimono, smoking by the window, who had caught him making bad change. Well, she hadn't caught him—he hadn't made bad change on purpose. But christ, she probably thought so. Shit. Feeling sick now thinking that this girl thought he was a liar, no better than the poser she was writing. She really was beautiful—a girl like that would never go for Ryan. He must know that. Was that why he wasn't here right now? He couldn't meet her—could *never* meet her. The moment he met her would be the moment it was over. When she would frown and say, *Oh. You?*

What was her name? He began walking down the drive toward the road, where he'd seen the girls handing out programs. He walked slowly, not wanting to lose his footing. And he couldn't keep his eyes off the stage for more than a few seconds. He kept turning around, looking for her. But she wasn't in the scene anymore—she had moved to the right side of the house where all the actors were exiting and entering the stage. One of the advantages of having a wraparound porch as a stage. Although it would be pretty funny if characters had to use the front door, if every few minutes someone cried out, *Honey I'm home!*

Edward smirked. *Maybe I should write plays.* His shoe skidded across a smooth surface, then crunched gravel again. He bent down, feeling around for—

He held the program up to his lighter, trying to read by the small flame. A word here and there, he was shaking with frustration. Too damn dark to read. He looked back at the gleaming stage. It was certainly bright over there. He could hide out in the kitchen, or maybe go upstairs? The cast and crew were collected on the right side of the porch. He'd sneak in on the left.

Walking up the driveway, keeping his eyes on the ground, not wanting the light from the porch to corrupt his eyes that had begun to see, just a little, in the dark. His shoe hovered above a swallowing spot, blacker than the rest. He pulled his foot out and placed it on solid ground—He heard her voice. Oh the fool he looked up. On instinct looked for her and felt two stabs of pain, excruciating, in his eye sockets. Mystery Girl, in a bright room. Mystery Girl, at the foot of a bed. A man, bundled up in the bedsheets, moaning.

"Do you know a song that begins, *I dreamed of a flower?*" he asked.

A fast, breathless voice shot from Mystery Girl. "Sure, why?"

"It would be so nice to hear it right now, if there were only someone to sing it to me…"

Silence, and then the soft clink of the whiskey bottle as she set it down on the floor. She sang with her head hung low.

"*I dreamed of a flower that wouldn't die, I dreamed of a love that would never fade…*"

Her voice was thin, airy. It cracked in places.

"*Aye, why oh why must flowers and happiness bloom for only one day?*"

The sick man said, "Hm. That was fine."

"What? You didn't like it?"

"It's just I wish you had been naked."

"Naked?" Her voice cracked.

"Yes."

Her shoulders slumped. She gathered up her skirts, pulling them up—

Edward's gaze shot to the ground. He swayed, dizzy, sick. She was weeping and he didn't want to see it. He grabbed the porch railing, steadied himself, then pulled himself up.

"No, don't cry. I wanted you to act crazy so I wouldn't die."

"You won't die now? You promise?"

Edward crawled toward the open window. A faint light filtered down to from it. He reached for the curtain and pushed it aside, peeking into the living room. Empty. Brighter. He craned his neck, looking for the light source, saw that light was coming through the curtained windows that overlooked the porch... He swung both legs over the sill, then sat back against it, opening up the program, flipping through to the section on the cast and crew. Photos on the left, bios on the right. At the top was the guy he'd seen on stage, looking very serious, very artistic, as the lead character *Henri Troppmann*.

Two pics down. Thick hair. Dark lips. One eyebrow cocked higher than the other.

MAY SHERMAN (Xenia) made her Icehouse debut as
Portia in The Merchant of Venice three years ago. Since then
she has appeared in nearly a dozen productions at the Icehouse
and was the recipient of the Young Actors of Michigan Award
in '79. This is Sherman's final performance for the Icehouse.
She is headed to the great Southwest where she plans to pursue
a career as a schoolteacher. We will miss her.

He'd never known someone named May. It wasn't a good name. Why name a person after a month? People would always be asking if you were born in that month, your name-month, and if you were, well la-di-da. And if you weren't then you'd always have to account for why your name was a month, *that* month, what an exasperating question. A modal verb. May was also that, too. A *helper* verb, good god, no wonder she was going to be a schoolteacher. Edward heard a small sound. A small sneeze. A chill swept through him. That wasn't a sneeze from the porch. On the porch, there was soft crying, a gentle murmur, but here, in the front room, a small sneeze. Someone was in the room with him.

Edward kept very still and looked directly ahead at the stairs that split the room in half. No one around him. They must be on the other side of the staircase… He crept forward just a little, just enough to see around the—the room changed. Brighter? Louder! Roaring in his ears, the crowd outside, hooting, hollering, the play was over? Edward leapt forward—he meant to step back, but he leapt forward and saw, across the room, on the other side of the stairs, a stranger sitting in the wing chair.

A bright thing in the stranger's lap. A bright, orange book. The stranger saw Edward and he grunted and his hands leapt up, holding the book to his chest. On the book's cover was the little white dog. It read, *Agatha Christie*. It read, *Dumb Witness*. Edward saw, peeking out through the pages, the edges of a white envelope.

Edward went cold. Holy fucking… It was him.

The front door banged open, and Edward jumped back. He saw the poser stuff the book between the armrest and the chair cushion, just as the actors and crew began to pour into the room.

"OK, people!" A girl with a clipboard shouted. "Fifteen minutes! That's a piss and a prayer! That's not a phone call to Mom. That's fifteen, now only *fourteen minutes!*"

"Are we letting anyone in?"

"No!"

"Where are they supposed to take their aforementioned piss?"

"Kyle told everyone in his curtain speech that restrooms were down the road, first left into the McDonald's after you've walked a mile."

"What! They'll just go in the yard!"

"Oh my god, Rhonda! You're right! You better do something about it quick."

Edward pressed up against the window curtains, hands twisting behind his back. Across the room, Mystery Girl—May—leaned toward the wing chair with her hand on the back, smiling broadly as she chatted with him, the poser. Edward felt sick. *All over, it's all over. This is how it ends…*

"Hey, you!"

Edward hung his head.

"You're not supposed to be in here!"

Edward looked up. The girl with the clipboard was pointing her finger at—

Someone else. Some dork in the doorway. He scratched his jaw. "Sorry, but like, is there a bathroom?"

The girl with the clipboard wagged her finger. "Nuh-uh. No. Get out."

"It's an emergency."

"Go-oooooo."

Beyond them, May pulled away from the poser. "Save that thought for later!" she said and began walking toward the stairs.

Edward closed his eyes. Lucky break, he got his one lucky… He opened his eyes again. The girl with the clipboard continued to scream at that guy. Dude was a goner. Guess who'd be next? Edward felt his heart race. *You gotta do something. Gotta save yourself…*

Edward stepped forward.

"It's OK. He's with me."

The girl whipped around. "And you are…?" She looked Edward up and down.

He gaped at her. "*Seriously?*"

Vertices in her forehead, little cracks of doubt.

"Uh, sure. Um…" she shook her head, muttering to herself as she stormed away.

The guy looked over at Edward. "Thanks. I owe you!"

"Try upstairs," Edward said and hung back at the windows,

fidgeting with the curtains. In the window's reflection, he saw the poser in the wing chair—his left leg folded over the right, his hands neatly folded on his knee. A long, delicate person, with very light, fine hair falling across his eyes.

The poser swept his hair back with a toss of his head. He coughed lightly into the palm of his hand, and then he spoke.

"I hate to be the bearer of bad news, but…" A small shrug. "There isn't a bathroom upstairs."

Edward turned from the window, now facing him.

"Who are you then?" the poser asked. A lightness to his voice, suggestive of friendliness, but Edward saw through it and scowled.

"Nobody," Edward said, a bitter edge to his voice. "I came here to piss, same as that other guy. But I didn't like how your friend was treating him, OK?"

The poser smiled grimly. "Ah yes, Ally can be quite tenacious about rules, certain rules. Well, all rules really, not just her own…"

Edward shrugged.

"She's very good at her job," the poser added quickly.

"OK."

"None of this was supposed to happen tonight but she threw it all together in basically a week, basically five days, six days, basically six or five days."

Edward muttered, "Yeah, that's a week *basically*."

The poser fidgeted as he spoke, his hands spidering around his knees, clearly wanting to reach into the chair cushions for the orange book, but refusing to so long as Edward was there. The realization that this was the poser's present dilemma spread a warm smile across Edward's face.

The poser sighed. "It's our last show. Everyone in the cast and most of the crew are seniors. We were all horrified when we thought that it was canceled. We've been practicing for months. I actually started working on this script a year ago."

"You're the writer," Edward blurted.

The poser colored. "Yes."

Edward reached for his cigarettes. His hands shook as he lit up. "Wow," he said, taking a drag. "That's really..." He trailed off, a frown settling in.

The poser bowed his head. "Oh, well. Thank you. But, of course, *Georges Bataille* is the one who really wrote it. He wrote the novel. He's the genius. I basically just wrote out all his dialogue."

"That took you a year?"

"It's in French. The book is. And I don't speak French. Or I try to, but my French is bad. Very, very bad. *Mon français n'est pas bon...*"

The right hand crawled out from the poser's lap. The fingers felt for the orange book in the armrest, its spine just visible in the crevice. Then the hand snapped back. The poser blinked and blinked at Edward. Huge eyes, watery blue and bloodshot.

"Hm, what? No? Nothing? I'm sorry. Plays! Even the ones I hardly write—I *hardly* wrote this and look at me. I'm a nervous wreck!"

Edward took a drag. Would he say it? Could he?

"It's good," he choked out.

The poser's face lit up. "You think so? What about it? I mean, what exactly?"

Edward gaped, smoke pouring out of his mouth and nostrils. What could he possibly say?

Then a shrill cry came from the back of the house.

"*Seven minutes, people!*"

Doors began opening, slamming. Vague cries, giddy shouts, feet pounding the floorboards.

Both Edward and the poser spoke at once.

"Do you mind if..."

"Whatdayasay..."

They both laughed.

"Sorry—"

"You—"

"No, you!"

Edward said, "Cool if I stick around?"

The poser nodded. "Oh that's what I was going to ask you! Please do. I would like the company…" His eyes seemed to spiral in his sockets, and his fingers, they couldn't stop fidgeting, groping the cushions, feeling for the orange book. "This house is so creepy, don't you think?" His eyes jumped to and fro, peeking over one shoulder and then the other. "I've never liked this house. No, I won't miss it."

Edward shouted, speaking over the feet thundering through the house, "Do you live here?"

"Hm? Oh yes! Four years now. Moving out this weekend. I won't miss it. No, no…"

The girl with the clipboard, *Ally*, strode into the room. Her gaze went from Edward to the poser in the wing chair, and then shot up the stairs. Coming down them was the guy who'd gone up for the bathroom. He was shaking his head. "I can't find a john anywhere!"

"What! You?" Ally pointed at the door. "Get out of here now!"

The guy stopped on the last step. "This is bull."

Ally threw her head back. "I am one second away from calling the cops. And you," she spun around, pointing at Edward, "I asked around about you. No one knows you. No one's ever seen you before." She strode over to the phone. "That's it. I'm calling the cops on you both."

The poser rose from the chair. "Ally—Ally, wait a second. This is my fault. This here is my guest. And the other chap, well, I don't really know him. But he seems like he's in a tough situation."

Ally dropped the receiver. "Everybody's friends with every-body. Lord, I'm not buying it." She wagged a finger at Edward. "Be very, very careful, you. There isn't a person here who wouldn't skin you alive for taking advantage of Jonathan."

The guy on the stairs cleared his throat. "But, like, where's the—"

"Get the fuck out," she snapped. She looked at her watch, threw her head back, and—

"PLACES, PEOPLE! IT'S SHOWTIME!"

The stampede of actors and crew pushed Edward into the back corner of the room. He flicked his cigarette out the open window. He wanted to jump out. The situation didn't feel right. It wasn't what he expected. Ryan. He expected Ryan. He could deal with Ryan, knew and hated Ryan. He wished—god fuck, why wasn't it *Ryan? Now what the fuck am I... Now how the fuck am I... Do I walk away? Just...walk away?*

Cheering out in the lawn. Loud applause. The play was starting back up, and Edward was straddling the windowsill, one foot in, one foot out.

From the shadows, the poser softly spoke.

"Hello. I see you there. If we keep all the lights out, and maybe kill that one upstairs, we could get away with opening one of the curtains. You could watch the play that way."

Edward pulled his foot back in.

"I'm Jonathan, by the way."

A chill crept up Edward's back. "Edward."

"Do you mind getting yourself a chair, Edward? There should be one in the kitchen." Jonathan looked back at the stairs. "I'll see about that light up there."

His skin remained cold, the chill settling in, as Edward stepped into the hall, looking for the kitchen. The first door he came to he opened. The smell of mildew hit him. Old things. Colorful coats and shirts and below, in a heap, shoes. He closed the door. He opened the next. Darkness. Lifting his left foot to step forward, he felt empty space, only air. Gasping, he pulled his foot in. If he had just gone on through, slipped through? *Down, down, down, in every successive moment expecting to hit the ground, but not hitting the ground, in every successive moment waiting to die and wishing you had never jumped...* That was...what? What was that? A line from a poem? Or maybe a song? Lyrics? But heard no music, whatever you called music, when it was inside your head. Chills raced through him.

He shut the door.

In the next doorway, he felt the wall for the light switch. Flipped it. The sight of the kitchen triggered a painful spasm in his stomach. Knifed in the gut, he felt so fucking hungry. He walked around a table, reaching the fridge. He gripped the handle, and he froze, eye to eye with a photo of the poser at the beach, completely covered in sand but for his blonde head and huge eyes—huge eyes swallowing up Mystery Girl. May. Splayed on a beach towel next to him. Inky one-piece. Freckles on cleavage. Sticky sand on thighs.

A fat cigar between her teeth.

"Lake Leelanau—"

Edward jumped.

"—last summer. We rented a cabin."

Edward's hands went for his pockets, feeling for cigarettes. His eyes lingered on Mystery Girl in the photo. "Who's she?"

Jonathan's warm, slightly perfumed body came up beside him. His lids extended over his eyes, then snapped back. "Oh right, right. You don't know everyone." He tapped the photo. "This is May, with the six-inch Louixs. She's in the play. And so are," he began tapping other photos on the fridge, forming a constellation of faces. "Daniel, Claire, and Marni…all five of us live in this house. One big happy—"

"And Ally?" Edward lit the cigarette.

"Not a roommate. But she will be taking over the lease this summer. She's younger than us, with two more years of all this."

That girl is younger? She'd treated them all like infants.

Jonathan nodded. Wait, what? Edward flushed, thinking for a second he'd accidentally spoken aloud. The poser murmured, "I know. I'm worried about her. When we're all gone, what will Ally do? She hardly relates to anyone outside our small circle. She's actually a shy person. Outspoken and shy. Yeah. That's a hard thing to be. I think that she went into college feeling so much older than everybody. I worry that she will go out of college feeling so much younger. What do I mean? Like she missed out on things, maybe the lessons we all learned because we were all a bit more open…"

Jonathan clapped his hands, jolting Edward, who suddenly felt a wetness in the corner of his mouth, a dribble of spit. He smeared it with the back of his hand, his gaze following Jonathan around the kitchen—

"A drink, a drink… That's what I need!" Jonathan went from cupboard to cupboard, opening them. "And what does Edward need? An ashtray for one. We'll get you that. Here you are. What else? Hm? This is scotch." He pulled a bottle out. "And in the fridge, we have beer, we have pop… Would he like any of these things?"

Why did he talk like that? What's the game? Holy fuck that scotch was Chivas Regal, a $100 bottle.

"Scotch," Edward said, and his stomach rumbled. He looked back at the fridge, at the photograph of May.

"Is she your girlfriend?" Edward asked.

"Who, Ally?"

"May."

Jonathan shook his head rapidly, hiding his face in a cupboard. "A friend. A good one. A girl and a friend, no more, no less…" He pulled two tumblers from the cupboard, gave them each a tall pour. Jonathan passed a drink to Edward, which he took with a nod, noticing Jonathan's longish fingernails curled around the glass, lightly pinging it.

Jonathan reached over Edward's shoulder and tapped another photo.

"That's my gal."

Edward looked over. He took a breath. She was lovely. Bangs. A wizard blonde. A small nose and a pretty turn to the lips. How did Jonathan manage to get a girl like that? Edward looked closer. Actually, she looked a lot like May. Except for the coloring, the bangs, wait…that was May, right?

"That's Monica Vitti," Jonathan said. "The actress."

Edward vaguely recognized the name. "So, not actually your girlfriend."

"Amazingly enough," Jonathan pushed the photos together, "they look alike, don't you think? We put up the photo of Monica Vitti to tease May. We put it up, she tears it down. We find a new photo of Monica Vitti—it drives May crazy." Jonathan sipped his drink. Then he smacked his forehead. "Oh! We're in here! And they're all—What's the matter with me? Do you mind? Would you grab a chair? I'll bring the scotch! *Quickly…*"

Jonathan sped out of the room, forgetting the bottle of scotch on the table. Edward set his glass down, poured another drink, picked up the ashtray and the glass and set them on a chair and lifted everything up and carried it out, all the while thinking, *Fuck this guy, fuck this guy, fuck this guy…*

Looking around for the little fucker, he saw him standing in front of the wing chair. "Where should I sit?" Edward asked.

Jonathan placed a finger against his lips. "We can talk, but quietly. Set the chair here." He gestured to the space in front of him.

The spot where Edward was to put the chair was about five feet away from a bright window. Facing this spot, and not the window, was the wing chair.

Edward whispered, "You're not going to watch?"

Jonathan's smile was cringing. "I'm sorry… I thought I could watch, but I can't…"

They both took to their positions, their awkward positions, Jonathan facing Edward, with a full view of Edward, only Edward, who faced the window, its blinding view of the porch. Was Edward supposed to be cool with this? *Sure, man, don't mind you watching me watch the play for the next—hour, hour and a half. Might go longer. I'm not doing that, fuck that. Can't see anything. Can't even hear them. But damn though. The poser, I can hear him breathing.*

Edward glanced at him. Jonathan's hand was draped across his face, thumb and forefinger slowly massaging his temples. The hand made a thorough mask of the face, no way to see through it.

But Edward never judged a person by his face. Never something as superficial as that. Choices, you had to judge people by their daily, mundane choices if justice was on your mind. You could start with the clothes. Shabby people, for really special occasions, always dressed up. They wore their most expensive, fanciest and therefore newest clothes, but the poser was dressed in the simplest way. He was dressed in the most elegant way—jeans, black. Thin laces on the shoes. And a plain shirt, black or dark blue, each of the three top buttons undone. Shabby people would look Jonathan over and say he was *shabby*, he was *misfit scum*, not realizing that they, in their mall clothes freshly clipped of tags—shiny shirts, pants smelling of plastic—were the spume. But Jonathan was money. He clearly came from *that world*...had dressed like he didn't give a fuck very carefully.

Jonathan's hands fell from his face, and Edward whipped his head around, believing that Jonathan had caught him watching. And Jonathan stared at him, and Edward stared at the bright window; and Jonathan stared at him, and Edward stared at the bright window. And Jonathan stared, and Edward looked back over, drawing his breath in to say, *HEY, do you mind not*—but Jonathan's eyes were closed. Jonathan hadn't caught him watching. Jonathan had an utterly symmetrical face. His cheeks weren't crooked, his nose wasn't—On Edward even nostrils weren't the same. But Jonathan's face repeated itself. A freckle below an eye balanced the freckle above another, on the eyelid. His bottom lip repeated the full, red, blossoming upper. There was a cleft in his chin, and one in his nose. That nose, a narrow shaft of equal width from tip to bridge, was probably the most perfect thing about the face. It was probably the most incensing thing as well. Edward wanted to rip Jonathan's perfect face apart, starting with that nose.

And now looking away, full of disgust for himself. *You start out judging a person, and then it turns on you, you hate yourself—*

Jonathan's voice made him jump: "What? Did something go wrong? No—don't tell me!"

Edward sucked his breath in, blinking at the bright window. "You know," he exhaled. Inhaled. "I can't really watch this play with you watching my face."

Jonathan sighed. "*Sorry*. It's the only way I can enjoy it. I can't enjoy it by watching it myself."

Edward glanced at him. "Then why do you even do it?"

Jonathan blinked. "Do what?"

"This." Edward gestured. "*Plays*."

A smile moved across his face. "I love it though. I love doing it with my friends."

Sensing an opening, Edward turned a little in the chair.

"That's...tough."

Jonathan nodded.

"And now your friends are all graduating..."

Jonathan kept nodding.

"Heading to the great Southwest..."

Jonathan frowned. "Hm? Oh right. It said that in the program. Yes, May is going to teach at an Indian Reservation down in Arizona. Apparently she'll be teaching every grade level. Probably have to drive the bus, too." He giggled.

"How about you?"

Jonathan exhaled. "Nope, nope, we're finally parting ways."

Edward arched an eyebrow.

"We grew up together, May and I," he said. "We're from the city."

Edward's breath caught. "You are?"

Jonathan nodded.

Edward's heart was racing. He had just caught Jonathan in another lie: "That's crazy! I thought I knew everyone in this town."

Jonathan blinked rapidly. "This town? God, I'm not from *this* town. Manhattan. We're from Manhattan. And you thought—" His eyes widened. "Oh, how funny! I said—And you thought I meant—" He coughed into his hand. "So you're from here? This, uh, city?"

Edward's face burned. "Yeah," he muttered. "I'm from here."

"And you go to the university?"

His jaw clenched. "Yeah."

Jonathan hesitated. "*This* might sound crazy, but—"

"You've never met another student who's from around here."

A sheepish smile. "Yes. Sorry."

"There's a few of us on campus."

Jonathan nodded, a look that Edward couldn't read passed over his face, and his right hand slipped into the cushions, feeling for the orange book hidden there.

Edward nodded at Jonathan's hand. "How are you liking that book?"

His hand sprung out of the cushions. "Book? What?"

"Isn't that a book wedged in there? A big orange one?" Edward reached over, and Jonathan shrunk against the armrest, blocking him.

"Oh yes, there's a book there, uh huh yes, I'm liking it…" he stammered.

"What's the book?"

"Oh, you mean the title?" Jonathan let out a nervous laugh. "*La Chute.*"

Edward frowned. "*La* what?"

The poser's eyes rolled. "Oh, well, yes, maybe you know it by its other title, *The Fall*. I'm reading it in the French you know, so it's a bit slow going. I'm a French minor, but my French is not great. It's actually *mauvais on s'excuse pas pas plus qu'on ne s'aplatit en poussant son interlocuteur à sortir son mouchoir*. Hey, how are you doing on that drink? Would you like another?"

Edward smiled. "That book, you know, is nothing to be ashamed of."

Jonathan nodded.

"A lot of people like it," Edward continued. "My mom, for instance? Huge fan."

"Oh, I agree. It's quite wonderful. Difficult, but wonderful. And maybe a bit hard to bear. The voice, I mean. The voice of an angry man can be hard to bear."

Edward grinned. "But I had no idea the author wrote in French."

"Pardon?"

"I mean she's British, right? But I guess over there people speak a bunch of languages. But hell, I'm assuming a lot. Maybe you're reading a *French translation.*"

Jonathan sputtered, "I don't—"

"I should suggest that to my mom. *Hey, it'll be like reading it for the first time. Only this time the big mystery will be what the fuck do all these words mean!*"

"*Albert Camus…*" the poser cried, "*…est très très français!*"

"Camoo? Who's talking about Camoo?" Edward asked, intentionally drawing out the author's name.

"We are!"

Edward shook his head. "I'm talking about Agatha Christie. She wrote—what did you say the title was?"

Jonathan went absolutely white.

"*Dumb Witness,*" Edward said. "Classic read."

Jonathan shrunk back into the chair. "You saw the book. You knew. I am humiliated."

Edward sucked his lips in, suppressing a smirk.

"You think I'm a jerk," Jonathan muttered.

No, just a sociopath.

"I love Agatha Christie," Jonathan said. "Maybe not *Dumb Witness,* one of her more minor works. No offense to your taste, but I don't think anyone calls it a classic. But she is one of the great female *genre-ists,* in my mind, at least."

"Seems like you're hiding it from me."

"From you? No! From people. From anyone. It's my habit to hide it, which isn't so hard to do, seeing as I rarely have the book with me in public. But tonight is…there's something I need to do once the play concludes, and the book, well, it plays a role in that. It has special significance."

Edward licked his lips. "And that thing you have to do, that's why you're so nervous?"

Jonathan nodded.

"The play isn't really what's upsetting you, huh?"

"Oh no!" Jonathan laughed. "That too. I really only lied about the book. I'm very sorry about that. It's just that I'm going to tell May that I love her tonight and this book—" His hand flew up to his mouth. "I told you." He started laughing behind his hand. "Oh my god. I just told you." Tears sprung from his eyes, and he was no longer quiet and demure and gently giggly but basically screaming with laughter.

Edward jumped up from the chair. He grabbed Jonathan's forearm.

"The kitchen," he hissed. "Come on…"

Edward dropped the poser into a chair at the kitchen table. Then he reached for the scotch and fresh tumblers, pouring them each a shot.

His hands trembled as he poured. He couldn't believe how well it was going for him. It had taken no effort at all to get Jonathan to admit that he was writing May. Now he just needed to convince the poser to keep quiet about it. How hard could it be? The poser was so nervous about the whole thing it should be a breeze.

Jonathan seemed not to notice the drink in front of him. He was looking around the table, finally turning and seeing the satchel hanging on the back of his chair. He reached around, undoing the flap. He dropped the orange book inside.

"May is my best friend," the poser said, turning back around. "My very best. My oldest…"

He blinked at the drink in front of him, while Edward leaned back, clutching his own tumbler.

Then the hand reached out, snatched it up—

Jonathan wiped his mouth. "I love her, but I have never told her so. A voice in my head says don't ruin the friendship that means so much to you both. And this voice that says no has always won the argument, at least until eight months ago."

Jonathan knocked back the refill that Edward had poured. Slammed the glass down.

"May gets love letters. They're from a secret admirer. She doesn't know that the secret admirer is me. Last week..." his voice broke. "Last week she asked *me*, in person..." He looked up. "Ah god, she asked me if she should try to meet this man she's writing. She said, *I might be in love with him, Jon.* Do you understand how terrible it was to hear that? When she said it, I felt as if she were admitting to being in love with someone else. I felt jealous. I was jealous of *him*. Isn't that absurd?"

Edward poured him another drink. "Who does she think she's writing?"

Jonathan shrugged, reaching for the glass. "She doesn't know."

"I mean..." He let out a hot spurt of air. "What's the name you use to sign the letters?"

Jonathan waved a hand. "Oh, some random name."

Edward put his hand over his mouth. Wow, OK. This guy would say just enough true things to make the lies seem real.

Jonathan placed the empty glass on the table. "Edward, you look upset. Why shouldn't you be? I'm telling you this terrible thing I'm doing to my best friend. But you see, I can only tell you this because I don't know you and you don't know me. You don't know May and you don't know our friends. My friends are wonderful, I love them, but I have never been able to talk to them about this.

"I didn't realize that this is what I needed. You. A perfect stranger. I suppose that is the Catholic in me. I need to confess to someone whom my confession will not be a burden. I hope this is not asking too much of you." His eyes widened. "No! What? Of course it is. I'm asking too much!

"My father does this. He loves to talk to strangers. If you meet my father at a bar, and he doesn't know you, then be prepared to learn everything about this man. He doesn't talk to his family. It seems he can't. An example—my parents and I are out to dinner. As usual, Father hardly says a word. When he finally does, it's to excuse himself to use the restroom. Twenty minutes pass and he isn't back—I get up to find him, and there he is, talking with the bartender. I overhear him telling him—but that doesn't matter. He's telling the bartender a very simple story. I ask myself, as I always do when I'm confronted with Father's bizarre behavior—*Why does he talk about his life with everybody but my mother and me?* I asked myself this question for years. Do you know what I finally realized? My father is a liar. This is also lying. It doesn't matter that every story he tells checks out as factual—his way of engaging with people is deceptive. If you can only have relationships with people who don't care about you, whose judgments of you have no actual bearing on their own life or yours, then you're fundamentally deceitful."

A film of sweat had built on the poser's waxy, bloodless face. His eyes were bright.

You little fucker, Edward thought.

"You think I'm terrible," the poser whispered.

Edward's jaw flexed.

"But do you know what I mean? Do you know people like this, like my father?"

"Man…" Edward scratched his throat. "What do you want me to say? Like, I'm talking to you, right? And you're saying you're doing the same thing as your dad, right? So am I supposed to be like, *Nah man, I don't know anybody like that*?"

Jonathan giggled and covered his mouth. "Sorry, I'm not laughing at you! Sorry, sorry!" He squeezed his eyes shut. He stopped laughing and began breathing deeply behind his hands.

A moment passed.

Jonathan rested his chin on his fists.

"Are you an actor, Edward?"

"No."

"Are you an artist?"

Edward shook his head.

Jonathan smiled. "What do you do?"

"What do I *do*?"

"Do you have…interests?" Jonathan immediately began shaking his head. "Sorry, strike that. Terrible question. *Insane* question."

Edward glanced at the fridge. "Man, do you have anything to eat?"

"Mm, yes. I do think there's some cold spaghetti in…"

Edward's chair made a long squeal across the floor. He pulled the fridge door open. A rush of cold air, head filling with the sour smell…

Don't let him rattle you, he thought as his eyes scanned the chock-full shelves—fogged jars, cartons with Chinese lettering, plates of uncovered, thinly cut meats. *Gain control of the conversation. Steer it back to May.*

Edward held up a plastic container. "This?"

"Yes, forks in the drawer."

As Edward fished around for one, Jonathan said, "You know…I didn't ask you about your interests to be nosy. It's just nice to talk to someone who isn't another actor or artist. An actual person. Do you want to sit?"

"Nope." Edward shoveled forkfuls into his mouth.

"I don't know how this whole thing looks to the world. I can *guess*…"

Edward chewed. "But like who does May think she's writing?"

"I told you—"

"Oh come on. She's a girl. You know she's making up stories about the guy."

Jonathan shook his head. "Truly, I don't know. There's nothing in the letters that's biographical—at least in the sense that we usually mean. Nobody ever mentions past history, family life, or even what they *did* that day. The letters are personal in a different way. It's all about what they think and feel about books, music, theater, film."

Edward scraped the sides of the container. "You know you keep saying *they*, right?"

Jonathan sighed. "I know. It's such a problem. I'm really beginning to think of myself as *two people* who are also *mortal enemies*."

Edward ran his finger along the inside, then licked his finger, lips, fork. "Wanna know what I think?"

"Yes."

"Are you sure? Because it's like you said, I'm nobody. I'm a stranger."

Jonathan leaned forward. "Yes. Oh please! I need an objective opinion. I need to know how this looks from the *outside*."

Edward set the empty container on the counter. He put his hand over his mouth, pretending to think but really he just watched Jonathan grow more and more agitated. The poser's face had no color, totally pale, basically cadaverous, but his eyes were wide, wild, bright, about to pop—

Edward said, "It's sketchy as fuck. It's fucking twisted."

Jonathan's eyes filled with tears.

Edward went for his scotch, and Jonathan also reached for his, sweat sprouting at his temples. They drank—Jonathan pulled the glass from his lips, sweating harder.

A shudder passed through him.

"Oh god." Jonathan covered his mouth. "I'm going to be sick."

Staggering up, knocking the chair over—

Jonathan escaped behind a door in the corner of the room. A sign read, "PISSES ONLY, SHITS/GIGGLES IN BASEMENT."

Edward leaned back in his seat, crossing his arms behind his head. He listened with pleasure to Jonathan retching in the background. Guys like Jonathan, they were go-go-go until they totally disintegrated. They were talking and laughing and jabbering mindlessly, until you knocked them over the head with a cinderblock. Hey. Not a bad idea. He imagined loading Jonathan into the backseat of Gran's car, driving out into the middle of nowhere, and dumping him in a ditch.

Edward lit a cigarette.

Get him so drunk he passes out. Then drive to the train crossing on Fremont, where the trains always stall. Up goes Jonathan's senseless body onto a freight car. Train moves on. Choo-choo!

The toilet flushed. Edward tensed, waiting for Jonathan to come back out. But the poser retched again, loudly, violently, and Edward smiled, driving to Lake Erie. *Put Jonathan on a cargo ship heading through the St. Lawrence Seaway to the Atlantic. Jonathan wakes up hours later. Water, water everywhere, nor any drop to...*

The legs of the table shook. Glasses and the bottle of scotch wiggling down the wood. And elsewhere: bangs, booms, shouts. People, a billion, thundering into the house.

Faces appeared in the kitchen doorway. Laughing, sweaty and flushed. They glanced at Edward, then turned away.

The next face was May's.

"Have you seen..." she stopped, listening. "Is that—?"

"Jonathan," Edward said, over the sound of vomit pelting toilet water.

May eyed him. "And you are?"

Ally appeared next to her, snapping her gum. "That's our mystery man."

May flushed.

"He just showed up out of nowhere," Ally said. "Acting like he owned the place. Maybe he'll tell you who he is. But I couldn't get it out of him."

May's eyes drilled into him.

"Jonathan's OK," Edward said. "He just drank a little too fast."

Her frown deepened, lips puckering. Edward thought of the photo, the fat cigar in those lips. How many times had Jonathan looked at that cigar and wished it was his cock?

Some other people came and stood in the doorway.

Ally snapped her bubblegum. "Earth to May?"

She sucked in her bottom lip, looking away from Edward to her friend.

"Let's *go-o*," Ally said. "Bus is leaving."

May's eyes returned to Edward, "What about him?"

"No," Ally cut in. "There's barely enough room in the car as it is."

"Ally," May murmured. "We can't leave him."

Edward frowned, listening to the girls quietly argue.

And then it dawned on him.

Holy shit. She thinks I'm Roger Ackroyd.

"May," he said, surprising himself.

She looked over. Her voice was breathless: "Yes?"

"I'll see you at the bar. We'll talk then."

What was that look on her face? Solemn or sad or—?

She grinned broadly, nodding.

"Don't you forget Jon!" Ally called over her shoulder, dragging May out of the room.

"Yes," May echoed. "Don't leave him!"

The toilet flushed again. The tap turned on. Edward took the last drag from his cigarette.

Put Jonathan in the trunk. Drive him up to Canada and dump him there. Dump him anywhere, really.

The bathroom door opened.

There was Jonathan, bouncing on his heels. "What? What's happening? Did I hear May?"

This fucking guy. He didn't even sound drunk anymore.

"The play's over," Edward said.

Jonathan looked around.

"Where is everybody?"

"Gone."

"Did they say where?"

Edward frowned, suddenly flustered.

Jonathan nodded. "They'll be at Michigan Bar." He looked at his watch. "Ten twenty-nine p.m. Well, it didn't run *too long*, considering the late start!" He looked up at Edward and smiled. "Well, shall we?"

Edward didn't move. "What are you going to do?"

Jonathan rubbed his stomach. "Well, the first thing I'll do is order a 7-Up to calm down my tummy!"

"No! What'll you do when you see May?"

"Hm, well I…" Jonathan's eyes widened. "Oh, I forgot! Oh, for one beautiful minute! Oh, I told you everything!"

Edward shrugged. "It's not like I held a gun to your head."

"Oh no, of course not. I'm the one who dragged you into this…*ugliness*. I'm terribly sorry, but thank you. I wish you weren't involved at all, but thank god you're here. I hate to ask for help, I'm really quite impossible at it. You can't imagine how terrible I am at just asking for the simplest of things from people." He slapped his thigh. "Well, shall we, *shall we*?"

"Jesus christ," Edward muttered.

Jonathan cocked his head. "Yes? What is it?"

"What are you going to do?" Edward cried out.

Jonathan laughed. "I don't have a clue! But it'll be OK! I don't know! I don't know why I know this. I get good feelings sometimes. I can be quite intuitive. Did you park far? Is it a far walk?"

Edward looked up at him. "You don't have a car?"

"Oh no. I'm a terrible driver. *Je suis un très mauvais conducteur…*"

I could push him out of the car, while clocking ninety, Edward realized, as they walked down Dunbar Road. *But he's the type to wear a seatbelt. I fucking hate him.*

Jonathan was rubbing his hands together, yammering on, "I don't know, I just don't know…"

Edward pointed. "That's my car there."

"I'm feeling excited." Jonathan laughed. "I have no clue!"

They slipped into their seats.

"So…" Edward said, pulling the car onto the road, "you're going to tell her then?"

"Maybe?"

Fuck motherfucker! Edward gripped the wheel. What the fuck should he do? Relax, think—but he couldn't relax, couldn't think—couldn't think until he was relaxing. Very tired. He needed a nap. A cigarette. No. One of the—

"Hold the wheel," Edward grunted.

Jonathan sputtered, "Now?"

"Never mind," Edward muttered, letting go and reaching into his pocket.

Jonathan screamed, "The road! It's turning!"

"Yeah…" Edward dug around his pocket, feeling for the pills. He took up the wheel again, the other hand holding the baggie out to Jonathan.

"Give me two."

"What are they?" Jonathan asked, taking the baggie.

"Quaaludes."

"*Really?*" Jonathan hesitated. "Can I have one?"

"Man…take a couple."

A rustling of paper. Edward felt two drop into his palm.

Then Edward heard a siren.

In the rearview mirror: red and blue lights.

Cops? For him? Edward felt his heart rise up, his spirits soar. Michigan Bar, that hell before his eyes, was vanishing, a new future materializing. Cops, cops were in the future. Never in his life had Edward been so happy to meet a pig on a country road. Edward's foot let up the gas, and Jonathan exclaimed, "What? That's not for us. Don't stop!"

Edward put his blinker on, then popped the pills in his mouth.

"But you weren't doing anything!"

"I'm drunk," Edward said.

"They don't know that!"

"And I'm on drugs."

"You didn't take them yet!"

Edward held up his empty hand.

Jonathan screamed.

Car off the road, engine cut, Edward watched the rearview mirror to see who was coming up. Anton or Steve? For the first time ever he prayed for Anton. *Give me the biggest asshole cop in the world. I need to make this last all night.*

Edward took his time rolling down the window.

"What are you doing?" Jonathan whimpered. "Roll it *down!*"

Yeah, yeah, Edward got it down.

An angry beam of light hit his face. "What'd I do?" Edward asked it, holding his hand up.

A heavy sigh. "Well, Eddie, let's see…"

Shit, it was Steve.

"Your tail lights are out. Both of them," Steve said.

Hell yes, Gran! Edward nearly cheered.

"Let's see your license."

Edward smiled weakly. "You know how I feel about personal identification."

"Uh-huh. Yep." The sound of drumming fingers on the hood. "I told you, Eddie, the next time I caught you driving without a license I'd take you in."

Edward affected a loud, sad sigh.

"But seeing as it's nearly graduation, I'll give you a present. Shoot, it's a present for both of us. Heck if it hasn't been a busy night." He patted the hood. "You're good to go, Eddie. Just tell your gran to get her tail lights fixed."

Shit! Shit! Shit!

"Thank you, officer!" Jonathan piped up.

"Eh?" Steve turned the flashlight on him. "What do you got there?" The beam quavered on the pills in Jonathan's hands.

Jonathan froze. "Oh, no—these aren't—"

Steve stepped back, hand on his holster. "Out of the car!"

John wailed, "No, no, no! You don't understand!"

Edward unbuckled quickly, biting his lip to keep from grinning. Steve was a softie about drinking, speeding—about pretty much everything. But he hated the out-of-town college kids and their out-of-town drugs!

Outside the car, Edward placed his hands on the hood and

watched Steve walk around the car to deal with Jonathan.

"I said put your hands on the car!" he hollered. Jonathan whimpered, slowly sinking to his knees.

Edward lost sight of them. He rose on his toes, trying to see. Suddenly there was a crack and an *oof*—then loud cursing, moans. Were the moans coming from Steve?

Edward squinted. "What'd you do, man?"

Jonathan stammered, "It was an accident! He bent over—I stood—"

Steve stood. His face slimy, dark blood oozing out of his nose and over his mouth. His nose looked all out of whack.

"You have—the right—" Steve wheezed "—to remain silent—"

Warmth rippled all down Edward's body. Ah, yeah. The pills. Finally kicking in. Feeling really fucking good and sleepy and very good as he wandered over to the patrol car and opened the rear passenger door. Edward got in... felt like just a minute later. Lazily Edward opened his eyes. Still in the patrol car, but there were street lights around them. Ahead, he saw the police station. He looked to the left and saw that the car door was open. Anton was peering down at him.

Steve appeared behind Anton. He held a bloody towel to his face. "It was the other kid."

Anton stuck his head in the car. "Hey, other kid. You're not very bright are you? Assaulting a police officer, that's not very bright!"

Anton reached in and grabbed Edward by the neck.

Into a bright yellow room.

A voice hissed, "They took my prints. Why haven't they come for yours?"

Staring at Steve's desk. On it was a photo of Steve's family and Edward's family. They all held fishing poles. He tried to open his mouth.

"… Edward, are you listening?"

It was dark. Hard lumps beneath him.

"Edward?"

Edward shook his head. "Who?"

"I've been thinking—" the voice continued. Who was that? "—about what you were saying earlier. Specifically, your question about who May thinks she is writing."

Edward smiled. It was the poser.

"What if she *does* suspect someone in particular? What if she tries to find this particular person while I'm in here?"

Edward, trying to sit up, found that nothing moved. "Where are you?" he called out.

"I'm in the cell with you. Did you hear anything I just said?"

"I can't see you."

"Your eyes are closed. Look, we can't have her looking for this person. She can't try to find him. If you get out tomorrow and I don't, I need you to go to her. Keep an eye on her. Make sure she doesn't find him."

Edward yawned. "Who is she writing?"

The poser exclaimed, "Me!"

Edward rolled onto his side. "Wrong answer."

Me, she's writing me…and Edward sat down on the beach towel next to her, feeling the sun, the sea drift. May took the cigar out of her mouth and dropped it in the sand.

WEDNESDAY

HE TRIED to explain things to her. Turned in bed and said, *This is how it is, this is what I did and why.* She listened to him, didn't interrupt, looking at him with those large black eyes that tore him up inside, that burrowed deep into him. *I love you*, he said, *I love you so much*, as he woke up with tears in his eyes.

This time, alone. Edward was cold, in dim light. His limbs were splayed out on the ground, no, bed—this was a bed. His fingers gripped an edge. His other hand slid up a smooth wall. As he turned his head to the side, tears crossed his face. There was a stranger across the room, prone in a narrow cot. Edward knew him. Didn't he? He knew the stranger's face. And the name was on the tip of Edward's tongue. Wanted to say *Roger*, but that was just his brain misfiring. He shivered. It was cold in this room.

This room? He scrambled to sit up. Edward saw bars, prison bars. *Oh fuck, what?*

He rose from the cot, staggering over to the bars. He placed his head between the cold rods, compressing his temples, jacking up the pressure in his head. This wasn't right. This didn't make sense. Confined. With him? He was really bad. Evil. Edward couldn't put his finger on why, or recall his name, but he knew the stranger wanted him dead last night, had tried to kill him. *It wasn't a fucking dream. He was going to kill you. And now you're in prison, actually gripping the bars, you jerk.*

Now Edward was shaking the bars. They did not move, they made no noise. He pleaded, "Hey, hey, hey?" Had to whisper— didn't want the stranger to wake—but he really wanted to scream, because this was terror. *Why, fucking god, would they lock me up? I did nothing! He's the violent one! His name is not Roger, Roger, Roger. Think, stupid. Fucking think. Think think think think*—

"Edward?"

He blinked, stunned, at the cop walking toward him.

"Yeah, so, you got to step back from the gate."

Edward stared.

"I'm letting you out, son."

Edward glanced back. "What about…"

"Let sleeping dogs lie." The cop pulled out his keys. "Your friend isn't going anywhere."

Edward shook his head. "He's not my friend."

"Hm."

The cop led him out the cell and into another room. Immediate strain to his eyes. Bad light. Like a dark bar at midday. Edward saw swivel chairs, messy desks, and felt a flurry of cooler air on his face. A floor fan ahead of him slowly turned its head.

Edward rubbed his temples. "Do you have any aspirin?"

"Got a headache, Eddie?"

Laughter. It seemed to come at him from all sides, compounding the pain in his head, his nausea. But throwing his gaze around the room, Edward saw there was no one else around but the cop who brought him in.

"Ah Eddie, you were born a little shit and you grew up into an even littler shit. By the time you're my age you're going to be a teeny-weeny pea-sized shit. About yay big." The cop held his forefinger and thumb apart a half inch. "A little bitty rat shit."

The cop held his belly, leaning forward as he laughed.

"Eddie Moses, the amazing shrinking shit!"

Ah fuck this guy. This guy, Edward knew this guy. He hadn't recognized him at first. He needed shitty lighting to see him properly. Without beer and cigarette stink, it's difficult to access most childhood memories. But Edward knew him. Yeah, he knew Bob, Bill, whatever dumbfuck name he had—he hung out at the Elks. A pathetic friend of his father, friend being all too generous of a designation, because his father was too fucking generous, too fucking careless, a practitioner of indiscriminate, mindless, and meaningless friendship. God this drunk was a cop? Bob was? Bill? Since when? Since always? Really? Always? In Edward's memory, the cop wore a Hawaiian shirt, bright red with big blue flowers on it. His knees kept jostling the poker table, spilling the chips, making Edward's dad and the other guys yell.

"Go on. Get your things, Eddie," the cop said.

Edward saw his wallet on the desk, along with his cigarettes, notebook, and pen.

"You're letting me go?"

"You wanna stay?"

Edward snatched the items up, cramming them into his jacket pockets.

"Don't forget your purse," the cop sneered.

Edward looked around, confused. There was a satchel on the desk. But it wasn't his. "That's—" *not mine* he almost said, but stopped. That satchel, light brown with two buckles. He'd seen it last night. Around what's-his-name's neck.

Edward frowned. "What's going to happen to…" and the name popped into his head, *"Jonathan?"*

The cop scratched his jaw. "Hm, well, I suppose there'll be a bail hearing in a week or so. Hope he don't got somewhere to be!"

Edward's grip on the satchel tightened. He remembered the wing chair, the orange book in Jonathan's lap.

Edward exhaled quickly.

"Yep. It's serious business," the cop said. "That boy in there assaulted an officer of the law. Other offenses, too." He began to count them off his fingers. "Resisting arrest, illicit narcotics, public intoxication. And we're also thinking he might be behind the recent spate of…"

Graduation was in a few days. Friday. If he was in jail, Jonathan would miss that. And by the time he got out, everybody would have left town. The Mystery Girl, May, would be gone.

"…thank your lucky stars you're not in there with him. I'd go find your old man and kiss the ring. If he hadn't come in here and explained things about your gran being how she is, you might be stuck in jail like your friend. And then where would you be?"

Edward blinked. "Huh?"

The cop rolled his eyes. "Gee, Eddie, you can pay attention, can't you? I'm saying there's no charges, I'm saying to thank your dad when you see him!"

Edward walked out of the station with a big grin on his face. Tingling all over—his knuckles, his lips. Free, free, free. And the poser was locked up! Even better, he had Jonathan's satchel. He hiked it up his shoulders, eager to find Gran's car, drive back to her place, and see what was inside.

He scanned the parking lot for the car.

"Yoo-hoo," he heard a familiar voice call.

He looked in the other direction and saw Aunt Amy leaning against Gran's car.

He frowned. "What are you doing here?"

Her eyes narrowed. "Careful."

She couldn't have driven in just this morning, just for him. Grand Rapids was about three hours from Monroe. And anyway, why wasn't she in New York City? Peter was graduating from Columbia this week. Or last week. What was today?

"I just meant—"

"Your dad couldn't stick around," she said. "Come on, get it."

He expected her to drive him to the college and drop him off. That would suck, just about the last place he wanted to be, but she didn't make the turn, kept driving straight. The car was headed…

out of town? Where was she taking him? He couldn't ask her. It'd only piss her off. Exactly the questions that shouldn't piss Aunt Amy off pissed her off more than any others. Why? Good fucking question. Edward closed his eyes, snuggling against the window. *Where are we going, Aunt Amy? — Wherever I want you to go, Edward. Wherever I and your mom have decided to take you...* Bright, loud images came into Edward's mind. A girl weeping, gripping the edges of her green glittering gown. A gruff voice, *Take it off!* Dread rose in Edward. *Take it off!*

Edward opened his eyes. Who was speaking? He peeled his slobbery cheek off the car window and blinked. The car wasn't moving, the engine was off.

Edward's eyes widened, registering the parking lot, the red brick buildings. They were at the county hospital, where they always took his sister. He croaked, "Viv? What happened to her?"

Confusion, then pain, flashed across Aunt Amy's face. "Oh no, honey. Your sister's fine."

But his mind was already there, in a terrible room with Viv. They had her in restraints. Sticking a needle in her. Her eyes rolled back.

But she's fine, he told himself. *Aunt Amy just said...*

"What'd you say?"

Aunt Amy rubbed her temples. "I *said* she's having some heart trouble. This morning, you know, there were problems. Luckily your mom slept at her house last night, so she was there to call an ambulance."

Edward shook his head. "*Who?* Fucking *who* are you talking about?"

Aunt Amy's jaw dropped. "Who do you think you're talking to?" She knocked him upside the head. "Hello?" She knocked him again, and he set his jaw, breathing in and out of his nose, hearing her, barely, over his seething exhalations. *Viv's OK, she's OK*—but what were they here for? Who had heart trouble? Which aunt? Which fucking aunt was up in there?

"…picking up your mom. She went over in the ambulance with her and doesn't have anything to get home in. It's ten a.m., Gran should be out of surgery by now."

Gran? Oh shit. "Gran is sick?"

Aunt Amy continued rubbing her temples. "Ah cripes, Edward. Coronary bypass. They were trying other stuff, but it wasn't working. I'll run in and get your mom. But if you want to come up… Yoo-hoo, would you look at me please?"

Aunt Amy gave his knee a hard, sharp squeeze that wasn't playful or comforting, just fucking menacing. When his aunt was mad, she looked exactly like his mom. They had the same little snot haircut, a goddamn bowl cut. Who got bowl cuts? They had a lot in common, his mom, his aunt, six-year-old girls, you know, they all had bad hearts. No bad hearts on Gran's side. On his dad's side, it was brain stuff and lung stuff. But there was nothing wrong with hearts on that side of the family—

He pressed his lips together, fighting back the urge to vomit.

"Are you coming?" she asked.

He shook his head, eyes darting around for something to puke in.

"Then wait here. I'll be back with your mom in ten minutes."

Aunt Amy got out of the car and began walking across the parking lot toward the hospital entrance. He couldn't wait—she was still in view but he couldn't—he leaned out Gran's car and it all just kinda came shuddering out, terrible taste, wonderful feeling. *Christ, I'm going to feel better.* He heaved a couple more times, then straightened. *Oh fuck.* His mom would see all that, would have to step right over the vomit, to get into Gran's car.

Edward scratched the back of his head, looking around. Could he just get out of here? Where could he go? Nothing nearby. This wasn't the city hospital where his dad worked, but the county facility built on the outskirts for the old people and the crazies. Ugh, he was so hungover. Didn't want to stick around for the bus—needed food now.

Poor Gran, he thought, walking up to the hospital. She

must be miserable. If he knew her, she wasn't worried about her health—just upset about all the meatloaves in her future. He remembered last year, after she had those so-called mini-strokes. *Oh they're calling this lasagna,* she had said, pushing her tray up, *but I know meatloaf when I taste it. Everything's meatloaves here, it's all meatloaves here, even the milk, you know, it tastes like—What, you don't believe me? Try it, try it!*

Ah Gran, I'm so fucking sorry.

He walked through the front lobby, straight to the cafeteria. He pushed in through the double doors and smelled coffee, syrup, hell yeah!—They were still set up for breakfast. He walked around the tables to the back of the cafeteria, where there was countertop after countertop of steaming buffet trays. He loved a buffet, any kind, where there was food laid out everywhere and you could have your pick, you could get anything and however much you wanted, toast *and* pancakes *and* bacon *and* sausage *and* ham *and* orange juice and pulling out his wallet he saw he had no bills in it, and sticking his hands in his pocket, he felt one coin, two, and in his other pocket, a gaping hole, his underwear. *Ah fuck my life.* His eyes scaled the list for anything less than, than…he checked the two coins in his hand…thirty-five cents. Milk was thirty cents. He went over to the cooler and found whole, reduced fat (bleh), chocolate, strawberry, hm. Strawberry? Eh. He took out a half pint of chocolate and went over to the register and paid for it.

Walking back through the tables, taking in quick little sips through the little red straw, he went directly past a woman with arms akimbo and realized, too late, it was his mom.

She grabbed his jacket, reeling him to her table.

"I forgot to ask Amy to fill up Gran's tank. Do you know if she did?"

Edward eyed the four red nails gripping his jacket.

"No," he said.

"No, you don't know, or no, she didn't?"

He gnawed on the milk straw. "I don't know."

She let go of him, sighing. "How will I get it all done? There's so much to do before your party this weekend!"

He sucked up the last of the milk. "Party?" he asked.

"Your party! Your party! For crying out loud!"

"I don't want a party."

"Oh of course you do! It's your graduation. Your aunt drove down here a week early to help out with it. Edward Allen, I swear, you're looking at me like you have no idea what I'm talking about."

"Right."

She rolled her eyes. "Would you sit? Would you do that? Would you sit? Would you?"

He tipped his head back. *Oh god, oh god, oh god!*

He would, he did. He sat. She was all business. Arranging things for his graduation. It was unbelievable to him. Not a word about Gran, how she was doing. His mom was a machine, *total business*, obsessed with his fucking graduation: there was Edward's ceremony in two days, *on Friday*. Then there was Peter and Edward's joint graduation party the following day, *on Saturday*. And his aunt drove down early, *last night*, to take care of Viv while Edward's mom spent *these last remaining days* arranging everything.

"And would you please not forget to get the extra graduation tickets. You get them *today*. You hear me?"

Edward stared at the completely untouched tray of breakfast food in front of his mom. He said, to that golden gleaming egg yolk, "I don't get why Aunt Amy is here."

"I'm going to strangle you! She's here for you. For your graduation."

"Right." His eyes moved over to her bacon. "Why is she here for *my* graduation? Her son, you know, you know Peter? He's graduating right now in New York City?"

"Peter didn't want anyone coming to that. He told her not to."

Edward made eyes at the buttered toast. "Right, OK. Then

we're operating on the same information. Peter doesn't want anyone coming to his graduation. I, too, do not want anyone coming to my graduation. Please respect that."

He watched as her face crumbled to little quivering bits. He wanted to say, but did not say, thinking instead—*all you care about is your stupid party and not that Gran is possibly dying.* And upon thinking this, Edward's eyes welled up.

Fuck man, Gran's not dying, fuck you for even thinking it!

"But the party…" his mom murmured, tears in her eyes too.

God the party, the party! Who cares about the party?

"*How's Gran?*" he growled.

She pulled the napkin off the tabletop, and blew her nose, wiped her eyes, god gross, wrong order.

"Gran's fine. Stable. Got out of surgery an hour ago. The doctors want to keep her for a few more days, probably until Sunday—oh, it breaks my heart. She was so looking forward to your graduation. Gran *loves* a ceremony."

He took a deep breath. "Well, what if we just did the party."

"Well…" She bit her lip. "I know things are busy with Uncle Joe right now. It might be better if he just drives down *Friday night*, maybe early *Saturday morning*, for the party. But are you sure," her voice broke, "that you don't want at least your father and me to come to the ceremony on Friday?"

His head shook. "Nope. No. Nope."

"I'll talk to your father." She looked at her watch. "*Shoot.* Your sister's at H.U.G.S. and I forgot to ask Amy—" Her eyes flashed up at Edward. "Oh no. Don't start with that." She reached for her purse. "Will I see you back here tonight? We're all meeting up in Gran's room at 7 p.m. Your cousin Dave is bringing Chinese."

He watched her food. "I thought I'd go see Gran right now."

"She's in post-op!"

His gaze stroked the untouched ham. "So, I'll stick around until she's out."

She snorted. "Uh-huh, sure. Say, how are your eyes liking that food? Taste good to them, yeah?" She pushed the tray forward. "Eat it. You look like…well, you look like crap."

Her hand flew to her mouth. "Edward Allen, you spent the night in jail!"

He gaped at her. "Yeah…?"

She shook her head back and forth. "You should not drive without your license! And as for *your friend*…" She leaned in, lowering her voice. "Eat your food, Edward Allen. You better just eat your food and *thank your lucky stars* we're giving you a free pass on this one."

Lucky stars, lucky stars, why did everybody keep telling him to thank his lucky stars?

Half muttering to herself, she continued. "All this craziness going on and we're all looking the other way, letting you get away with—" Her eyes sharpened. "What're you up to, hm? What exactly is going on with you?"

"Oh enough," he said, shoving toast into his mouth. "H.U.G.S., Ma. You've got to check my sister out of the institution."

She grabbed her purse, standing. "And would you take a *shower*?"

He chewed her toast and bacon. He grabbed his mom's coffee and drank it down and frowned at the empty cup. He hated coffee. His mom loved coffee, and he always hated it. Hated her coffee breath, haunted by it all through his childhood, as well as by toilet bowls filled with her stinking coffee pee. And while a human could survive a week or so without drinking water, his mom would die in the first hour of the morning if she didn't have two to three cups of coffee, at least two cups of coffee, one wasn't enough. By the afternoon, she'd be taking slow calculated slips from the cold dregs of a third or fourth cup until the moment her head fell into a pillow at night. All day long her body ground down into bits, and the bits were what went to bed at night, and for three hours every night, she slept totally still, totally debilitated, until the beans in her blood and bones and brain and muscles began weakening, dimming, and the pain began building, lighting up each individual tooth in her head, until her head hurt so much, she had to get up. Coffee, she needed coffee, get moving, quit hurting, have coffee, get moving quit hurting have coffee go go keep going or you're dead.

He shouldn't have had that cup of coffee. His legs were jittering. He bolted up, got out, around, walking from the table, through the exit, through the lobby, out the double doors, down the sidewalk to the bus stop, shaking his fists at the wrists, bouncing in the soles of his shoes...feeling close to Gran, closer than ever. Waiting for the bus to come, thinking about how all through breakfast there was a tight, sharp ache in his chest. And closing his eyes, he immediately started to dream. Loud, bright images, a girl in a green dress, incredibly beautiful. He knew her, of course. He wondered what Mystery Girl was up to right now.

What did she think when he didn't show up to Michigan Bar?

The satchel, he touched it, hanging at his hip. *Patience*, he told himself. He'd open it up as soon as he got to Gran's. And if he wasn't ready to see what was inside...well, at least he had it. The head of his enemy. His trophy. The bus pulled up. Edward fumbled with his wallet, getting out his pass. The doors to the bus opened, and he ran right up and held out his pass. The driver looked at it. Then stuck his bottom lip out.

"Expired," the bus driver said.

"What?"

"Expired."

Edward frowned, still holding it out. "No, no, this doesn't expire, this is a student pass. It lasts all semester."

"Expired," the bus driver said, and Edward looked down at the pass, knowing full well there was no date on it, it lasted the semester—but there it was, the expiration date. 05-23-80.

"Aw, it can't be more than a day passed this," and somebody elbowed him, hard, from behind, and he craned his neck around to glare at the person pushing him aside. Some dumb chick. She was talking to the bus driver—and then she turned to him.

"Look," the girl said. "I got your fare."

Eh, what? She got his—? OK, weird. "Um, thanks."

She rolled her eyes. Snapped a fat wad of bubblegum. "Man…" she drawled and looked past him. What the fuck? He didn't ask her to help him. Fuck that. This town, man, fuck it. It sucked, the people sucked. He wanted to like them, but they were all terrible.

He took a seat by the window and looked out. Oh look a red barn. Hey, there's hay. Hay. Hey there. Haaaaaaaaaaaay. Who would live here, who didn't have to live here? Who would live here, who had a degree that would let him work anywhere? But Edward's dad, after he finished up his medical program, chose to move back to the town he grew up in. His dad could have stayed on in the town he did his residency in. Traverse City was better. Not much better. Remotely. For no other reason than you could see the bay from most places. You could walk to the water. Stand on a shore and forget about the land behind you and all the members of your family standing behind you. But Edward's dad moved back home to southeast Michigan, chose to do it. Edward didn't have a choice like that. Did he? Probably not. His brain felt like a dead root, keeping him firmly planted in Michigan.

The bus lurched, and Edward saw he'd overshot his stop by a block. He jumped up from his seat, screaming, "Stop!"

At Gran's, the kitchen was a mess: he recognized his mom's handiwork, probably from cooking dinner for Gran last night. Tomato-sauce handprints on the cabinets, the fridge. Dry pasta shells crunching underfoot as he passed by the sink—four different dirty sauce pots in the basin, along with two plates, one licked clean, the other crusted over with bloody spaghetti. Christ, she even got sauce up on the ceiling. Probably what gave Gran the heart attack in the first place. No one liked a clean kitchen more than Gran, no one hated cleaning more than Gran. She wouldn't cook for fear of dirtying a sponge. He left the kitchen for the bathroom.

Took a shit with the satchel on his knees. Contemplating opening it. Beginning to think this was a bad idea. *Better to throw it out? Forget all about it…?*

His hands had another idea, already undoing the buckles and peeling back the flap. There was the orange book. Agatha Christie, *Dumb Witness*. At least he knew what he was getting into.

He cracked open the book to the short stack of letters inside it. He picked up the first letter in the stack and opened it.

```
THINGS KNOWN ABOUT ROGER ACKROYD

1. He lives at Fernly Park in King's
Abbot (England)
2. Fifty years old, give or take
3. At the mercy of his housekeepers, who
all want to marry him.
4. Successful merchant of (I think) wagon
wheels.


. . . and also,


5. A poet who writes for the Daily
Bobcat.


. . . Well, Roger, am I onto you?


I think so.


If you dare, put your reply in the
library book about you.


Sincerely,
Mystery Girl
```

"Holy shit," Edward muttered. This was it, the first letter. *Put your reply in the library book about you.* That line reminded him of something the poser had said last night: the name came from Agatha Christie. Could that really be true?

Hands shaking, Edward turned to the next letter.

This was different from the first. Handwritten. On lined paper ripped from a notebook. A draft maybe?

Things known about Mystery Girl:
She is a girl / she is a mystery

Things unknown about Mystery Girl:
Why she writes me / Everything else.

Sincerely / Roger Ackroyd

God. This guy. You sound super fucking cool, I mean, I want to fuck you, Edward thought, crumpling up the letter, tossing it. Then he lifted up off the toilet seat and snatched the balled-up letter. He sat back down, unfolding and flattening it across his knees. He read it again, going over it slowly, muttering, "Yeah yeah, fuck…" at once ripping the letter to pieces, realizing he was actually throwing the pieces down onto the tile and letting out a cry, basically crying, *fuck this shit, I don't need this shit, you don't have to read this shit!* and he looked down at the two unread letters on his left knee… Several minutes passed. He stared, barely breathing, body aching, he clenched every fucking single muscle in his ass and head, stared, stared, and then actually read the first line of Mystery Girl's reply.

Dear Roger,

He bit his fingers.

I got into another argument about you with my friends last night. They say that anybody could have done what you did. A child could have done it.

Probably, Edward thought.

I could probably ignore them if that's all they said about you, but their views are even more ridiculous than that. They think you are out to destroy poetry! "Roger Ackroyd proves that future poetry is doomed to replication and repetition.

He proves that, finally, there is nothing
new under the sun."

Boring, boring, boring. Banal, banal, banal.

It's one thing for our parents to snub
their noses at our generation. Old
people always say their contributions
are superior to ours. But I cringe every
time I hear someone my age say that we
have nothing new to look forward to. When
my friends say that you are destroying
poetry, I say you are clearing the way
for something new.

Ah god, Mystery Girl wasn't just presumptuous. She was a
kiss-up. Disappointing.

The cherry on top is your name! Roger
Ackroyd! I love Agatha Christie's novels.
THE MURDER OF ROGER ACKROYD is one of my
favorites. I felt like the name was a
clue into who you are and what your true
purpose is.

Edward shook his head. He couldn't read any more of this. It
was totally absurd—

Who are you? Why did you write "The Waste
Land"? What did you mean by it? I hope
you write me back again. I'll look for
your reply in another Christie novel. How
about PARTNERS IN CRIME?

Sincerely,
Mystery Girl

Edward tossed the letter aside. It slid across the floor, scattering
the torn-up pieces of the poser's first letter. He had one left. The
poser's drafted reply. He scowled at the salutation:

Dear "Mystery Girl,"

Oh wow. From the beginning, the poser slapped you in the face with his unoriginality. He could only mock, only belittle Mystery Girl, knock her down to size, with those stupid scare quotes around her name.

I don't relate to any of your (or your friends') concerns.
I'm not thinking about any of your (or your friends') concerns.

I'm concerned with the work / how to create the work / how to throw

my
mindbodysoul

into my work
for the rest of my life.

No, Edward thought. *You ONLY care about what other people think, you fucking phony.*

I don't want to be like my parents whose
work ≠ passion.

They strived & failed & failed & strived / they hate work & their lives.

Maybe I am crazy
alone / creepy.

I don't know you seem like a nice girl
& you liked my poem

but maybe you are like them
& don't get it

Edward couldn't read another word of it, not another word. He'd explode if did. *I hate him, hate him, I want him dead, dead, dead,* Edward thought, jumping up from the toilet, nearly falling forward from the pants around his ankles. He turned around and stood above the toilet bowl, ripping the poser's letter to pieces, and throwing them in.

He agreed with Jonathan, basically. Other people had a lot of stories about you, and if you didn't believe those stories yourself or at least live them out, other people wouldn't have anything to do with you. You hated their stories, and yet you did everything in your power to make their stories come true. You went above and beyond to make them accept you.

Edward looked down at the pieces of paper floating in the toilet, now telling himself that he was different from Jonathan. Edward understood, perhaps he alone understood, that no one created things, they only sifted and sorted the junk heap. There were no artists who were the headspring of invention. There were sifters and sorters—people who went elbow deep into the junk heap to pull out new arrangements of things. *If only I didn't think that way*, Edward thought. *If only I were another dumb artist who told myself I was a genius, would I be happier?*

Edward flushed, pulled up his pants, and stumbled out into the hall, dragging his hand along the wall to keep from stumbling. When he made it into the guest room, he flopped onto the bed and said, "The poser is neutralized," emphasizing the last word, neutralized, then saying it again, "neutralized," then again, "neutralized," until he was shouting, "NEUTRALIZED, NEUTRALIZED, NEU— " but then he fucked up and stuttered and said *neutered*, not neutralized, and fell into silence, stunned. Why the fuck was he in bed anyway? He wouldn't be able to sleep. To sleep he had to extinguish his thoughts and to extinguish his thoughts he needed pills, a cudgel—he remembered the caffeine he had earlier and knew he was doomed. He'd lie like this for hours and bicycles, he's bicycling down a long country road, alongside infinite dead fields, looking for the farmhouse where the Mystery Girl lived. He had to see her—he had a confession to make. The words were on the tip of his tongue. *I'm Rah—I'm Rah*—Dying to tell her. Now that he'd decided to confess he couldn't wait to do it, had to do it now, but where was the house? The farmhouses all looked the same—

His body jerked: he was up, walking quickly away from the bicycle, cutting through tall, brown grass that came up past his shins.

He looked around, terror building in his chest.

What if I die here?

Waking, wanting to leave the house, he walked down into the basement looking for the bike. He eyed a wheel in the corner. Handlebars. He walked over to the bike and squeezed the front tire. Flat.

He left the house on foot, telling himself he wasn't going anywhere—just a short walk to stretch his legs. In his condition, with all his energy, the only thing for him was walking, smoking and walking, both at the same time, one cigarette after the other, one foot after the other. It was really beautiful out. The not-too-warm air, the sun lowered to a late afternoon angle.

When he got to the house on the corner, he stopped. A million cars in the street. The smell of fire and frying and the sound of laughing ecstatic people in their backyard. It's Wednesday. The day of Jim and Carol's fish fry. He'd been invited to it, sort of, when he'd run into Carol last week.

He recalled that Carol's eyes were narrowed, almost accusatory, as she looked him up and down. *It's pretty freaky,* she had said, *that I should run into you twice in the same day, when I never see you anywhere.* Edward knew exactly who Carol was the second time he saw her. But the first time, hours earlier, he hadn't recognized her. She could have been any fat person at the pharmacy. Seeing Carol this second time, at the grocery, he realized that his old high school friend wasn't actually fat, just terrifically pregnant.

Edward coughed into his hand: *When are you expecting?*

Oh, any minute now! Carol said with a laugh, and he coughed harder and she said that her pregnancy was the occasion for an upcoming fish fry, *our last hurrah—once this kiddo comes out, who knows when we'll have time for friends.*

Edward frowned at that. He hadn't seen Carol and Jim for years, not since high school, even though he was one of their friends, even closer to them than Ted, who, no doubt, had been invited to heaps of fish fries over the last four years.

Teddy can't come to the fry, she was saying. *I hope we get to see him, though, before his big move to N-Y-C. I'm just thrilled he got a job at an important newspaper!*

No, Ted might move, he might have a job, nothing's final, Edward didn't say out loud. Instead he said, very casually, that he himself was moving permanently to Cambridge.

Carol looked surprised. *Really?*

Yes, yes, Cambridge, Massachusetts, he said, completely red-faced because it was a lie, a sort of lie. Christiane didn't know yet if she were going to Cambridge, and even if she were, there'd been no mention of Edward coming with her, no expectation or hope or question. How embarrassing that Edward had just lied to Carol, who didn't matter anymore. *What the fucking fuck, you fuck*, and he went on to say—

Yeah, my girlfriend got a job at Harvard.

Carol's eyebrows shot up even higher: *But what will you do there?*

Edward's jaw tensed.

She laughed. *Sorry! I just can't think of this place without you! You Moseses are everywhere in this town. You know I see your mom nearly every week? It's her I'm always running into at the grocery—at the grocery or the pharmacy—and we always talk about how I never see you!*

Edward realized right then that when he had seen Carol the first time—although he'd walked her out to her car and carried her bags and said it really sucked none of the old gang got together, going on about how much it sucked for minutes—she had not invited him to the fish fry. And upon this realization, he firmly resolved, right there in the frozen food aisle, to not only skip her stupid fish fry, but to never say hello to Carol again.

Now, days later, standing on the sidewalk outside Jim and

Carol's house, which really reeked of propane, Edward thought of how neither he nor Carol wanted him here. It was guilt and embarrassment, guilt and pity, that had eventually driven Carol to invite Edward to her celebratory fry. *Bring your girlfriend*, Carol said, and Edward all but clicked his heels, only agreeing, of course, to get away *at once*; and he ran out of the grocery store, throwing open the door to Christiane's bedroom: had there been any news while he was out? Any letters from Harvard? And before Christiane could say *Still no news!*, Edward told her he wanted out of this town, he wanted out of this state: *If you get the job at Harvard, I'm coming with you.*

In front of Jim and Carol's, Edward started pacing. He lit another cigarette. "Christiane? Eh? Is that what's bothering you?" he muttered. Wasn't worth worrying about. The relationship was over, dead, finito. He washed his hands of Cambridge within days of agreeing to go to Cambridge.

A car rolled up and parked in front of Edward. A pizza delivery guy got out. He had on the stupid Tito's outfit: red polyester pants and polo and bright white trainers. The pizza guy stood on the sidewalk for some time, staring up at the house. He was Edward's age, and that should have put them in high school together. But Edward was certain he'd never seen the guy before. Guy must have moved here for college but then dropped out. Damn. Even worse than being born here—you moved here for college and got stuck.

The pizza guy looked at Edward. He pointed at the house.

"Is there a party going on? Like a barbecue?"

Edward nodded.

The pizza guy read the order slip taped to the bag in his hand.

"Rain," he said. And then he frowned, said another thing. It sounded like, *blah-blah.*

Blah-blah? No...

"Rainne Blaha," Edward said.

"Oh yeah? *Rain Blah-Blah* ordered this shit to a barbecue?" The pizza guy scowled and turned back to his car. "Fucking wasting my time..."

Edward called out. "Just go around back. She's definitely there."

The pizza guy looked back at Edward. "Oh yeah?"

Edward nodded.

The pizza guy shook the bag. "Gimme five-fifty!"

Edward let out a surprised laugh. "What?"

"Five-fifty!" the pizza guy yelled.

"But I didn't order that! Rainne Blaha, she like exists, man!"

The pizza guy stepped back onto the sidewalk. He went a few steps past Edward and then whipped around.

"Well? Are you going to point this chick out to me or what?"

Goddamn! Edward felt guilty, actually guilty, as if he had done what the pizza guy thought: phoned in a fake order with a fake name. Someone would actually do that to the pizza guy? Yeah man! Just look at him. People phone in fake orders to fuck with the pizza guy all the time. It's like once a day, twice a day, this shit happens to him. Damn, why does *Edward* feel bad? This wasn't his problem. Turn around. Stop walking *into* the backyard. Turn back now before someone sees—

Oh, there she was.

"Hey," Edward said, pointing Rainne out to the pizza guy. "That's her. The tall one."

Fucking Rainne. Ordering pizza to a fish fry. God.

Edward stuffed his hands in his pockets and found himself in the dead center of the party, staring at these old buddies of his from high school, a few with babies clenched to their chests but other than that, looking as they always did—plump, shabby, happy, reaching out onto the picnic tables laden with platters of fish, stuffing fry after fry in their mouths, consuming a lake's worth. He heard snippets of their conversations, no different from any conversation that their parents or their parents' parents had at these things, those about riding lawn mowers and births and deaths and recreational fish ponds. Also, this food: "Everybody knows that perch is the best fish to fry, and Erie perch is the best perch to fry, no perch is like Erie perch, no fry should be made with anything but Erie perch," his former friends from high school said as they ate and ate and ate and said and said and said this same fucking thing about how everybody knew that Erie perch was better than all other perches, and as they talked, they showered their environment with fish bits, and if they noticed a fish bit was on their person, they spotted it up with a moistened thumb and re-ate it, and Edward stepped out of the center of the gathering to the side, anxious to not go nuts. He had almost forgotten about these people. It seemed like a miracle that he should have avoided this group throughout his four years at the college, considering that a mere mile separated the campus from this very house. Staring at them, he had the terrible notion that this was all they'd been doing these past four years. While he had been in college, learning things, etcetera, his old buddies were here, eating fish.

Edward shrunk against the side of the house, still watching them as he reviewed the numbers: fifty kids in their high school graduating class. A mere *three* went to some brand of college. Edward and Ted went to the college in town. Rainne was at Bard. Or, more accurately, she had just graduated from Bard with a major in...what was it? Psychology? Philosophy? Poly sci? Something that started with *p*, although Rainne might as well have been just another English major...

Portuguese?

Perhaps. She went to Bard or maybe Barnard, and majored in Portuguese and was now sitting next to Victoria who had gone nowhere. They were sitting backwards at a picnic table, leaning against the tabletop edge, their knees pointed out toward Edward who was yards away. He watched Rainne pay the pizza guy. From the plastic bag she took out a small cardboard box. He thought about calling out to her. He could say—

"You ordered a pizza?" Victoria asked. "To a fish fry?"

Edward choked back the words. He wouldn't have said that. He would have said something funny: *What? Too good for fish?*

Victoria leaned forward and looked down into Rainne's takeout box.

"What's all that?" Victoria asked.

Rainne stared too.

Victoria said, "Shredded cheese, cucumber, a tomato." She paused. "Wait. You ordered a salad?"

The only remarkable or interesting thing that Edward could think of about Victoria was that he had never had a single conversation with her, even though they were in some of the same classes all through grade school. Edward didn't get her enough to say that she was dumb. Did she have a sense of humor? He'd seen her break out weeping just when he thought she was coming to the punchline of a joke, or while being completely serious, she would explode into roaring laughter.

It was a problem of language, probably. Edward looked around the party, certain he spoke a completely different language from them. His head was filled with English and their heads were filled with fish. Dogs were better company, he thought, looking around, than these people whose heads were filled only with fish and fish thoughts—real actual fish and strategies of how and when they could next stuff their heads. But Edward was not like that. Rainne was not like that. They always stood apart from these fucking people.

"What's *that*?" Victoria asked, her loud voice bringing Edward's attention back to them.

"What?" Rainne said.

"Is that *egg*?"

Rainne placed a forkful of salad in her mouth and began chewing.

Victoria asked, "You got that from Tito's?"

She swallowed. "What the fuck isn't adding up for you, Victoria?"

Victoria turned bright red. What she said to Rainne was too fast and soft for Edward to hear, but the tone was nasty. Rainne covered her mouth, shaking with laughter. Victoria gave her a poisonous look and stood and walked away with her neck craned around to glare at Rainne the whole way, only looking ahead when she reached the next picnic table that was packed, unlike Rainne's, with people.

He tried to remember the last time he saw Rainne. Was it a year ago? Longer? She visited home a lot in the first few years of college, coming into town for two days, three days max. The first thing she would do before laundry or sleeping or even saying hi to the stepdad who'd raised her was go to Edward's apartment, Ted and Edward's apartment. Rainne came to see Ted, who was awful to her. Rainne liked Ted. Had since kindergarten. But Ted liked small girls, he liked them cutesy, and Rainne looked like a horse, Ted said, and she was five foot eleven. Every conversation or comment led back to her height, her long neck sloping down into her shoulders or her forlorn, otiose face. Edward would sit smoking in uncomfortable silence, trying to think of something banal but useful to ask her, to change the subject from her unusual body and Ted's obsession with it, but it was hard for Edward to remember anything but how best and how hard to bash in Ted's face.

"Hey," Rainne called over to Edward.

He pushed off the wall and walked over.

"Maybe you can help me out with something," she said, gazing up at him from the bench.

"OK." He lit a cigarette.

"See that guy over there? In the gray V-neck?"

Edward glanced to where she was pointing. He saw brightly colored sundresses and then, amidst them all, the Mickey Lolich jersey that Jim always wore.

"You mean the Tigers jersey?" Edward asked.

"Now look very carefully at his face."

Edward looked immediately away.

"The left side looks totally melted," she said, much too loudly.

"That's *Jim*," Edward said quietly.

"Jim?" Her voice was vague, as if she didn't remember him. Then she sucked her breath in. "Whoa. *Jim.*" She leaned forward. "What happened to his face? It looks—oh, I can't see! Would you move?"

Edward didn't budge. In a low voice, he said, "You don't know?"

"What don't I know? *Why,*" she asked, voice rising, "*would I know?*"

He told her as quickly and quietly as possible: "Two years ago, Jim and Carol went to a music festival in Toronto. They did a bunch of acid and Carol was OK, but Jim had a bad reaction."

"And?"

"He was in a coma for three weeks and, when he came out of it, he had some brain damage. Still the same nice guy. Like, he's all there. But he can't do some things. He can't move his face."

"Jesus," she murmured. "That is horrible. Do you think Carol got knocked up by someone else?"

Was she joking?

"I mean, if her husband can't move *his face…*" Rainne giggled.

He laughed nervously.

Rainne smiled. "You know, I had a dream about you."

Edward's heart, already racing, leapt into his throat.

"It's not a sex dream," she added.

His eyes rolled up. "Christ."

"Well." She grinned. "It's kind of a sex dream. Would you like to hear it?"

He shook his head. "I hate dreams, Rainne. I hate mine, I hate other people's. I hate hearing people talk about their dreams."

"Do you dream about me, Edward?"

"I dream about aliens."

"It's more of a *memory* of you than an actual dream. But if you don't want to hear it…"

"Christ, christ," he said softly, the blood rushing to his feet.

"You die," Rainne said, as he joined her on the bench, "before you're able to finish your latest book, a novel that includes so many actual events in your life that I wonder if it isn't autobiographical. The novel is about a young man who goes to France—"

Edward let out a barking laugh, and his knee knocked against hers.

"—and lives out his life there. And midway through the novel, there is a huge, defining conversation that changes everything for the character who is so very much like you, but the details of the conversation are only indirectly described. No one seems to know what was said. Critics all disagree about the meaning of conversation. For my part, I wonder if this defining conversation was real. Did you actually have this defining conversation? If so, what was said? But you are dead, so I can't ask. Instead I go to France to find out for myself." She paused. "So far so good?"

"Yeah, sure," he said.

"In France, I track down a friend of yours, an artist who has video footage of you, taken just before your death. And three or four hours into it, I finally see you. Your back is to the camera, you are facing a woman whose face is blurred. This is it! This is the defining conversation you wrote about in your novel, and what I have been trying to verify as real. You are telling her the story of when you first met her, touching her shoulders and face as you say, *I can remember the first time I ever saw you. It was in New York City and you had on seven coats and were speaking French, which I didn't understand.* Oh, I realize, the woman was homeless and insane when you met her. But this is something you do not realize. Then, this woman utters something in a thick French accent."

Rainne hesitated.

"The woman, she says to you," she leaned forward, whispering loudly in Edward's ear, "*I'm still not going to have sex with you.*"

Rainne burst out laughing. Tears squeezed out her eyes as she pointed at Edward. "Oh god! If you could see your face!" She wiped her eyes. "After I had this dream, oh, about a year ago, I turned it into a short story. A lot more interesting than what I just told you." Edward opened his mouth, but nothing came out.

"I wrote about you," she said, clarifying, and all the feeling in Edward's face drained out. "I have it here, in the latest *Bard Times…*"

Back in high school, he used to listen to Rainne talk for hours about how she hated this town and she hated these people and one day she was going to get out of this town and away from these people and write about them, and they weren't going to like it. Edward would get by the way Rainne limply gestured that she meant *all this* in the sense of this town, this place, these people. But he never thought she meant him. He wasn't supposed to be part of *all this*.

She thinks I'm just like them, he thought. *I'm no different from everyone else at this party.*

Rainne twisted around, reaching for her backpack on the table. But Edward stood up, right up from the table, and walked away before she could show him the newspaper.

A hand grazed his shoulder as Edward stalked past the other tables, back to Gran's. "Hey, Eddie!" Carol called, but he kept going. There were no places to protect him, there were no people to protect him, every place was harmful, every person was harmful, looking for some way to use him, looking for some way to extract what was most private and important about him for their own use. *I was actually fine before this,* Edward thought. *I was really fine.*

He walked up Gran's steps, unlocked the door, found the gin and poured himself a double, taking the drink and the bottle into the living room. Edward sat down on the couch. He knew exactly what to do.

THURSDAY

NOT SMART. Clueless. Wore glasses. Wore uniform. Named Steve.

"Here is Steve who is a...first lieutenant?"

"First lieutenant."

"First lieutenant. I couldn't tell if they were gold or silver. They are silver, you are a first lieutenant, and this is the next item up for bid on *The Price Is Right*!"

"A pair of Robot Lamps!"

Steve blew air out of his mouth. Yeesh...

"From Florino Lamps and Tables comes the look of tomorrow, today, with these Robot Lamps."

Plastic female bleh model presented robot lamps, ironic yet positive. Big smile wink wink.

"Lieutenant Steve, what do you bid on those lamps?"

Steve looked over his shoulder, at screaming human mass.

"You know what, Steve? This is one of the greatest shocks of my last few weeks. A lieutenant in the Marine Corps looking out there for advice?"

Steve bowed his head. So much shame in this life.

"I should think that you have long since learned to make decisions in moments of stress."

Fuck Bob Barker. Shithead.

"Now what do you bid on that, Steve?"

Steve concentrating, concentrating. Like prairie dog.

"Three hundred dollars."

"The actual retail price of the lamp: three hundred and twenty dollars! The winner: Lieutenant Steve! Come up here to me."

Steve ascending. Joining stage, Bob Barker, mannequin controller.

"I think that my little lecture was just what you needed. Steve turned around and made up his own mind and won the lamps."

Like American hero.

"Now I'd like to try to give you all this!"

"A three-drawer chest, a pair of rockers, a range, and a sewing machine!"

A car door slammed. Edward's gaze cut away from the TV screen. Through the picture window, he saw two cars in the driveway, two women stepping out. It was his mom, his aunt, and Edward fell to the floor, hands and knees flattening the Ring Ding wrappers. He grabbed the empty box of Lorna Doones and began cramming the wrappers in. Looking for the remote. Where was it. Where was it. There. He crawled across the carpet to the TV set and pressed down the power button, but for some reason, the screen wasn't turning off, so instead he tried the volume, glancing over his shoulder, seeing the sofa, the carpet, the damages—god god, wrappers, cum tissues, cigarettes and ash and empty cans. The mess was bad enough. But what would he say when his mom and aunt asked *why* he was camped out at Gran's?

… *Ted kicked me out.*

… *Christiane left me.*

… *I'm not graduating.*

He had no excuse. While Gran was in the hospital, he was here, living off the fat of the land. He glanced up at the TV set, and Steve's head hung. Defeated. Steve walked away, reluctant. Crowd cam pan. Now commercial. "Why not try this great—" Fuck, fuck, Edward reached around the set and pulled the plug.

Peeking out the window, he saw his mom nod. She turned away from Aunt Amy and began cutting across the lawn, approaching Gran's porch, the front door. *That's it, finished, my life is over.* He bit his fist, ready to vomit. She was going to be so pissed at him, but also, if he were totally honest with her, if he told her right off the bat he was here because of x-y-z and didn't pussyfoot around, she would be totally enraged by what *they* all were doing to *him.* There was nothing more terrible to her than injustice. And nothing that had happened to him in the last few days had been fair. Tears filled his eyes. He heard her jingling keys. He sniffled. The next sound would be the key turning the lock...

"Oh, Amy!" his mom called out from the porch. "It's not even here though. The punch bowl is at home, in the garage. I can picture the exact box it's in."

Ah, christ, no—"Mom," he moaned, falling back on the carpet. "Mom..." His eyes glazed over.

Car doors opened.

He took a deep breath.

"*MOM!*" he shouted, shocking himself and then, just as involuntarily, burst out laughing. He clamped his hands across his mouth. He was laughing, he realized, just how his mom did: silently, violently, at the mercy of slaphappy and totally inaudible convulsions. Seconds passed. The car drove off, and his tremors flat-lined. He was rigid, tense, both hands covering his mouth.

The room slowly dimmed, the sun setting. He closed his eyes, seeing Bob Barker's face, the Big Wheel ticking, bold bands of green, white, black, the red ticker falling on the fat 100. Edward glanced over his shoulder. A smile on Rainne's face... She held up a sign. He squinted to read what it said...

Edward swallowed, wetting his lips with his tongue. He murmured Rainne's name and opened his eyes. The room was dark. He sat up quickly and his neck spasmed. Rubbing his shoulder, looking for Rainne and seeing faint outlines. Sofa. Rocker. No Rainne, no of course not. *Hurts, don't it? Thought you cut her leash, didn't you? Yeah, you're a fool.*

He staggered up. He needed something to drink, something to

kill the pain gathering in his head. He gently kicked this and that, playing putt-putt with all the soft discarded matter on the floor, reacquainting himself with the wrappers and packages of assorted snack cakes, knocking around a few empty cigarette packs and then, finally, he stubbed his toe on the empty gin bottle. White light flooded the room. The headlights of the passing car lit the room, the driveway, and he saw Gran's car, right where his mom and aunt had left it.

In the kitchen, Edward borrowed some money from Gran's wallet and lifted his jacket off the kitchen table. He pulled on his shoes, then stepped out the front door, onto the porch. He froze, his eyes on a lightning bug vanishing and re-vanishing at his right shoulder, at his left shoulder. His hand plunged—caught the bug first try, brought it up to his eyes in the cage of his hand.

The bug tickled around his fingers, no glow to it. He breathed in. The cold air felt so good. He was already feeling better—just the thought of having the car back was instantly reassuring. He could count on his family to do certain things, always close cabinet doors, always turn off the lights. If you borrow the car, bring it right back. And of course, leave Gran's keys in the ignition. He liked that he could expect these things. He could expect to be right. Something in the world made sense to him, and it was probably the strangest thing in this world, the weirdest and most unreasonable and irksome people in the world. *But my people*, he thought, and he let the bug tumble to the grass. He opened the car door up. The keys were not in the ignition. What the fuck. He took a seat at the wheel and felt around, groping the area, the sides of the seat and under the seat and beneath the pedals. Crumbs. Dust. Air. Why hadn't his mom done what they always did—leave Gran's keys where she could find them, where she wouldn't lose them? In less than a minute he tore apart the glove compartment, and the seat and floor, absolute chaos, so many fucking pepper packets, why the fuck were there so many, and crumpled-up salts, god, that's what these little balls were, one thousand depleted packets of salts along with disgusting, flattened ketchups. Which uncle or aunt hated pepper but loved ketchup and

salt? Ha! Trick question, they all did. He checked under the passenger seat, riffled through all the pepper down there. He did not find
them. He was in a really awkward position, and it was not obvious
how to get out of it without snapping his neck, but then he just kind
of popped out totally upright. He rubbed his neck, kicking open the
driver's side door to get out and crouch beside the car. He checked
under the driver's seat. Just a paper napkin. He remained outside the
car, crouching, panting, thinking this is idiotic. The keys were in the
car. They had to be. *My psycho mom has hidden them.* He scrambled
back into the driver's seat and yanked down the sun visor.

"HA!" he cried, snatching the keys-on-chain clipped there,
beside the reflection of his bloodshot eyes.

He drove down the street to the Villa Party Store. There was
no where to park, so he pulled back out of the lot, back up the
street, and parked in the neighborhood. He got out. He could
see, looking down the street, Gran's mailbox under the glow of a
streetlamp. He smiled to himself: *what we always did in high school.*
The shortest distances, who could get a car and go the shortest
distances, the absolute shortest distances. You did not want to go
far, you did everything you could to get a car, you lied or bribed or
guilt-tripped your way into your parents' or your friends' parents'
or your girlfriends' aunt's cars, and then you used it to go basically
nowhere. Edward drove the family sedan one-quarter mile every
day in the twelfth grade to get to his first period. But his personal
record was bested by others in their group—Ted, by backing out
of the driveway, could immediately back into the high school
parking lot. Edward smiled. Some things weren't so bad about
high school. Certain aspects were not enormously irritating, he
thought, walking into the Villa Party Store.

Inside, he passed the single row of wine to get to the seven
rows of hard liquor in the back of the store. He fingered the

ten-dollar bill in his pants pocket, reminding himself that, since it was Gran's money, he needed to use it for gin. Of course, he could still afford bourbon for himself if he got Gran this bottle of, he squinted to read the label, Schenley. Idly he put the bottle back, hearing familiar voices. He was sure it was Carol and Victoria and...was that Dan? Fuck 'em. They were clearly talking about him, Edward, about his *performance* at the fish fry yesterday.

"His performance was just, wow, I mean if he didn't want to come—"

"Oh that's just how he always is—"

"Really you're actually going to defend him and his weird—"

"No no no all I am saying is—"

"What are you saying?"

"All I'm saying is it's not so amazing that—"

"Eh, you're right, he's always been a loser."

Edward's face burned. They didn't know, they didn't fucking know what was going on with him. He stepped out of his aisle and into theirs, ready to tell them—

He saw two people he didn't know and a third who kinda looked familiar, but only because he had that jaw, that snappy kind of jaw, the kind you could just run your fist into.

"What?" the girls snapped in unison. And this guy, this fucking guy, laughed.

Edward's face burned. "I need something," he said gruffly.

The guy leaned back into the shelf, settling in. His gaze challenged Edward—*Oh yeah, nerd?* But the girls smiled broadly, snapping their bubblegum, and stepped aside, revealing the shelves they had been blocking. Condoms. They were standing in front of condoms.

One of the girls leaned over and asked, "Which size are you gonna get?"

Edward turned on a heel, walking quickly away. He continued to hear their laughter even as he reached the door. "Fucking morons," he muttered. These were the sort of people that Rainne had always hated. How could she think he was anything like them?

Out in the parking lot, he kicked a stone, sending it shooting into the dark street. He slowed his pace, thinking Rainne was dead wrong about him. But could he blame her? He hadn't given her any evidence to the contrary that, although he was born here, raised here, and went to college here, he wasn't like anybody here. Edward took a step forward, realizing it was wrong to not have told her about Roger Ackroyd. He walked faster. It wasn't too late—the poser hadn't confessed to anything yet. Edward just had to get to May first.

Edward Moses is Roger Ackroyd, May would tell her friends...

Edward Moses is Roger Ackroyd, May's friends would tell theirs...

News would spread to Ted, then to his friends. They'd all be speechless.

Edward cut across a neighbor's front lawn and went around to the back of the house—jumping out of his skin when a pack of dogs showed up in the windows and howled. He quickened his stride, running down the fenceless border between the neighborhood's backyards. He was moving forward but steadily sinking into the boggy grass. Each time he lifted his foot, it came up heavier. He used extra force to kick back his heels, trying to shed the muck and mud that had collected on each of his soles. Passing now from grass to stone, from lawn to paved lot, he rose and emerged tall and crooked. He scraped and kicked and stomped his shoes against the gravel to get off the mud. He jumped up and down like some deranged bogie and limped, his shoes still uneven, toward a door near the dumpsters, partially blockaded by them. The door had no handle, a steel plate in the brickwork, and to the uninitiated it looked impenetrable, but Edward just had to hit it hard with his shoulder and give it a swift kick, and he was inside Michigan Bar.

He hated the place: thick with beerstink, humid, every passageway clogged by another game of pool or another immobile

centipedal connection of girls and girls or girls and boys with their
faces mashed together. Their voices mashed together too, a morose
continuous drone below an unbearable blah blah blah. Everybody
was saying, Edward realized, their goodbyes. The night before
graduation, of course everybody's here.

No room at the bar. He waited by the water jug for an
opening—then saw one and went forward. A girl cut him off—
smashed his toes, elbowed his ribs. Now she stood in his space on
tiptoes, calling out an endless drink order. He was inches behind
her. If so inclined, he could grab her by the zippy ponytail and
yank her back. Instead, he slipped into the narrow space beside
her—didn't even touch her, didn't even graze her elbow—but
her jaw dropped just the same. He called out his order—in a flash
the whiskey neat was in front of him. He shot it down, while she,
the cutter, glared.

"Move, go, move, asshole!" She whacked his shoulder. Edward
shrugged her off and turned, faced the bartender—

"What's the scene?"

Joey said, "Started out as a frat party. Now everyone's here."

Edward glanced back. "Any townies?"

Joey snorted. "Yeah… *You*."

The girl gave Edward a sharp pinch, asked what it took to get
a drink.

"Who's the girl?" Joey asked Edward.

"Fuck if I know."

"So, you're free then. Wanna make a buck?"

"Can't," Edward said.

"Nothing to making drinks. Everyone's so drunk they don't
know what you're putting in it."

Edward leaned closer. "Have you seen any theater kids tonight?"

"Eddie, I'm dying here. You gotta help me out."

Edward grabbed the handle of Jameson and poured an inch in
his empty glass. He pushed it toward Joey.

Joey waved a hand.

Edward gaped. "You're the only bartender I know who doesn't drink while he's serving."

"When I drink—"

"You want to enjoy it." Edward downed the shot.

"Drinking with this crowd just makes me—"

"Miserable." Edward said, wiping his lips.

"Christ." Joey dragged his hands down his face. "Goddamnit."

The pinching in Edward's arm had stopped. Now there was a rough, relentless tugging on his jacket sleeve.

"Can you believe this girl?" Edward asked.

Joey shook his head. "Different chick, man."

Turning around, he noticed how sharp her nose was this time, how long and pinched. Probably this was why she didn't act for the Icehouse Theater, why she reigned behind stage, clutching a clipboard, snapping out orders. And her name was...

"Ally, right?" Edward asked.

Ally folded her arms across her chest. Her mouth was moving, but he couldn't hear her.

He leaned forward. "What?"

"*What have you done with Jonathan!*"

He heard her—he thought of the poser in the jail cell. But he shrugged and tapped his ear.

"Can't hear you!"

"Jonathan," Ally yelled. "JON-A-THAN!"

Edward turned his hands up, shaking his head.

Ally's eyes bugged out. "Listen, you..." She jabbed her finger in his shoulder, but he nudged it away, pushing past her. He'd already spotted May at the water jug, arms crossed and slouching.

He leaned toward May's ear, shouting at little: "Hey—we met last night!"

A nod.

"You want to talk?"

A faster nod.

Ally yelled to May, "Is he taking you to Jonathan?"

May nodded, then looked over at him. "Is it far?"

Edward shook his head, confused. Jonathan had somehow slipped back into the conversation. His eyes bounced from May to Ally to May. He started to say, "Actually…"

May touched Ally's shoulder. "Stay here, OK?" Then her hand slipped into his. May walked toward the door, pulling Edward along behind her. People looked at her, then to him. Eyes ping-ponged between this woman, and *that?* This beauty, and *that goon?* A dark freckle on May's nape, made darker by the bar's red light, distracted him. He felt a little moan slip out. Did she hear it, feel it on her neck? His mouth was ear-height to her, his breathing agitating her hair. If he stumbled, he'd be eating her bun… More, more of these dark incredible stars were clustered between her shoulder blades, falling, scattering, down her naked back. She wore a halter top. Her large tits jiggled behind it as she shouldered open the door.

"Oh thank god," she sighed, letting go of his hand and flexing her wrists in the cool night. "Eh, ooh…" She moaned and lifted both hands up over her head. She undid her hair. It fell and she flipped it over her head, gathered it up in her fingers, tying it up. He shivered. It was cold out. Clear. Stars, blue, red, white, visible when he looked up.

"…just so dramatic," she was saying. "He probably thinks the play went terrible last night and is hiding."

Edward had no idea. He stared.

"Is that it?" she asked.

He blinked. "You're talking about Jonathan."

"Yes."

"You don't know where he is."

"*That's right…*" she said in a voice that he supposed she thought sounded patient and cheerful, but only reminded him she was days away from becoming a schoolteacher.

Edward shrugged. "He's locked up."

Her eyelids fluttered. "What?"

"He punched a cop."

A cool, dead look. "Really," she said.

"I think he was high on pills."

"That's unbelievable."

He nodded.

"No, I mean that's unbelievable. I don't believe you."

Edward's jaw flexed. "You think I'm *lying?*"

Eyelids neither closed nor opened but vibrated as she sucked her upper lip in and simulated an underbite. A look he had no chance of reading. She stepped past him.

He turned, eyes following her. "Where are you going?" he called out.

She yelled over her shoulder. "He's in jail, right?"

He jogged to catch up. "Yes!"

"Then that's...!" She threw her hands up, not finishing the sentence.

Shit. He had to stop her, or at least slow her down. Should he tell right now?

"Who are you anyway?" she asked.

His heart sped up. He licked his lips, trying to find the words.

"Not an actor," she said.

He flushed. "No!"

"Not Jonathan's friend."

His flush deepened. "*No.*"

She laughed. "Honestly, you don't have to answer." She cocked her head, and her pace slowed. "Not an art kid." Her smile grew broader, and she stopped.

"So what was a *townie* doing at the play last night?"

His face was on fire. Here it was, his opening, but he felt too humiliated to speak. Staring at his feet, he heard her voice: "You were supposed to meet someone at the play, but..." Her voice faded. He jerked his head up, catching a glimpse of her red hair as she rounded the corner, then disappeared.

Shit, shit! He stumbled forward, nearly tripping on his own feet. He grabbed the corner and propelled his body around it.

May was crossing the street, headed toward the police station. He jogged until he was at her side again.

She sighed. "So Jon's really in there, huh?"

Edward panted. "It's late, nearly midnight." Was it? He added hastily, "They won't let you see him."

She fluttered her eyelids. "Oh, I can be very persuasive."

His heart went cold.

"Stay right here," she touched his shoulder. "No running off like you did last night. You and I have a lot to talk about."

He watched her run up the steps to the station, sandals smacking the cement. Through the little windows of her armpits, her breasts bounced. The door to the entrance slapped shut. Anger swept through him. He groaned, and pulled the hair down over his eyes. *What am I doing? Why did I let her run in there? I should have said to her...fuck! I should have said...goddammit! Ah shit!*

His only consolation was that it was late—the night officers would never let her see him, no matter how much she fluttered her eyelids... Right? Edward was smoking, pacing, muttering aloud. The bell finally tolled...ten times...eleven...twelve! Midnight then! But ages had passed since she went inside. What was taking so long?

Edward stopped pacing, put his hands on his knees, and vomited into the bushes.

A car grumbled up. Edward spat into the bushes, then straightened. He knew that car. He knew that guy behind the wheel... That's the Tito's pizza guy, squinting into the pull-down mirror. The pizza guy was evaluating his junkie pallor, his bloodshot eyes. *What's the destruction, how blazed am I?* His fingers went into the pocket of his red Tito's windbreaker. He pulled out a little bottle of Visine. More than ten seconds of drips in the left eye, and then in the right, an insane amount of drips. Dude was zoning out. Already did the left, but now he's back at it, doing it again. His life is a comedy. Or tragedy. Edward didn't know which as he watched the pizza guy leisurely slap each of his cheeks.

Now the pizza guy shook out his cheeks, blubbering his lips, and rolled his head around. An idea came to Edward—no, an *instinct*, which felt like a good idea, but it didn't give him an overall working plan, only each action one at a time without point or purpose or a thought to the end. So, Edward sucked in some air—not knowing that next he would hold his breath, next he would whistle, next he would attract the attention of the pizza guy who, by this time, was stepping out of his car. When Edward rubbed his chin, he hadn't known beforehand he would do that. When he muttered, "Well, well," it was a total shock to him.

"Brave!" Edward bellowed.

The pizza guy jumped, looking around until he saw Edward on the sidewalk. He rubbed his nose, looking back at Edward nervously as he opened the trunk of his car.

"I respect your bravery man!" Edward yelled as the pizza guy pulled a red pizza carrier out of the trunk. "But I wonder..." Edward scratched the back of his head. "Yeah I wonder, just kind of..."

The pizza guy slammed the trunk shut. "Goddammit, *what?*"

Edward waved his hand. "Nah. Nothing."

The pizza guy walked around the car with the pizza carrier in his arms.

"It's just..."

He stopped at the curb. "What, man? What? What?"

"Eh, you know what you're doing."

"You're tripping...you're just...you're messing with me!"

Edward held up his hands. "Hey, no judgment. I smoke, too. Just not before delivering pizza to the police."

Pizza guy rocked in his shoes. "You're saying...shit. What are you saying?"

Edward scowled. "Man, you look high!"

He jerked his head to the side, eyeballing the grimy car window. He was staring at...his dark reflection? His upper lip began to tremble.

Edward cleared his throat. "I guess, I mean I could help you out. Deliver that pizza for you."

Now his whole body shook. Edward wondered if he'd heard him.

"I said, I could run that pie in for you, no problemo."

Words, fucks, flowing freely from him, he dropped the pizza carrier on the sidewalk. More moans and curses. *Fuck life* was the gist. To Edward's surprise, the pizza guy's red hat flew off.

Then the red Tito's windbreaker.

Then the red Tito's tee.

The pizza guy kicked off his white sneakers, muttering, "Unbelievable! Letting a hobo deliver my pizza!"

Edward blinked. "Hobo?"

Pizza guy stepped out of his shiny red track pants. "Oh no, don't try—I don't wanna hear your fucking story man. Just deliver the pizza and like, don't fucking steal my pizza bag. And I want my shoes back—you're just getting the tips, OK? Don't try to—I'll be outside and I run fast, so don't you, just don't—" He flinched at Edward.

Edward stepped back. "I don't need the clothes!"

Pizza guy trembled, voice rising in pitch, "Man put the fucking clothes on. Put them on! Don't let them find us out!"

Pizza guy stripped down to his socks and tighty-whities, then shrunk into a squatting position. Edward laughed nervously and looked around, over his shoulder, deciding... *Shit. Best to get this over with quick.* He shed his jacket, then unbuttoned his flannel shirt. Cold air hit his chest, making him shudder. He moved even faster, shaking the sleeves off his arms, then grabbing the red shirt, stuffing his hands and head in. He yanked it down. He reached for the red track pants at his feet. Soft, silky. He wouldn't put them on though, fuck if he'd wear the pants. Edward dropped them, reaching for the jacket—

Pizza guy shrieked, "Wear the goddamn pants!"

Funny, frightening. Edward didn't know what else to do. He undid the button to his jeans. They dropped lickety-split to his ankles. Goose pimples spread across his legs and his dick shied into itself and he imagined May walking out of the station to discover him mooning her. He stepped into the track pants and pulled them up. They didn't fit. As best he could, he cinched them, but still there was enough room to stick in another Edward. The fuck? Edward wasn't so thin, the pizza guy wasn't so fat. But he didn't want to think about it, what this meant, potential problems to his thinking vis-à-vis bodies and so on—He rolled the waistband up and up, and they stayed up, pretty fucking precarious though. He put the jacket on, stuffing his wallet and keys in his pockets, then put on the virginal white tennis shoes and red cap. From his new clothes wafted a hint of aftershave, onion, and cat piss.

Edward walked into the police station, pizza carrier held high, red cap tipped low. He looked for May in the waiting area—didn't see her. A solitary officer at the front desk, leaning back, penciling in a crossword puzzle. He looked up as Edward approached. Gave the air a sniff.

"That'd be for Maloney. He'll be at his office, salivating."

Edward stepped toward the door.

"Hold it!" the cop cried out. Edward froze.

"Pepperoni?"

"Clam. Pineapple. Anchovy. Mushroom..." Edward babbled. The officer recoiled. "Good god!"

Edward passed into the main room, eyes darting around the unoccupied desks. In the back of the room, a cop slept kicked back in his chair with his feet on the desk. To Edward's right, three cops stood with their backs to Edward. Edward could hear May on the other side of them, wailing loudly, "But it's graduation!" In her voice, Edward recognized the histrionics of Wednesday night's theater performance. The cops were responding in overlapping platitudes—"there there!" "now now!"—like nervous dads confronted with the kid they only saw on Sundays. Edward was immediately soothed. May could wail all she wanted, but the cops weren't going to let her see Jonathan.

Edward's eyes returned to the sleeping cop across the room. Crumpled burger wrappers littered his desk, along with a few scattered French fries. His gaze moved to the door the cop guarded. It would be so easy to slip in, say hi to Jonathan. Just a few minutes alone together to catch up.

The cop didn't stir as Edward came up to his desk and set the pizza box down. Glancing over his shoulder, he saw May's teary profile. The cop directly in front of her leaned in, blocking her face. Edward grabbed the door knob and slowly turned it. He opened the door an inch, then another inch. May exploded, "It's *almost* like you're not listening!" Edward shot a panicked glance to the sleeping guard—he was as still as death—then opened the door a few more cracks before squeezing through.

The room he'd entered was dim and warm. He inched the door closed again, then turned, squinted. A cage was lit by a white flickering light—he looked around, looking for more cages. In his memory, this had been a prison. But this was the only cage, barely smaller than the room it was in. Jonathan was inside, lying on a cot. Edward waited, watching him, letting his excitement grow.

Jonathan lifted his head slowly, squinting. Then he bolted upright.

"Edward?"

Edward stepped forward to the cage. "May is here too."

Jonathan's eyes filled with tears. "And my father?"

"We're all here, buddy," he said as gently as possible, and Jonathan's tears spilled.

"This isn't happening. This isn't real! I fell asleep, I'm dreaming…" Jonathan remained seated in the cot, blinking rapidly.

Edward covered his mouth, struggling to hold back his laughter.

"Are they letting me out?" Jonathan croaked.

"Any minute now. May is talking sense into them."

He exhaled. "That's just…this has been…" He gave his head a shake and began laughing nervously. "Your outfit! I thought—I don't know what I thought. Pizza? Delivery? This has all just been—"

"Jonathan, *May is here*. Have you thought about what you're going to tell her?"

He shook his head. "Frankly, my head's just a little *mmm*, well, frankly I'm a little—" He laughed. "You'd think I'd sleep? Nothing to do for days I just might, but the cops told me I wasn't graduating because of these *charges* against me which is just... *hello!*" A smile spread across his face. He lowered his voice to a false whisper. "How mad is Father really? At the police, I mean. Has he gotten President Chiseler involved? Who did he bring from the Board?"

Edward shook his head. "Dude, May is about to walk through that door!"

The smile froze on Jonathan's face.

"What are you going to say to her?"

He giggled nervously.

"The thing is," Edward stepped closer to the bars, "she's been saying some really wild things. She's telling people that she's been corresponding with...well, *Roger Ackroyd*."

Jonathan swallowed. "Guilty as charged," he said weakly.

Edward clapped his hands together. "Wow! I am such a huge fan. I have so many questions for you. Like, I really want to know *why* you wrote those poems. What do they all mean?"

He rubbed his eyes. "You can't really expect me to answer that. Not right *now*."

"Aww," Edward whined. "Just tell me about *how* you wrote the poems."

"Listen...are they coming?"

"Eh, not for a minute or two." Edward leaned forward. "Did you mix the poems up at random, or did you work them out line by line, choosing each word carefully?"

Jonathan leaned to the side, trying to look around Edward to the door. "Because if May is coming, I really don't think we should be talking about this."

"So it's random then?" Edward said.

"It's a creative process! I can't unpack it for you."

"Try."

Jonathan lowered his voice. "Look, if you want to understand why I wrote the poems, read the poems. Everything is there, in the text. And if you want to know *how* I wrote them, well, that's frankly impossible to explain in the time we have."

Edward barked, "How long?"

Jonathan leaned back a little. "Eh?"

"How long did it take you to write 'The Waste Land?'"

"A night, a few nights…" he stuttered. "It wasn't easy. You can't imagine how difficult it is to reimagine a work of genius like that. I had to use every word in it."

Edward closed his eyes. "I would you; / I the my the that's you whining ever to door / Your to you telling. / You the unheard. through among fattening wants mountains turn undesired. / Over key, earth." His eyes opened. "Section four, line 659."

Jonathan was gaping. "You…memorized it?"

"Yes."

"I'm honored." He frowned.

"I also know your other work—'So You Want to be a Writer,' 'Howl,' 'Canto LXXXI,' 'The Road Not Taken,' 'Do Not Go Gentle into that Good Night,' Hamlet's soliloquy…" Edward cleared his throat. "Want me to recite all that, too?"

Jonathan slowly shook his head.

Edward's forehead grazed the bars. "So, Roger, tell me about the name."

"You mean, where does the name come from?"

"Yes!"

"*The Murder of Roger Ackroyd*… It's by Agatha Christie. One of May's favorites." Jonathan cleared his throat. "Listen, if May is about to come in here—"

Edward let loose a stream of curses.

"You lying fucking—" Their eyes met. "—I could kill you—" Edward heard himself saying and grew aware that he had for a while now been repeating this, working his anger up, getting panicked enough to shout, "*You are NOT Roger Ackroyd!*"

"Yes...I am," Jonathan said weakly.

Edward leaned forward until his forehead was pressing into the bars. "You're going to tell May that you've been lying to her. And if you don't tell her, I'll tell her. And she'll believe me because I have the proof. I have the proof and you don't, you lying piece of—"

Edward cursed him, pulling back from the cage. He reached for the door knob and his wet palm slipped on the steel. He swore loudly, pulling the sleeve of the windbreaker over his hand, turning the knob.

The air was drier and colder in the office area. Edward pulled his cap down low and kept his head down, weaving through the desks, at which one, two, three cops were seated. He looked for May... didn't see her... He walked faster, was almost at the door, when—

"What the hell?"

"Did he just come from—?"

Chairs toppled, papers flew up and spilled across the floor. Edward was running, running, punching open the door, now skidding across tile, falling onto his hands, then up, springing up, springing out—He felt a hand snatch at his windbreaker. He felt fingertips, but not the grip, not the capture, because he was out of the station, sprinting down the sidewalk.

The pizza guy was hanging out of his car, his bare legs splayed out on the curb. Edward leapt over his feet and kept running.

A right on 1st Street. A left on Jeffers. Sirens in the distance. Those were for him? He got to 4th Street and took a right into the alley, leaping over trash and trash and a cat, maybe a rat, and the alley spat him out in front of Michigan Bar.

It was even more packed than before. He entered the crush, for once incredibly grateful for red and white strobe lights, the stoned crowd, this head-crushing music. He had to get out of these clothes, it was all he could think about, until he got out of the red polo and jacket and pants, he was a sign that screamed *Arrest me!* But when reached into the men's room, he realized he had nothing else to wear. Edward gritted his teeth. Trapped.

He pushed his way to the front of the bar.

"Still need a hand with serving?"

Joey high-fived him. "Get back here!"

For a while there, Edward was taking shots of everything he served.

Then, deep into the night, he looked over and saw her in a haze.

"I've been looking all over for you," she said in her sexy, throaty voice.

"Oh yeah?" he asked.

Fucking brilliant. He fucking loved her. He poured her a tall drink of…shook and he shook and he…he said

And she

They laughed

But then

then…

what?

What did he do?

FRIDAY

His FINGERS on occasion slid into vision and he was aware of them and then they slipped out of understanding and he stopped thinking about *fingers*, sinking back, deep into the space between his brain and these pages. These pages were again crawling with fingers, suddenly his ink-stained, overlarge fingers were taking over every conceivable inkling of thought—he thought that maybe before he'd been writing, writing and thinking, possibly writing and thinking and typing, but now he was fingers, all fingers. He jumped up from the desk, tipping over the chair, now tripping over and falling into and onto and over and through god-knows, this room was a war zone—to get to the tiny bathroom in the far corner... Inside, after locking the door, he began wondering where he was, that is, who owned the things on the floor and from whose head came all these long brown slimy hairs? *What was I doing before I sat on the toilet? And who was that person in the other room with me?*

He had no news for himself. He had nothing to tell. He finished quietly shitting, then jacked off, then splashed cold water on his face. He turned off the tap and stared at the water winding down the drain. Drops of water fell into the suds at irregular intervals, the sound, the perpetuation of pause-drip, drip-pause-drip, drip, pause, dripdripdripdripdrip, was not anything that would drive him insane, not him.

He went out and saw what the mess was for. All the things, the billion fucking things, were set out to be packed into the suitcases and bags and boxes and book boxes also on the floor. He loved book boxes. This flap went over that flap went up into that, with a twist, he loved that, how it all just worked, who did that, who thought of that, he wanted to do what that person did, he wanted in the coming years to be useful in ways unequivocally benign. He said this maybe out loud, but he couldn't be sure, couldn't be sure if he had thought any of it *in my head*, but she didn't stir. Drool connected her lips to her pillow. Crust connected her eyelids to her eyebones, whatever they were called, you know that ridge on top of your cheekbones. Cheekbones. Cheekbones? Cheekbones were lower on the face he thought, but feeling his face he felt maybe he was wrong. He had never taken anatomy, he absolutely hated the medical sciences. There was something he would never do in the coming years: go into the medical sciences. The worst thing about the medical sciences were all the crooks in the medical sciences. If you could go into the medical sciences without first being yourself a crook or without, in the end, becoming vaguely obliging, with nebulous scruples, he would still not have gone into the medical sciences because the second worst thing about the medical sciences were all the people in pain.

Katie's face was humorous while she slept. She bore a striking resemblance, in sleep, to his Great Aunt Jane, an ancient lady who had so far kept all her elephantine (elegant) white teeth and who snoozed with her eyelids vibrating and jaw dropped. Katie looked amazed by her dreams. If only he had a camera. Was there one lying around? He started to look, then noticed the condom wrappers on the floor, the destroyed condoms on the bed with her. Dread rose in him. He looked down and saw he wore nothing.

Edward began to sweat, or grew aware that he was, profusely, from not just the usual places (armpits, hands), but through his cheeks, through his neck, milky rivulets running down his naked chest. He mopped up his body with the red track pants, continuing to pat himself off as he looked for the shirt to match the pants: the red polo with *Tito's* embroidered or printed on the left breast. After minutes of searching through Katie's piles, he found the polo and dressed himself in this stupid, totally public costume. He wouldn't be able to walk out of Katie's dorm room without attracting the most obnoxious kind of attention to himself. Was there nothing else to wear? Absurd question. His eyes searched the room anyway. They lingered on the desk. They moved on to other things.

His eyes were back on the desk, fixed to the desk, taking in what was there. He had been there. At that desk, he'd been at that desk. Seated there for hours. Edward hadn't written a word in months, been too occupied for months, too distracted, without the time or inclination or ideas, without the privacy, to write—but he'd written, last night, this morning, he'd found it in him to put words down on pages, plural. *God, I had a prolific night.* He stared at the papers on the desk and on the floor, covered in something like his own handwriting. He picked up a page at his feet and couldn't read a word, his handwriting transfigured by whatever drugs he'd been on—likely blow, given the tininess of his scrawl. Each compact letter partially overlaid another. He would later have to unspool these dense pages, disentangle each letter if he wanted to understand even a word.

In the typewriter, there was a paper with text on it. He snatched it out and read with surging alarm—

May had been waiting for Roger Ackroyd these past eight months, but she wasn't impatient. In the last possible moment, he would come to her and they would finally be together.

She found him on her doorstep, the morning of Graduation Day.

"Can I help you?" May asked the stranger, then smiled, recognizing the orange book in his hands. DUMB WITNESS. That cover

art. If she turned to the last page,
she'd see her name neatly printed in ink.

So this was Roger. He was how she
thought he'd look: dark wavy hair. Not
tall, medium. A sharp nose. Smart-look-
ing. She'd seen him before — it wasn't a
big school, a thousand of them mulling
around. She had paid attention to them,
to the males, often playing the game, Is
it you?

She took the book out of his hands and
inspected it.

"This one always was my favorite." She
tapped the doggie on the cover with her
nail. "Adorable."

Then she opened the book and flipped
through it, finding nothing inside, no new
letter for her. She sucked in her bottom
lip, took a deep breath. As she exhaled,
her teeth slowly released each red wet
bit.

"So, are we all done with letters then?"

He said, "Yes."

She lowered her chin. "Very good."

This was insane. This wasn't his voice or style; this wasn't to his
fucking taste. He avoided prose, never wrote it or read it, despis-
ing novels more than anything, long newsy novels with characters
and plot and the other things. But this was it, his story. Bourgeois
storytelling was his deep unconscious art.

He dropped into the chair. His head was pounding. His eye

sockets ached with a sudden, alarming intensity. He'd not only created this stupid little scene, he'd written himself into it. That was *Edward* at May's doorstep. That was *Edward* with the Agatha Christie book, agreeing to be not just Roger Ackroyd the poet, but Roger Ackroyd the letter writer, and for what? For love? For May? To *date* her? This wasn't just absurd, this was fatal, against his nature. Blueprints for a future in which he committed soul-murder. What kind of life would he have ahead of him?

Edward's gaze returned to the pages on the floor. Hundreds and hundreds of tiny compact scribbles. Without nicotine, coffee, soft comfortable clothing, and the privacy of Gran's basement, the writing was as indecipherable as hieroglyphics. It was all there though. *His* future.

Edward gathered up the papers, creating several piles on the floor. When he found a shopping bag among Katie's things, he stuffed them into it.

Muffled shouts, a commotion outside. Edward went to the window and looked out. Graduates, in black gowns and caps, were coming out of the dormitories and gathering in the yard. A few broke away from the crowd, headed in the direction of Ibsen Field. Graduation was sometime this afternoon. Two p.m., or three. The sun's position above the commons indicated that it was beyond morning.

He turned and looked back at the bed. Katie was now face down in a pillow, her arms at her sides. She looked like a floater, dead.

"Katie," he said.

Nothing.

He stepped to the edge of the bed. "Katie…" He tugged on the fitted sheet.

She slowly turned her head, revealing red slits of eyes.

"What?"

But he had nothing to say to her.

She closed and opened her eyes. She looked at the shopping bag of pages in his hand.

"Did you start it?" she said in a weak, groggy voice.

He stared at her.

"Your novel. You got this incredible idea. You had to write it down."

"I don't remember any of that," he said.

"But you've been writing all morning—"

"*I don't remember last night.*"

His response put a new look on her face. Her lip, the top corner, curled, and one eye grew smaller, half the size of the other. A bizarre look he supposed meant to express sarcasm, contempt, but he didn't really think she was feeling contemptuous, didn't know Katie to ever feel an emotion stronger than self-pity and even self-pity she killed off quickly, with weed, boozing.

She rolled away from him, saying nothing more and refusing to look at him as she took baggies of hash and tobacco and rolling papers out from a bed-stand drawer and began rolling a joint right there on the mattress. The sheet had slipped off her shoulders. Edward was aware of her nakedness and his own absurd red costume as well as Katie's small round breasts and, on his chest, the word *Tito's*. Her heels were tucked near her pussy and his pants were rubbing up weird on his thighs and her tongue he watched curl over her top lip—dread surging in him again. What happened last night? Should he ask her? What good would come of that? It seemed to him that people never said what happened, just what they wanted to be true. They said, *I remember*…and then talked about themselves and the past as though history were an ideal situation and not their own confused current involvement with things.

Looking at Katie again, he realized she didn't look so good. Her face looked yellow and her hands couldn't be still. She was trying to light the joint she had rolled. He snapped his fingers. Immediately she handed him the lighter and joint. He saw, examining the joint, she hadn't rolled it right. There was too much hash on either end. It would all burn too quickly, or fall out. But Katie fidgeted in bed, looking so impatient and upset that he figured she'd burst into tears if he asked her to wait while he rolled her a new one. He flicked the lighter, holding the open flame up to the hash until it started to bubble and then he tipped his head back and lit the whole thing, the paper burning and she went up on her knees for it. Carefully he handed it back to her. But as she held the thing in her hands some of the hash fell out onto her mattress. He watched her pretend like it hadn't happened. She continued to pose like she was actually toking, like this was actually helping and hash wasn't perpetually falling onto her bed, like she was, inhalation upon inhalation, getting to OK. No, he wouldn't ask her about what happened last night. He didn't want to. And didn't need to. He held in his hands the shopping bag, and in the shopping bag, the start of a novel. He knew the gist. He'd written a possible future in which he tricked a beautiful woman into thinking he was the incomparable genius who had written her the love letters. A future in which he was the artist who loved, and was loved by, a really special chick. Christiane would have a lot to say about this. Christiane, who understood nothing and would always understand nothing about him, would clap her hands, thrilled: *This is your deep unconscious speaking! Let's really think now about what it all means…*

"It's all fucked."

Edward looked over at Katie. She lay back with her arms thrown over her face. The joint had burnt down to her bitten, chipped-paint nails. Again he grew aware of his highly visible red costume, her nakedness which she had done nothing to conceal. She looked as exposed and pathetic as he felt. He dreaded the moment he had to join the graduates gathered outside her dormitory as the Tito's Pizza Guy.

Hanging from the back of the door was Katie's cap and gown.

"Are you walking?" he asked, staring at the garments.

Katie began coughing. When she stopped she said, "No."

He looked back at her. "I forgot mine."

She stared at him for a moment. Maybe she already knew he wasn't graduating. But then she waved a hand.

Relief slipped out his voice: "Yeah? It's cool?"

She shrugged. "We're the same size."

No, she was shorter. She only said that because she was hurt he wouldn't stay and fuck and get high with her. And now, as he took the graduation gown off the hanger, he heard her in the bed gathering the sheets up to cover herself.

"It's weird," she said. "I'm never going to see you again."

He said nothing, putting on the cap and gown, patting his pockets to make sure he had everything...*wallet, keys, smokes... notebook...*

It was all there. He picked up the shopping bag of pages and crossed the room.

"Eddie?"

He had one foot out the door.

"I hope you do finish it. I would love to read a novel by Edward Moses."

Another graduate, another girl, was coming out of a room a few doors down, and Edward slammed the door shut on Katie too loudly or too furiously because the girl in the hall looked over her shoulder, with surprise or—given the wide whiteness of her eyes—with actual alarm. "Oops," said Edward and the girl looked quickly away and he felt like an idiot. He was feeling more and more like an idiot, each step more an idiot, because he had to walk behind her, had to be careful not to walk too close. They were both walking to the stairwell door at the end of the hall, and he had to give her space and walk more slowly than he was accustomed to, nearly halting after each step, holding his breathing, counting *one...two...*then taking another step forward. He watched her fists clench and unclench at her hips. She glanced back at him, and the toe of her shoe caught on her other heel, but she caught herself and fell into a faster pace, nearly jogging to the stairwell door. He quickened his steps, in a hurry to get past her. He wanted to outstrip her, to run up to and then beyond her, to prove he wasn't following her or doing anything weird. She sprinted for her life. She got to the door first and flung it open. He reached for the door but it shut on his fingers and, kicking it back open, he cursed and the sound echoed down the shaft with a ghoulish reverb as the girl's high heels clattered down the steps.

He gave up. He was at the top of the stairs, and she was at the bottom, punching the push-bar open. He took slow steps down the stairs and wondered what the fuck was going on. He wondered if what she thought had happened would be the story of what happened, if she would repeat it to all her friends and if they'd repeat it back to her in amazed question form. It was all so overwhelming. *One thing after another, it's one thing after another,* he thought. And not one thing because of another, just one thing after another. He knew there were causes, that everyday there were causes, myriad fucking causes, for the shit he got into. For the shit that happened to him. But he had yet to find a cause with the same relationship to effect as he had to his daily accidents. He was, he thought, merely pretending that his life wasn't an ongoing fuck-up.

Bodies outside the building blocked the stairwell door. He managed to open it a foot and then squeezed out. His back pressed against the door, he couldn't see faces, just black gowns, black caps. He couldn't hear voices, just a blank, depthless roar. He managed one step forward, and instantly bodies filled the space behind him.

In the crush of people, he began thinking again of what Katie had said just before he left, that thing about wanting to read his novel... He told himself to forget about it. If you were smart you ignored compliments. It seemed to Edward that the day you were told you had a nice voice, or that you looked good in blue, was the day you were ruined forever. You were everyday always paying attention to your nice voice, trying to use it more, and you were perpetually wearing blue. Never stopped wearing blue. Or you took a different tack. Somebody complimented your cooking, why, you could even cook professionally, and you never boiled another potato in your life. With every compliment came a wish for a different, more optimal you. Inside each compliment was the threat your voice would crack, you would fail to finish your novel... *The only time anybody ever really complimented me without an agenda to change who I am was by Christiane, last Sunday, shit. Christiane had said...* How had she phrased it?

Edward felt his eyes and nostrils burn: Christiane's words were at once bright and terrible in his mind. She'd said to him, *I am not worried about you.* And with that truest compliment Christiane seemed to scrub all the self-pity off him. She scrubbed all the self-doubt off him. Edward didn't say another word to her. He left the room.

Edward, in the crowd of graduates, was jostled, his shoulders knocked and his calves scraped. He buckled at the knees but was prevented from crumpling totally by grabbing the back of the person standing ahead of him. Edward straightened, did not let go of the shoulder that had saved him, holding onto the shopping bag of pages with his free hand. Hands gripped his own shoulders but he didn't look back. The crowd of graduates moved, he had no choice, he had to go along. Voices rose up. Hundreds. Singing.

> *If I could attain but one wish,*
> *I'd never leave my friends at Monroe,*
> *My dear old friends at Monroe!*

Edward wished he hadn't left Christiane at the table. He should have asked her what she meant—*What do you mean you're not worried about me?* How different this week might have played out if he hadn't pushed aside what she said. If he had remembered what she said and *not* the words spoken at Sunday dinner—if he'd reflected only upon her encouragement and *not* obsessively upon the discouragement served to him during the usual after-dinner walk, which he always took with his father, then Edward might be marching to Ibsen Field with his classmates not as a phony and a failure, but as somebody about to fucking graduate.

Your mother tells me that you want to move back home for the summer, that you are writing something, and any sort of work you might do, any sort of job for hire, would kill the project immediately, his father said on their after-dinner walk. He and his father had been kicking a stone back and forth, shooting it down the sidewalk. On the graduation march through campus, Edward took tiny steps and felt soft gold tassels lightly swipe his cheeks.

I think you should get to work immediately, he remembered his father saying. *You need a job. You especially need a job—*

*You are self-absorbed enough as it is. You are dependent upon your mother and me enough as it is. Spending a summer of writing will only make you more self-absorbed, more dependent—*and his father kicked the stone too far, sending it hurtling into the street.

…I think staying in Monroe was a mistake for you, he remembered his father saying. as tassels hit his face. *I blame myself, I saw this coming, when you first expressed a wish to follow in my footsteps, I told you to think long and hard about what it would mean for you to stay in town and go to a school so close to the family. You had plenty of opportunities elsewhere, but you told me emphatically that it was Monroe, Monroe is the only place for me.*

Edward remembered how, when they reached the end of the street, where they usually turned right to head back to the house, he did not go right but turned left, leaving his father standing on the corner. Edward remembered walking on through the neighborhood in the direction of Christiane's apartment. Shaking with pride. So proud—*delighted*—that he hadn't lost his temper. He had said nothing to give his father the upper hand.

Edward and the graduates stepped off the pavement and onto the soft sponge of Ibsen Field, coming to a stop under the bleachers. Edward, having left his father, came up to Christiane's apartment. The landlord's dog was twirling, gasping, in the yard. Loops of metal chain were wound around its slick shaking body. Edward froze at the gate, at first not understanding. Then he looked up. Kids in the windows were throwing stones. The stones hit the ground, hit the dog's head. Edward was on his knees, his fingers clawing the ground for the stones so he could fling them back up at the rotten children. He was on all fours, picking up the—M&M's. M&M's, not stones. He hurled the candies back up at the kids in the windows. They giggled, shrieked... And soon after, Christiane had appeared in a window a floor above them. Holding a hand to her eyes, calling down.

Edward?

He stood under the bleachers with the graduates. His eyes glazed over, not seeing any of them. He saw the dog in chains, Christiane in the window. The kitchen table. Champagne on ice and thick wedges of frosted cake on paper napkins. They got very drunk very quickly, celebrating Christiane's new job at Harvard.

...Did I ever tell you, Edward had said suddenly, waking Christiane, who had been drifting off, sinking slowly into her last glass of champagne, *about the time my father drove us up to Traverse City?*

She shook her head. Or she stared at him.

Or asked, *Where is that?*

My dad talks about Traverse City like he ran it while he was there, like he knows everything about it. Goes on and on how those were the best three years of his life. As a kid, I often wondered why he left. I always kinda suspected that something terrible must have driven him out of there.

He finally took us up there when I was in middle school. It's a four-hour drive, four-and-a-quarter tops, but it took us six hours because my mom kept saying, 'Your turn is coming up,' and my dad would immediately throw the wheel and make the turn and my mom would scream, 'I didn't say turn here! I didn't say turn here!'

Christiane laughed.

When we got to Traverse City, Dad drove at a crawl while my mom hung out the window, pointing things out to me and my sister. My mom kept pointing out the places and things important to him, all the places that he had been to, that were 'his places,' while he smoked through an entire pack of Marlboros and did not stop the car once, even though my sister and I were dying to use the toilet. My mom would say, 'This is where your father did his dry cleaning' and she would say, 'This is where your father got break-fast.' 'This is where your father rented an apartment' and 'This where your father found a fifty-dollar bill.' *'This is where your father bought the bread and pickles and peanut butter on which he lived for three years and, oh lord, there it is, this is the hospital where your father did his medical training'* while my father kept a finger on the wheel and smoked and smoked. Near the end of it I said, *'Seems like a nice place to live. Why did Dad ever leave?'* You see what I did there, of course. I asked the question as if he wasn't right there in the driver's seat. I wanted to piss him off. I wanted him to *fucking speak.* He hadn't said one word since we'd reached Traverse City.

The story ends with my dad finally stopping the car outside city limits and with me running out into the woods to take a piss and not getting into the woods in time—but that's not the point. The point of the story is that my dad took us to this place he had talked and talked about all my life and nobody got out of the car once. He drove us up and down the streets, while my mom, who'd never even lived there, pointed things out. And when SHE had nothing left to say, we turned around and headed home.

Christiane shook her head. *Hey! You're leaving something out!*

Edward said, *Huh? What?*

What was the answer?—Why did your dad leave?

Someone in the crowd of graduates began calling for attention. Directions were shouted. Time for everybody to line up according to last name. Letters of the alphabet were cried out. The crowd loosened, scattered...

...Christiane had reached across the table and tightly grabbed both of Edward's hands.

Oh, but that's your father, that's another person you're talking about. That's his mistake, his life. Not yours!

I'm not worried about you, she added, and Edward pulled away. His chair tipped as he stood. He fell into bed and reached for the lamp switch. Christiane then said something—but Edward was listening to the dog in the yard. It hadn't let up. It had been continuously barking all evening.

That dog, that dog, that dog! he seethed...

On Ibsen Field, Edward felt a tap on his shoulder.

"Don't you know where to go? What's your last name?" The marshal nearly jabbed him with the roster.

Edward swallowed. He loosened his lips with his tongue.

"Your name?" the marshal shouted.

"I'm not worried about it," Edward said.

The marshal blinked hard, chapped lips quivering. But now someone nearby was shouting: "*Roger Ackroyd?* Is there a *Roger Ackroyd* here?"

Edward drew in his breath.

"The A-Line is missing an *Ackroyd, Roger*! Anybody? Anybody?"

Rustling gowns and rotating heads. Whispers behind hands, a few snickers. Further down the field, the marching band was warming up: discordant brass, strangled woodwinds. Then, a snare—symbols crashing—

A graduate broke free from the D-line.

He cried, "Here I am!"

Cheering broke out. The fake Roger pumped his fists in the air, and the cheers swelled into joyous uproar. Other graduates jumped out of their lines to clap him on the back. Audience members stuck their faces between the bleachers, laughing and calling down. Eventually a girl chucked her graduation cap at the poser's head. "Nate," she laughed, "you're so stupid!"

Directions now, a voice telling everybody to take their places. And that guy... *Nate*... went back to the D-line, and everybody let out a collective *Aww!* Edward hung his head, terrified that he would now cry. He had pictured this moment: his commencement. On this day, he would finally be better, smarter. He would feel really fucking hopeful. At last he could go out and be anybody—do anything—but he felt like nobody and was capable of nothing and was bewildered, utterly, by how much time he was about to have on his hands. What was he going to do? With the summer ahead? With *the years* lined up before him?

You can do anything you want at any given time, except for most things, he thought. *Anybody at any given time is doing anything, but not Eddie fucking Moses, who is stuck thinking the same things again and again.*

"Hey, Edward!"

He looked up, startled. There was May, stepping out of line. A fresh vanilla scent hit him, and he found that she was hugging him, holding him close, with her full soft breasts against his rib cage. May stepped back. She looked him dead in the eyes. "What happened to you last night? You weren't outside the station. Instead there was this... I had the strangest conversation with a pizza delivery person."

May gave her head a quick shake, laughing.

"Anyways, thanks. For telling me about Jon. I wasn't able to actually talk to him last night, but I did get ahold of his father in New York, and to make a long story short, Jon *should* be getting out today. In fact, I was sort of hoping he'd be here for the ceremony. Have you seen him?"

They both looked around. The field was crowded now, the bleachers filling up with parents. May gripped his arm and shivered

"...so, so exciting!" she was saying, and then she said something else, which Edward couldn't hear, because the band had started playing Pomp and Circumstance.

May shouted, "So I'll see you there?"

"Where?"

She stepped back into line. "Nine p.m., Michigan Bar!"

Then May's line moved. She began to walk, flashing him a thumbs-up.

He held up his thumb too, and then a shoulder slammed into him. A second shoulder hit him, then another, another, and now all the lines were surging forward, while he took his first steps against the graduates marching. He plowed through their lines, slammed into the marshals with their clipboards, and eventually broke free onto the main drag through campus. He was trembling, his heart beating triple time. He was glad? Jonathan would soon tell May the truth, and May would spread it around to her friends. Soon everybody would know that Edward wasn't some waste of space...some *zero*...

The news would spread quickly around the bar.

Ted would shake his head. *Holy shit! Everyone is saying that Edward is...*

Rainne would frown. The Poet's name sounded familiar to her, but she couldn't quite place it. Then it dawned on her.

Edward, you dummy! Why'd you never tell me?

Edward would smile.

No.

Wink at Rainne.

Ugh, no.

He'd push her away. Put his arm around May...

The shopping bag of pages rustled as Edward adjusted his grip. He took a final drag, then flicked his cigarette into the bushes outside the Secret Garden. The band was playing the school song. How long had he been wandering? Half an hour maybe. He was hungry and tired and wanted to be in bed with a box of Ring Dings and a handle of Jim Beam. He did not remember, he suddenly realized, where he had last parked Gran's car. Last night, when he left the bar with Katie, had they walked? Driven?

He lit up his last smoke, walking over to and now wandering through the visitor's parking lot. After seeing many grimy little cars and after going through row upon row, he had not found his gran's car and was approaching the parking lot's entrance. He halted. He knew that car. That was his mom's car. Her little red coupe. Chills raced through him. He looked over his shoulder, expecting to see her jump out from between the cars...

Gotcha!

He looked back at her car. But was it hers? She had promised to skip the ceremony. He stepped closer and saw—

Ah hell!

Viv was there. His mom had locked her in the back seat again.

Fucking hell, it wasn't normal. Edward ran up to a side door and began yanking on the handle, but it was locked.

"Viv!" He rapped on the window. "Open the door!"

She was plugged into her Walkman and didn't look over. Just smiled and hummed and bobbed her head along with whatever music she was listening to. It sounded like…"Summer Nights?" The *Grease* soundtrack?

He rapped harder.

"Viv!"

Her humming, did it just grow louder? He rapped the glass one last time. "Viv, it's me! Open up!"

She stared straight ahead. "I can't," she said.

He nodded enthusiastically. "Of course you can. Just push up the lock."

"No," she looked over at him and grinned, "I can't *hear you*."

He blinked quickly, then started laughing at her joke. He set the shopping bag on the ground. "Where's Mom?" he asked.

"Taking pictures of you!"

Fucking hell. Christ. "And she locked you in here, huh? How long ago did she leave?"

"She'll only be gone five minutes."

"But how long ago have you been waiting?"

"She'll only be gone…"

"Yeah, yeah," he muttered, patting his gown. *Wallet, notebook, lighter*…he felt the keys in his jacket pocket. Yes! He parted the gown, pulled out the keys, and plunged the car key into the lock of the driver's side door. Instantly the horn began blaring, the headlights flickering on, off, on. Shit, he'd used the wrong key. He glanced over at Viv and saw her eyes were wide, her mouth a small o. An instant later she was shrieking, hands pressed against the headphones on her ears. She rocked back and forth and he swore and swore, fumbling the keys in his hand, looking in vain for the right one—except these were Gran's keys, not his mom's keys. *Oh my god.* In the haze of noise he slumped forward, his forehead on the glass. He watched Viv sob and rock. He felt his eyes sting.

…The alarm shut off.

Viv still wept, rocked.

His forehead was still pressed against the glass. "Sweetie," he said, voice cracking, "listen. What do you hear?"

She didn't answer, tears streamed down her face.

"Do you hear any birds singing?"

She said nothing, trembling.

"Do you hear a cat, any cats meowing?"

He waited. Then he said, "Do you hear any fish, *glub a glub*—"

"Stop! I don't hear that!"

He feigned surprise. "Then what do you hear?"

"You! My baby brother."

He wanted to break down and cry. He forced a smile on his face and eyed the Walkman.

"What are you listening to?"

She didn't answer.

"Is that the *Grease* soundtrack?

Still she ignored him. He stared miserably at her through the glass, imagining all the things he'd say to his mom when she came back to the car. *Quit locking her in cars! You wouldn't even do that to a dog!*

He imagined her retort: *Of course I wouldn't do it to a dog. A DOG would chew up the upholstery. Your sister, however—*

Is a person!

The sound of an approaching car. Edward looked up. A police car had just pulled into the parking lot. It disappeared behind parked cars, crawling slowly toward the university entrance.

He tapped the glass. "Viv?"

She said nothing.

"Don't go anywhere, OK?"

She shrunk in the seat, chin doubling into her neck. "I know," she murmured.

He stepped back and his foot crushed the shopping bag behind him. He snatched it up, cramming in the papers that had fallen out and went forward, striding rapidly through the rows. He got to the first row in front of the university entrance and stopped, hanging back between two cars. A cop was just letting Jonathan out of the patrol car. He held a shopping bag and wore rumpled clothing—the same long-sleeved shirt and dark slacks and worn boots from the night of the play. His pale blonde hair was flat and greasy against the sides of his head.

Edward waited for Jonathan to get far enough ahead that he wouldn't see him, then began trailing him. Jonathan started off down the main drag, headed toward Ibsen Field. Did he really think he was going to make it in time to graduate? An hour must have passed since the ceremony had started and, from the field, nothing could be heard. No band music, no speeches, no recitation of names. If the ceremony wasn't over yet, it was about to be.

Jonathan stopped at the fountain in the center of campus. It was a large circular pool with a tall sculpted spout in the middle. Edward noticed for the first time that the carvings on the spout, which had always registered as abstract lumps and swirls, were actually writhing fish. Little trout. Jonathan dropped the shopping bag on the ledge. He reached inside and pulled out a long, black graduation gown.

Distantly, music. *Pomp and Circumstance*, for a second time. Jonathan smoothed his gown, adjusted the cap on his head.

Edward cleared his throat. "You're too late. Graduation is over."

Jonathan looked up, startled. As his eyes hardened on Edward, a shudder passed through his body.

"Better just head back, wait to tell May later when she's alone. Less embarrassing for all of you."

Jonathan ripped off his hat and threw it on the ground.

"Who do you think you are?" he yelled. "Telling me what to do! Who do you—"

Edward's face heated up. "I'm the guy who—"

"Nobody! You're nobody!"

"I wrote the poems," Edward croaked.

Jonathan threw his head back and laughed.

Edward felt his chest expand. "I have the letters—all the ones May sent to Ackroyd and drafts of his replies. There's nothing to stop me from telling her that I'm him."

Jonathan stopped laughing.

"I'll fucking marry her," Edward growled. "I'll spend my whole life with her. We'll have kids, and every year for Christmas we'll send you a fucking card."

Jonathan shrugged. "OK. Do it."

His chest tightened. "Or I could just tell her the truth. I wrote the poems, but you're the miserable fuck who lied to her."

Jonathan smiled grimly, looking down at his hands. He picked a bit of dirt from his fingernail. "I gather you have proof of that too?"

"Yup!"

"Drafts of the original poems?"

"Every single one."

"And I suppose," the poser grinned at him, "you kept all this in a shoebox and wrapped duct tape all around it to keep it safe…"

Jonathan reached into his shopping bag and pulled out a box wrapped in duct tape. It looked exactly like the shoebox in which Edward stored all his poems. There was a difference though: this box could be opened. The tape had been sliced through. As Jonathan lifted the lid, Edward thought, *No, no, it can't be.* He'd left his shoebox in the trunk of Gran's car.

"Seems like they got our possessions mixed up over at the police station," Jonathan said. "Where is my briefcase anyway? There's a book in it that needs to go back to the library."

Edward began to see red.

"I haven't had too much time to look through the box yet, but it seems obvious enough that whoever has all these drafts and originals is the real Roger Ackroyd." Jonathan riffled through the papers. He pulled one out. The paper was covered in dense blue scribbles.

Edward dropped his shopping bag, lunging at Jonathan. Easily Jonathan leapt aside, his gown whipping behind him. Edward lunged again, and Jonathan raced around the fountain. Edward caught up, his fingertips grazing the sleeve of Jonathan's gown—the poser jumped onto the fountain's ledge, now grinning and jumping from foot to foot on the cement lip. Just as Jonathan cried out, "Finders, keepers!" Edward scrambled up onto the ledge and jumped on him.

They both fell back, and the box flew up. Edward watched dark water zoom toward him, then his shoulder hit water, cement. The left side of his body smarted from the impact, and his clothes grew instantly heavy.

Jonathan, beside him, flailed and splashed and nearly stood, then stumbled, weighed down by his sodden graduation gown. Edward too found that it was hard to stand under the weight of his garments, and so he turned onto his back and watched papers flutter down from the sky. One landed on his face. He peeled it off and held it up. It was an early draft of "So You Want to be a Writer"—

if it doesn't come bursting out of you
in spite of everything,

do it.

Jonathan's screams, hysterical and distracting, turned Edward's attention toward him. The poser grabbed the sides of his head, sank to his knees—the problem, Edward realized, was all the ink was bleeding off the papers. Lifting a poem up from the water, Jonathan watched in horror as all the blue ink ran down. He crawled forward, dredging up paper after paper and draping them on his arms.

"What is wrong with you?" Jonathan screamed. "Help me!"

Edward exhaled and sank under the water. He could still hear Jonathan's splashes, but they were far away, unimportant to him. More distantly he began to hear other voices. He rose above the surface again, wiping his face. He couldn't believe what he was seeing.

Gathering all around the fountain were graduates just coming from the field. A sea of black gowns, black caps. Amused faces.

Then a cry—

May broke through the crowd.

"Jon! What are you doing?"

Edward pulled himself up, scarcely aware he was yelling, "He isn't Roger Ackroyd!"

At the other end of the fountain, Jonathan shouted, "You can't prove it!"

May came to the ledge. Her face was flushed. Edward pulled one of the papers up from the water and held it out to her. "This is my handwriting. Oh my god, this is mine!"

The blue ink was streaming down, all the words illegible.

"I am Roger Ackroyd!" Edward shouted.

May gave him and the poem a passing glance. Her gaze fixed on Jonathan.

"Is this true?" she asked.

Jonathan's mouth hung open. No words came out. Then he whimpered.

May groaned. She sat down hard on the ledge of the fountain and put her face in her hands. Some graduates broke away from the crowd and crouched down at her side, putting their arms around her. Her friends stared hatefully at Jonathan, but everyone else around the fountain was looking right at Edward. He felt the urge to flee. To leave all these papers and all these people. He began to move his body slowly through the water, keeping along the ledge. He was several feet from May, about to pull himself up, when he froze. May was speaking again. To Edward? Or Jonathan?

"I knew OK? I knew from the beginning, or at least I thought I did. That's why I gave you the first letter and asked you to deliver it to the paper, instead of doing it myself. I figured if you were Roger like I suspected, then you'd hold onto it, write back to me yourself..."

Edward looked between May and Jonathan, who was seated on the other side of the fountain, facing May with his head in his hands. May sat with her back to him, staring at her lap as she continued. "And when the reply came, how could I not recognize your voice in the letters? I've been reading your stories and plays since we were kids. And all those hints you dropped when we were together…" She looked up from her lap. Her eyes flickered over the crowd gathered around her. Then she fixed her gaze on the top of a building.

Then Edward realized: *Oh, she's acting. This is acting.*

"Don't you get it? I was excited! I was waiting for you to tell me that you liked me, that you…" she lowered her head, "…*loved me.*"

Then she looked over her shoulder.

"You didn't have to lie, Jonathan. I don't know why you lied."

Jonathan's face was gray. He stared ahead at May. But Edward didn't think he was looking at her. Edward imagined him looking inward, weighing her words, trying to figure out if he still had a chance with her. *Idiot. Doesn't realize he's lost.* Then, another thought occurred to him: *Jonathan has finally stopped pretending.*

But May stared right at Edward. They all were, actually. The entire crowd around the fountain—a hundred eyes turned toward him.

May said, "So you're the guy, huh? *Roger Ackroyd.*"

Look at her, just at her. But he couldn't. His head dropped, and he stared at the water, scarcely nodding.

She snorted. "Big whoop."

Jonathan chuckled. Edward tensed, spinning around, ready to—

"I don't know why *you're* laughing," May snapped. Then, she groaned. "The both of you are pathetic."

She got up.

Jonathan cried out, "May, wait!"

Ranks of friends enclosed around her. "I don't want to hear it!" she exclaimed as Jonathan scrambled after her.

Edward was left alone, standing in the fountain, with all his ruined poems. A film of ink covered the water. His bare skin, where the water had touched it, was stained blue. He swallowed. He didn't care. It didn't matter. He would gather up this fucking litter and he wouldn't care. He took a heavy step forward.

Then he heard the first click.

Click-flash!

Then another click–flash, then more in rapid succession.

They were snapping pictures of him. The graduates and their parents, armed with cameras. They held them up to their faces and took his photograph.

Edward knew, staring blankly into the flashing lights, that this was not as low as he would go. He had not hit bottom. This was not as far as he would plunge in this life.

EPILOGUE | SATURDAY

AWARE OF failure the moment he woke. Waking was failure, noises and chemicals and his cells, the thriving billions, forcing him to exist again against his will. He hated every part of himself. He was horrified by his capacity to eke out more new mornings. And he knew before opening his eyes that somebody was with him. He didn't know who. He kept his eyes closed and feigned deep breathing.

A poke to his shoulder, sharp prodding.

Edward grunted.

Fingers snapping at his ear.

Edward's eyes opened to slits.

And he saw, leaning over him, a face so like his own that he became very afraid. A cigarette dangled from the lips of this face. The eyebrows were arched. A mocking, critical grin.

"*Peter?*" Edward croaked.

Peter widened his expression. "Rise and shine, cousin!"

Edward pushed up on his elbows. He looked around Gran's living room for the other relatives.

Peter quietly laughed. "Just me."

Relief flooded Edward. He swung his legs around to the floor. Rubbing his eyes, he looked up at his cousin again. He reached out his hand, palm up.

"Give me," Edward said.

Peter tossed over the smokes.

Exhaling, shaking his head, Edward stammered, "I'm at Gran's because...well, you know she had a..."

Peter grinned.

Edward looked up from lighting his cigarette. "*What?*"

"I'm just imagining what you'll do, once your mom gets to be Gran's age," Peter said.

Edward gaped at him. "Why bring that up?"

Peter taunted, "Will you crash in the lobby of her nursing home?"

Edward chucked the smokes at his head, and Peter ducked as the pack whizzed by, striking the TV screen.

"So how is she?" Edward waited. "Gran!"

"She's ninety, Ed. So I'm sure she'll be fine."

Edward puffed away, watching Peter saunter over to the TV. His cousin kicked the pack up with the toe of his shoe, catching it on his fingertips. Edward's face flooded with heat. Envy or admiration or—delight, just pure delight to see his cousin, who walked over to Gran's chair by the window and said nothing about how ugly it was, with its canary yellow and purple roses. He merely brushed imaginary crumbs off and sat, gently, with his legs crossed.

Peter's head turned from side to side. "What did you *do* in here?"

Across the carpet were cookie and cake wrappers, bottles and...

Edward shook his head. "Nothing. I'm cleaning it up."

"But yesterday," Peter fidgeted. "At the graduation ceremony. Did you actually..." His voice trailed off, and Edward's stomach melted, a bright flash of fright in his head.

"What do you know?" Edward asked.

"Oh—" Peter moved his hand around in the air.

"Oh!" Edward moaned. He was ruined, ruined!

"All morning your mother was calling your friends up, trying to find you," Peter said. "She got ahold of Ted, but he didn't know where you were. Said it'd been months since you lived with him."

"Then what?" Edward asked.

"She went out."

"*Out?*"

"In her car…"

Edward threw back his head.

"It was mentioned by someone in the family that you might be over here." Peter gestured. "But then my mom said, *Oh but he isn't.* Seems that they both came around the other day, and you weren't to be seen."

Edward frowned. "But you thought different."

"It's where I'd hide," Peter said with a shrug, and Edward narrowed his eyes. Peter tapped ash into a tray that until now, Edward hadn't known about. But there it was, next to the crystal candy bowl, filled with butts and the sides clouded.

Peter continued, "But we're getting ahead of ourselves now, because before I came over, I went for a drive with your mom and sister. And we're driving past the college when Viv comes out with this thing about seeing you yesterday, at your graduation."

Peter uncrossed and crossed his legs.

"Your mom nearly crashes the car, looking back at Viv to ask if she's sure. Oh, yes, she's very sure. Well, what does Viv remember? Only that you were wearing a dress, which makes your mom ecstatic. She turns to me and says, *Well, that's weird! So weird! I didn't see him on the field, and they didn't call his name!* And here her eyes grow evil. *Say, Peter. What do you know that I don't, hm? What are you hiding from me?*"

Edward yawned loudly, nervously.

"*Oh nothing, Auntie Josephina,*" Peter recounted. "*Just got in from New York, haven't seen Ed since Easter.* But then your mom sticks her neck out and goes—"

"*Huh,*" Edward exhaled.

"Right. And I wasn't lying. I hadn't seen you. In fact, when I got into town last night, I went to Michigan Bar, hoping to see you. Instead, I ran into your friends."

Peter paused, glancing at his cigarette.

"Amazing things they were saying," he added.

"Yeah," Edward grunted. "Skip over that part."

Peter shrugged. "Nothing much more to tell you, then. I told your mom that I had no reason to think you didn't graduate. And that if Viv saw you in the car wearing a gown then you probably had. *Could it be, Aunt Josephina, that you are being too hard on young Edward?*"

Edward rolled his eyes. "Of course you said all that."

Peter leaned forward. "*What happened yesterday?*"

Edward tapped ash into the candy bowl. He frowned. Switching to the ashtray, he said, "Woke up, graduated, came here."

"No shit? Because a lot of people at the bar last night were saying—"

Edward shuddered. "I don't want to talk about it."

Peter lifted a hand. "All right. That's all to the story then. After failing to find you around town, your mom drove us home. She had to finish getting things ready for the party. And then I got into my own car, came here."

Shit. Edward had forgotten about his graduation party.

"When's that thing happening?"

Peter blinked several times. "Now."

"Shit, shit." Edward stood up, searching for his pants. "Shit," he muttered, kicking around the wrecked living room.

"You don't have to go."

Edward shook his head. "Better now than later. My mom won't ask me so many questions with everyone around." He hesitated. "My dad, though…"

"Had to drive to Ypsi to deliver a baby."

"Perfect," Edward muttered, snatching up the jeans behind the TV.

They both finished their cigarettes and headed for the front door. Peter paused in the entryway, sniffing him.

"Ed, you bathed!"

Edward reached for the doorknob. "Eh, not exactly—"

The car in the driveway wasn't one Edward recognized. A Camaro, popping red.

"What happened to your Volvo?" Edward asked.

Peter grinned. "Do you like it?"

"Are you like officially an asshole now?"

"I could make you walk," Peter suggested.

Edward got into the passenger seat. It smelled wonderful in his cousin's car.

"Strawberries," he said.

"Sorry?" Peter asked.

"Nothing. You're very clean."

Peter started up the engine. "Try not to touch anything."

They pulled out of the drive. Edward looked around, marveling at the order and cleanliness. He opened and closed all the compartments. They were spick and span, the car documents collected in a labeled leather binder. *Peter would make a damned good roommate,* he thought.

"How long did it take you?" Edward asked.

Peter stuck his neck out. "Eh?"

"To drive here from Manhattan—the city."

"Nine, ten hours?"

Huh. Not bad.

Edward reached into the cup holder and pulled out Peter's cigarettes.

"Out the window," Peter said, and Edward rolled it down.

He hung out the window, enjoying the cool air on his face. But Peter cleared his throat.

Edward looked back at him. "If you don't want me to smoke…"

Peter shook his head. "No, it's not that."

Edward waited, feeling uneasy.

"There's something I should probably tell you."

Edward's heart twisted.

Peter said, "Your friends are at the party. They're all waiting for you."

Edward covered his face. "Who?"

"Ted. And others…"

"Rainne?"

"Yes. And some others I met at the bar last night."

They came up to the turn to his parents' house. Panic surged in him. He couldn't go to the party now. Absolutely would not do it. He had managed to avoid them all yesterday. He had escaped everybody after the fountain. It would be the last nail in his coffin, if he saw his friends now.

"Don't turn here," Edward said.

"What?" Peter asked.

"Just drive, just drive!"

Peter looked at the road. "OK…"

The car accelerated.

They drove past the turn.

Peter cleared his throat.

"So where are we going?"

Edward gaped at him. "What does it matter?"

ACKNOWLEDGEMENTS

I'm indebted to my editor, Leland Cheuk, and to my mentor, Bruce Bauman. I'm grateful for readings by: Brian Evenson, Seth Blake, Susan Henderson, Diana Wagman, Mehtab Kaur, Charlotte Simpson, Anna Clark, and Ante Vulin. What's best in this book I owe to you, Drew.

7.1BOOKS